Old Flames and Brimstone

Mark Croswell

Cover photo by Dhivakaran S as found on Pexels.com

ISBN: 978-0-9980428-0-0

Chapter 1

"I'm scared, Darla," Margie whispered.

"No reason to be, honey. You've lived a good life, raised a wonderful family. You always trusted in the Lord."

"I know, but I'm scared. I'm just not ready to go."

Darla put her hand softly on Margie's forehead and stroked her gray, thinning hair. Margie Thumpacker had once been the envy of every woman in town with thick, beautiful hair, but her failing health over the last three years had turned it to wispy at best. It wasn't Margie's hair, though, that Darla McGee cared about. The words Margie had just uttered were like blood in the water for a woman like Darla, a woman with a shark-like sense for weakness. Darla could smell it a mile away, a skill finely honed over the years by watching her Southern Baptist father go to work on the guilt and sin of his congregation. Every problem was an opportunity to use the gospel as a weapon, a self-serving gift that Darla exploited often. Unfortunately, Darla was also in a hurry this morning and was struggling to be patient.

"Now don't you worry," Darla said. "Heaven's gates are open for you, waiting for you to come in. You can hold your head high, not an ounce of shame to hold you back as you parade proudly into the Promised Land. You've left everything behind, no stone unturned, no little sin hiding that you haven't asked to be forgiven for. I know that's true. You know that's true, don't you, Margie?" Darla asked as she kissed her forehead. Margie began to weep as Darla looked at her watch for the third time in ten minutes.

"Almost, I.... Just one thing, Darla, but it was so long ago. I feel like I've been punished many times over for it but it still just hangs out there like a big neon sign, taunting me."

Margie began wiping the tears from her eyes as Darla tried to suppress a smile. Darla licked her lips, carefully setting up for the kill.

"Honey, if there's a burden like that hanging around your neck, why, you have to get it out in the open. It's an anchor, keeping your spirit in place. My daddy always told me we weren't fully forgiven until we had openly confessed and put our trust unto our brothers and sisters. Margie, don't hold back. Tell me what is troubling you so badly. Ask to be forgiven so that nothing holds you back from the reward you so rightly deserve. You don't want that neon sign hanging over the pearly gates, do you?"

"Darla, you'll think I'm horrible."

"No, honey, never! We've been close friends for so long and I'd be devastated if you passed without driving this demon out of your soul. Margie, quickly now before the Almighty's angels sweep you away and you lose the opportunity."

Margie continued to weep as she turned her head away from Darla. Darla felt she'd maybe pushed her a little too far, but then Margie rolled her head back and looked Darla in the eye with determination.

2

"I've been strong my whole life. I've always done what's right, I was always faithful to my husband and my kids and my friends. I'm strong enough to do this," Margie said. She took a deep breath and continued. "Remember that week, back when we were in high school, that Joan ran away from home and said she'd lived out in the woods for five days?"

"Yes," Darla replied with a curious look. "Wasn't that the day after she'd spent the night at your house, when she'd gotten a little tipsy at the class dance?"

"Yes, well she didn't stay out in the woods. She was at my house the whole time. I was hiding her there because she didn't want to go home."

"So what? A lot of us didn't want to go home at that age. I would've loved to have found a place to get away for a week, or two for that matter. Even now I find myself sometimes wanting to be in two places at once." Darla checked her watch again as Margie wiped her eyes.

"Well, I didn't want her to go home either."

"Of course not, you were good friends. You two did everything together and—"

"We kissed on that first night."

"You what?" Darla asked, startled by Margie's admission.

"Kissed. And then hugged, and then—"

Darla gasped, putting her hands up in hopes of slowing Margie down. The words, no matter how slowly they came out, were more than Darla could digest. But Margie kept going.

"— she shared her body with me, and I did the same."

"Be quiet for a minute," Darla said. "Just be quiet."

"It's all out there now," Margie said with a huge sigh, "I don't need to say anymore."

"But what all did, I mean, what happened?"

"What all did we do? Everything two girls could do without boys. I don't have to tell you, you can probably imagine."

"I just don't understand!"

"We didn't understand it either. We didn't think we'd get caught, but we did."

"Who? Who caught you?"

"My mother. She sent Joan home, told her that if she ever came by our house again she'd kill her. Called me a filthy slut and then got drunk."

"Your mother? Drunk?" Darla asked, shaking her head. She was dumbfounded by Margie's recollection of the entire event.

"And called me a filthy slut, thank you! For three days."

"I can't imagine! What were you doing when she caught you?"

"Darla! You make it sound like a dirty movie. God, I'm sorry I told you anything. I should have given this at confessional years ago like my mother told me to."

"Why didn't you?"

"To Father Russ? Can you imagine what my penance would have been?" Darla nodded in agreement.

"Look, Margie, don't be mad. I'm not judging you, I'm sorry. You surprised me and I didn't expect it. So, was that the end of it?"

"No, Momma brought a boy home to stay with us, made the two of us share a room," Margie said.

"Why did she do that?"

"I don't know. Maybe so he could keep an eye on me, tattle if I did anything wrong. Sometimes I wonder if she wanted me to have sex with him so I'd know what I was supposed to feel like."

"I knew your mother, she'd never do that."

"It didn't matter, we hadn't done anything anyway. Not then."

"Who was it?"

"I'm not telling you. Jesus, if you aren't the nosiest woman!"

"Okay, I'm sorry. It doesn't matter."

"Damn right it doesn't," Margie said, and then caught her breath. "Okay, I feel better now."

"Good, good. Why don't you get some sleep?"

"I'm going to. Maybe the good Lord will finally take me in my sleep."

"Don't talk like that."

"Mind your own business. And look, don't go gossiping about this and don't ever tell Joan I told you."

"Do you want to pray?"

"No, I want to sleep."

"Alright, honey."

Darla stood and smoothed Margie's hair back. She was trying to remember Margie's face as it had been when they'd played together as little girls, but that was seventy years ago and it wasn't easy to recall that sweet, innocent little face after what she'd just heard. All she saw was a woman who'd aged quickly in the last three years, succumbing to everything nature could throw at her. But her mind was still sharp and Darla believed everything she'd said.

Darla had just cleared the exit doors of Fallon Memorial Hospital when the angels took Margie, ascending high into the heavens as the needles in Darla's head inevitably began to knit their sinister blanket of guilt and shame to be spread out for others to see. Deep down Darla knew it was wrong but rationalized that by reporting the testimony of others, she would, by proxy, perform the final act of washing away their sins. It also gave her information that kept her enemies at bay. She looked at her watch once again and felt relieved that one of her lifelong ambitions would be achieved in less than an hour.

*****

Eloise Laine thought she'd be the only person out at the old retreat that morning. Unlike many others, she didn't have anything against the old building, she just enjoyed watching things go up in flames. Her son, Champ, dutifully pushed her wheelchair to a nice grassy spot on the hill and set an umbrella over her to keep off the sun. He sat impatiently in a lawn chair next to her, wishing he were somewhere else.

"So, what's the fascination with this building, Mother?"

"It's nothing to me, I've never been inside. I just like watching fire trucks and buildings burn."

"You're the only one, then. Half the town is sorry to see it go, the other half can't wait. I'm surprised Darla isn't here lighting the match."

"She'll be here, don't worry. Darla sees this place as a monument to everything she hates. It's just a damn building but you'd think it was an altar for sin."

"It was a swinger joint, what's the big deal?"

"In our day it was a really big deal. We weren't open like everyone is today. People swapping wives and having all those sex parties out here. I heard there were drugs and gambling, but that wasn't what shut it down. Darla told me one time she was afraid to even touch anything in there because of all the disgusting things she saw."

"That was a long time ago, why all the fuss now?"

"Because it changed the whole town. Or at least I'm convinced it did. There were several people in my class that worked there cleaning or being valets or whatever and I'm telling you it changed them all."

"I heard it was just for rich people who liked that kind of lifestyle, kind of a secret society."

"I think it was supposed to be, but it wasn't just rich people coming out here, some of the locals were showing up, too. The whole damn town just became more curious and wild when they learned what was going on out here. And what did I care? Let people do what they're going to do, but it seemed like everyone was unhappy after it. They just couldn't settle down and I think half of 'em couldn't believe that something like that could go on this close to us right under our nose."

"I still don't see what the big deal is."

"That's because your generation was all about smut if you asked me. Brother McGee would have been standing on your chest and ready to drive a stake through your heart with half the shit you kids did."

"That I did?" Champ said as he laughed. "I didn't do anything like that."

"The hell you didn't. Kids do what kids do, don't think I don't know."

"That was Darla's dad, right?"

"Yeah, Brother McGee. I swear he invented fire and brimstone, but I think even this place wore him down. The harder he preached against it, the worse it got. For ten years after this place closed down he attacked everyone he thought had a link to it. I think he was just fanning the flames, bringing more attention to it. My understanding is that he was pretty hard on Darla, too. She swears it killed him. He had a heart attack in mid-sermon, yelling and slamming his fist on that pulpit and then he dropped to the floor."

"Well, he left the business in good hands. She seems like a chip off the old block."

"She wasn't always like she is now. Something in there changed her. She was a pain in the rear before, but after the big blow-up she spat venom from then on."

"Speak of the devil," Champ said.

Darla's car came roaring up and stopped close to Eloise and Champ. She got out of the car, concerned as she looked down the hill at the retreat.

"Why isn't anything moving?" Darla asked angrily.

"Any what moving?" Eloise replied.

"The machines, the men? Don't you think somebody should be doing something down there? The fire trucks should be here by now, what's going on?"

"I don't know, they don't call me for permission."

"I'll light that thing on fire myself if I have to."

Darla opened her trunk and began taking out hand-painted signs stapled to wooden stakes. There were ten in all and she laid them out side by side and then pulled out a small mallet that she had trouble lifting.

"Here, Champ, help me put these signs up."

"What do they say?"

"It doesn't matter, just hammer them down in the order I have them."

"Go help her, Champ, before she starts getting all high and mighty," Eloise said.

"Yes, ma'am."

Champ took the mallet from Darla and walked along the row, reading the words on each sign. He shook his head, looked up, and saw a line of cars heading toward them. He grimaced, knowing everyone would see him putting up the signs with bible scriptures.

As the cars parked, people began congregating in the area around Darla and Eloise to watch the spectacle. Darla paced back and forth, looking down the hill at the building that she swore was looking back, mocking her. As more people gathered, the crowd became louder with laughing and light-hearted conversation and she became infuriated.

"What are you people so happy about? Nothing is being done and none of you care a wit!"

"Calm down, Darla, for God's sake. It'll happen," Eloise said.

"Don't use the Almighty's name so carelessly, Eloise. And I'll have you know that I paid for the legal fees and insurance myself so the fire department could practice by burning this building down. Now I want to see some movement and I want to see it fast."

"Well, it isn't going to happen today," a voice said from behind the others.

Everyone turned around to see the young man making his way to where Darla stood.

"What are you talking about, Alton?" Darla asked.

"Someone bought the building last night before it could go into foreclosure," Alton replied. "He paid all the back taxes and fees and it isn't going anywhere."

"I don't believe you. Nobody around here has that kind of money and what would they do with it anyway? This place is going to burn today, by God—"

"Ms. McGee, I sold it to him myself. It's done."

"You did? The grandson of my best friend sold it out from under me? You knew I wanted this place gone and you, the worst realtor in the county, kept the devil's lair of lust alive and well...." Tears were forming in Darla's eyes and her voice quavered with emotion.

"Well, I'd say he did a good job," Eloise interjected. "Good for you, Alton, good for you. I hope you made a nice commission for yourself."

"No shit," Champ said, with a measure of awe in his voice. "Who the hell did you sell it to?"

"Stop encouraging him! What is wrong with you people? As long as that building stands this town will never heal."

"Let's just give it some time, Ms. McGee," Alton said defensively. "Mr. Kranz says he has some plans for the old place."

"Kranz? Kranz who?" Darla's eyes became wild and round.

"Edwin Kranz. He said he stayed there one night and—"

"I didn't think it could get any worse." Darla's face reddened, matching her hair and her temperament. "Of all the people that have no business in this town or with this piece of property, he would be at the head of the line. It can't be, I won't allow it."

Darla walked calmly to her car, got in, and began driving down the hill toward the retreat. The news of who had bought the place started a whole new conversation of excitement and intrigue among those standing around, except for Eloise, who watched as Darla's car got closer and closer to the retreat. She reached over and tugged at Champ's hand to get his attention.

9

"Hey, better go down there and stop her. She'll damn well burn that place down."

"Well, what do you want me to do about it, Mother?"

"You're the damn cop, go down there and arrest her or something," Eloise said.

Thirty minutes later Darla had her own escort detail of one police car in front of her and two behind to ensure she left the area without being arrested. A warning was also given about returning after everyone had left. But at the top of the hill where everyone was still gathered, Alton tried to answer everyone's question about the newest interest in town, Edwin Kranz.

That evening, Alton regretted having said anything at all. Edwin had asked him to keep his name confidential, but since the sale was already complete, Alton didn't feel a need to keep it quiet any longer. Before the end of the day, the whole city was buzzing about what would become of the old retreat.

*****

Ellie Mintzer rushed up the jetway, her heart pounding from both excitement and exertion as she prepared to see her father. Though they'd spoken often by phone, she hadn't seen him for four years and had grown concerned about his health. His excuse was merely a matter of their schedules not aligning but she wasn't so sure. But today was supposed to be a turning point for them, a new beginning that she'd begged for for years and he had finally relented. They were going to spend a week together in his home town, where she hoped to learn how he ultimately became a grouchy, headstrong son-of-a-bitch.

As the jetway opened to the concourse, she found a hole between some of the passengers to shoot through. Her flight was two hours late and the connecting flight they would share to Houston left in thirty minutes. Ellie stopped at the desk of the gate attendant, waiting impatiently behind a passenger who was arguing loudly. Ellie looked around for a clock but didn't see one. She got out her phone to look at the time and became more frustrated. The argument didn't seem to be resolving and she looked around for another gate attendant. She picked up her bag and turned to rush down the concourse when it occurred to her that the man's voice sounded familiar, very familiar. She turned and looked again at the desk and there he was.

"He chewed his goddamned gum with his mouth open the whole time and had his headphones turned up so loud I couldn't get to sleep," Edwin Kranz complained.

"Sir, I'm sorry that happened, but I'm not sure what we can do about that."

"Make a damn policy or something, for Pete's sake. No gum, and the blasted headphones ought to have limiters or something."

"Dad?" Ellie said nervously, with a huge grin and her arms wide.

Edwin didn't hear her and the gate attendant pointed over to Ellie to redirect his attention. He looked over his shoulder, annoyed with being interrupted.

"Dad, it's me, Ellie!" she exclaimed, her arms still extended.

"Hi, I'll be with you in a minute," he said and turned back to the attendant. "Now who the hell do I talk to so we can get this changed?"

"Well, you can go to our website and contact—"

"And that's another thing, I couldn't get a damn connection with my computer—"

"Dad, we're going to miss our connecting flight," Ellie demanded.

Edwin turned and looked at her again, this time studying her and her words, and finally picked up his attache case.

"We'll pick this up at another time," he said to the flight attendant. He turned toward Ellie who was shaking her head with her hands on her hips. "You're late, what the hell took you so long?"

"I don't fly the planes, Dad, and it's great to see you, too."

"Guess it couldn't be helped, then. Good to see you."

Edwin finally held his arms out and embraced her. Ellie became emotional feeling his strong arms hug her and pat her on the the back. Edwin neither looked nor acted his eighty years and Ellie found it to be a relief. She wanted all the time she could muster with him and while he was still able to do things that she wanted to do.

"You look great," she said as she wiped her eyes. "I don't think you've aged one bit."

"I still run and ride my bicycle. Sometimes I swim. I don't eat very good, but I don't care. You're looking good. You look tired, though. Do you get enough exercise? Don't you and Gary get out and do things?"

"Larry, Dad. His name is Larry. No, I'm not the exercising type, I suppose. He isn't either, I guess we're two peas in a pod."

"I see. Well, let's get to the right gate so we can get out of here. I never did like Dallas. I never really liked Houston either, but it's better than here. Have you eaten yet?"

"No, I didn't—"

"We can grab a hotdog on our way."

"A hotdog?"

"Yeah, what's wrong with a damn hotdog?"

"Well, they aren't very good for you."

"Neither is not exercising. You get a carrot or whatever you like, I'll get a hotdog. Unless I find donuts."

"Jesus," Ellie mumbled as they walked.

It wasn't hard for Ellie to understand why her mother had only put up with him for two years, but Ellie still adored him. He had tried to visit at least once a month as she grew up and she'd never wanted for anything. The only thing she ever knew for certain about him was that he worked long, hard hours and travelled often for his job. He was in the oil industry, but she wasn't sure what he did, and to her it didn't matter. To her, he was what she always wanted to be. Always in charge, always sure of himself, and always able to withstand any challenge. He could also be very stubborn and smug, and impossible to follow through an airport.

"Dad, would you slow down?"

"A bit much for you? Sorry. Let's go here, they've got those fries with chili on them."

"I'll pass, maybe I'll get one of those yogurts instead."

Edwin shook his head in bewilderment.

"So, is your daughter normal?"

"What?"

"Your daughter. Does she eat bacteria, too?"

"It's good for you. It's good for your digestion."

"So, are the chili fries, they'll go right through you."

"That's your measuring stick?"

"One of 'em."

"So, this surprise you have for me. It isn't a restaurant where I have to eat something like this, is it?"

"No, where we're going you can order anything you want."

"Really?"

"Really. You can order what you want, you can decorate any way you want, you can even be your own boss."

"I don't get it."

"You will. Come on, get your cup of germs and let's go."

Ellie smiled. It might take some time, but she was determined get used to his abrasive nature. She also hoped that he might mellow some once they had spent a day or two together. None of that was important now, she was going to focus on their trip to Fallon, Texas where she could learn all about his early days.

*****

Karen Trimble stood in the doorway of the manager's office, determined not to lose her temper. She watched in anger as the two women in the office chatted about a television sitcom while the nurse call bells chimed endlessly and the yells for help echoed down the hall of Fallon Nursing Home. Karen couldn't think of a polite way to interrupt and had never been known for subtlety.

"You don't hear those?" she asked calmly.

The two women ignored her and continued to talk.

"Excuse me? The alarms? You don't hear those?"

"I'm sorry, what are you asking about?" the woman sitting behind the desk asked.

"I'm wondering if you hear those alarms and all that yelling?"

"Yes, I hear them. What are you doing about it?"

"I'm trying to keep up with them, but I don't have a lot of help."

"I put ads in the paper and online, I don't know what else you expect me to do."

"Call in the temps, that's what they're for. And until then, it would be nice if you would help out. This is a nursing home and you're still a fucking RN, aren't you?"

"Karen, don't swear at me. I'm doing my job and if I'm on the floor, I'm not getting that job done."

"What job is that, sitting on your ass and bullshitting all day with the cook?" Karen looked at the cook, who was trembling in fear. "No offense, Grace, but her time would be better spent working than shooting the shit with you."

"I suppose I should get back to the kitchen—" Grace replied as she stood.

"I don't think I like your tone," the manager said.

"I don't think you have time to like or dislike my tone. It's almost four o'clock and the visitors will be arriving soon. I've got four people that I know need their diapers changed, two that have been vomiting for a while, and one pair who were making out in the chapel."

"What? Who were they?"

"It doesn't matter," Karen replied. "If you're that worried about it then go see for yourself."

"You just left them there?"

"Damn right I did, they're the only two people in this building who seem happy. Look, I've got work to do and maybe you can find time between stories to hand out meds."

Karen walked out of the door with her head held high, predicting to herself that within a week she would storm out of there again but with her final paycheck. It was the principle of the matter and finding another job had never been much of a challenge. She smiled as she passed the old couple holding hands while sitting on the porch swing by the entrance. They returned her smile, and it gave her a sense of hope that some day she, too, would find someone, even if it was for a short time in the back pew of a chapel.

*****

Ellie sat in the window seat, looking down at the trees and small ponds as they approached Houston. Edwin had insisted on sitting in the aisle for more leg room, which meant that a defenseless elderly woman was forced to sit between them.

"It's very pretty out there. When was the last time you were in Fallon?" Ellie asked.

"About twenty years ago, I came through while traveling," he replied.

"Traveling? Where all did you travel?"

"All over."

"All over where?"

"All over the United States," he grumbled. "You know, I sent you the pictures."

"Yes, pictures say a thousand words. Thank God, because you don't seem to have many today," Ellie sniped, but Edwin only nodded as he continued to play solitaire on his computer.

The woman between them sat motionless, doing her best not to get in harm's way. She thought about suggesting they exchange seats again, but as she looked over at Edwin, his stern demeanor quelled the idea.

Edwin's lack of communication wasn't new to Ellie, and his irritation with everything that moved made things even less tolerable. His nature ran contrary to everything for a man his age; he was active, driven, and terribly independent. He was quiet but temperamental and had an air of sophistication that could be misconstrued as arrogance. Ellie hoped that someday she would feel as confident as he looked. She reached her hand across the lady between them and gave his arm a light squeeze. The woman smiled approvingly.

"I love you, Dad."

"I know. When we get there, I've got a few things to do so I won't see you until tomorrow morning. Breakfast at eight in the lobby?"

"Yeah, that sounds good. And Dad?"

"Yes?"

"I love you."

"I heard you a moment ago. Thanks."

The woman between them sighed.

Chapter 2

Darla drove down the hill and parked her car behind an excavator at the old retreat. It was early, and she didn't think anyone would be coming out there now that the commotion had died down from yesterday. She desperately wanted to burn the place down but knew she'd be the first one they'd look for if she did.

Today, she thought, might be the last day she'd be free to look around the old place without being noticed. She'd been out here hundreds of times, scouring every nook and cranny for more of the 8mm films like the ones she found right after the place had closed. She knew there must be more of them, and maybe a lot more, but there was only one, maybe two that she was interested in. She made her way into the back door where the chain gave away just enough for her to squeeze in like she'd done almost daily for the last fifty-plus years.

Darla sat down on one of the old chairs inside, trying to decide where she might look today. She couldn't think of anywhere she hadn't looked, at least not in any of the obvious places. In fifty years, she could have torn all the plaster board and paneling off of every room in the retreat but she never had, and now she was too old and frail to do so and she regretted it.

Her emotions began to overwhelm her, remembering the things she'd seen on the old films. They didn't make movies like that back then, not that she was aware of and certainly not in Fallon. The sex, the perversion, and every kind of lust imaginable were on those films and they had been enough to incriminate at least a dozen people. She remembered well-to-do men and women exposed and shamed on the front page of the paper, their actions and offenses smeared across page after page of the Fallon Courier. That was when she had first begun to panic, after she'd seen what happened to so many people when she gave the films to the police to take the spotlight off of her. Since then she'd spent a few hours every day looking for more tapes, hoping to get rid of them, hoping to keep anyone else's past from being discovered.

*****

Edwin sat in the motel lobby eating his third donut in five minutes. He hated feeling rushed but his run had taken longer than usual because of a cramp in his right calf. He'd showered, shaved, and gone over his stock portfolio much faster than he would have liked, all in an effort to be down in the lobby on time. Edwin looked impatiently at his watch. He had just stood up and brushed the crumbs from his mouth when Ellie rounded the corner, still in her pajamas.

"What are you doing?" he growled.

"I came to get some breakfast, what are you doing?"

"I'm ready to go. I thought we agreed to meet here at eight for breakfast?"

"Yeah, it's a quarter after eight. I'm going to eat, take a

shower and fix my hair, and then we can leave. It won't take that long."

"Alright, call me on my cell when you're ready and I'll come pick you up," he replied. She knew he was irritated and decided she would try to appease him.

"Dad, I'll grab a bagel and get a quick shower."

"No, take your time." Edwin purposely tried to change his tone to mask his obvious frustration. "I've got plenty to look at, I can pick you up later."

Without waiting for a reply, he pushed his chair under the table and hurried through the door. Ellie sighed, knowing she should have gotten up with the wake-up call. She'd known exactly what he meant when they agreed to meet but had gotten distracted by emails and doing web searches, and now she regretted it. The confrontation was another in a litany of failures at trying to get his approval. She picked a few things from the continental breakfast, no longer feeling as hungry as she had just moments ago.

Ellie's phone rang and the caller ID showed the picture of a little boy with the name "JACK!" below it. His voice was just what she needed to cheer up.

"Hello, Jack," she said.

"Hi, Grandma. Where are you?" Jack asked.

"We're in Texas, where are you?" Ellie replied.

"We're at home, mom got me up early so I could call you before I went to daycare. When are you coming back to see me?"

"Soon, buddy. We're going to be gone for about a week and then I'll be back."

"Good, I don't like daycare, I'd rather stay with you."

"I know," Ellie said, feeling her heart sink a little. "Well, I promise when I get back, I'll let you stay with me for a few days. How's that?"

"Okay. Mom says I gotta go. I love you, Grandma."

"Love you, too. Be good for your mom."

"And my dad."

"Yes, and your dad. Bye now."

"Bye."

Ellie closed her eyes, now with something else to worry about. She'd taken some personal time from work and had spent a few weeks watching Jack while his mother worked. Only recently had Jack become close to her and nobody could explain why. As a toddler, he'd shunned Ellie which had pained her. Now that he wanted her love and attention, it would be difficult for both of them when she went back to work. He'd be starting kindergarten soon, but there were still those off days where some sort of daycare would be needed. His father refused to watch him during the day, claiming it kept him from focusing while he searched for a job, and it frustrated Ellie.

"Hello, miss," a voice said. An elderly woman with a pleasant smile stood beside her with her hands nervously clasped. Ellie recognized her as the motel clerk who had checked them in the night before.

"Hello," Ellie said.

"Was that your father that just left?"

"Yes, is anything wrong?"

"Edwin Kranz?"

"Yes, that's him."

"May I ask what your mother's name is?"

"Excuse me?"

"Oh, I know it seems like I'm being rude, but I was curious to know what your mother's name is. We knew Edwin and we wondered who he might have married."

"Really?" Ellie replied. It was an odd request yet the sweet and almost childish manner in which the woman asked made it impossible for Ellie to resist. "Her name was Lydia."

The woman frowned, puzzled by the response.

"Are you sure?"

"Yes, I'm quite sure."

Ellie had an urge to smile, the innocence and inquisitive nature of the woman was charming. Ellie refrained, not wanting to seem rude or condescending.

"I don't remember a Lydia. Was she from around here?"

"Uh, no, she was from Utah."

"Utah? Well for heaven's sake I would have never guessed. What on earth would he be doing in Utah, I wonder?" she asked with a laugh. "True to form, he did get around."

"Did he?"

"He was a dashing young man, your father was. Sort of."

"I am surprised."

"And what is your name, honey?"

"Eleanor, but I go by Ellie."

"Oh," the woman sang as she put her hand to her mouth. "That makes all the sense in the world! He would have loved that name because of…. well, we haven't seen Edwin in ages. What brings him back to Fallon?"

"He's just showing me where he grew up, kind of taking me on a tour of the city. What is it about the name Ellie—"

"How nice, getting to know his roots and yours, too! Do you like it here?"

"I really don't know, we just came in last night. We flew into Houston and drove up. The people here certainly seem nice."

"Well, thank you. My name is Ruth Zingg, by the way. May I?" she asked, pointing at an empty chair next to her. Ellie nodded. "I guess we all wondered what became of Edwin. Some said he was in the service, some people thought he might live overseas now. You know, some people thought he might've wound up in prison."

"My dad? That's funny. He's Mr. Straight-laced himself. No, he might get locked up for being a stuffed shirt but never for doing anything criminal."

"Really? Edwin Kranz?" Ruth asked with a doubting look, but she knew Ellie was sincere. "Well, of course not, bless your heart!"

"Yes, Dad was in the service for a while and after he and Mom divorced, he went to work for some oil company."

"I'd love to talk to him. When is he coming back?"

"I'm supposed to call him when I'm ready."

"I can have my nephew take you out to him, I'm sure he wouldn't mind."

"I have no idea where he is."

"I'm pretty sure I can guess. If not, then you can call him and my nephew can take you to meet him."

"Well, I don't want to put you out or anything."

"Oh, it's no trouble. My nephew would be glad to. Hold on here and I'll go ask him."

Ellie sat holding her coffee, sorry she'd said anything. Now she felt trapped and wanted desperately to run out of the lobby and to her room. Ruth was by the waffle maker talking to a man who looked to be in his mid-twenties. Both looked back at her as they talked and after a minute they came to her table.

"Ellie, this is Alton Chandler, a realtor and a good family man," Ruth said.

"Ms. Zingg, I really don't think this is necessary," Ellie said, but Alton had already extended his hand.

"Forgive my aunt, she gets all excited. But she told me who your father was and I'd be glad to help. I'm really looking forward to meeting him."

"He'll be coming back to get me, I just don't know when. Did you have an appointment with him or something? He didn't mention meeting anyone."

"Oh, uh, I thought he might be wanting to meet out at the retreat. I didn't know he'd be coming to town so this it's somewhat of a surprise for me."

"A retreat? I don't know anything about a retreat. Are you sure we're talking about my Edwin Kranz?"

"Yes, ma'am."

Ellie looked at the ground, frowning and trying to put the pieces together. None of this made any sense to her except when she considered how anxious her father had been to get out and about this morning. Ruth took the opportunity to nudge Alton and put her finger to her lips to keep quiet. After a moment, Ellie looked up at Ruth, who seemed like the least harmless person she'd ever met, and Alton, who was the essence of a spit-and-polish realtor and decided that there wouldn't be any danger in taking them up on the offer.

"Tell you what, I'll take my rolls up to my room and get cleaned up and meet you back down here in about twenty to twenty-five minutes?"

"I'll finish my breakfast," Alton said with a nod.

*****

The Fallon High School Class of '54 stuck together like glue. Even those who didn't like the rest were somehow sucked into the perpetual vortex that held them and their memories captive as the years went by. Even in death, their memories and scandals would live either like perennial flowers or open wounds. There was only one notable exception: Edwin Kranz. He'd walked away years ago without the courtesy of letting the rest of them get their pound of flesh before his departure. But that was about to change.

Ruth Zingg used her smile and a few nudges to make her way past the mourners to get to the end of the pew. Everyone who mattered in their clique was congregated on one side of the church where two windows had been opened. One allowed fresh, morning air in and the other provided Hester Jorgensen with a place to throw up from her psychosomatic withdrawals. Margie Thumpacker's funeral was scheduled for ten in the morning, precluding Hester from having her customary first drinks of the day. Darla McGee and Belle Chandler were sitting in the middle pew while Belle's husband, Cary, sat with Joan Campanella in the row ahead. Darla tried to keep some distance between Cary and Belle to avoid any public spats between them. Joan seemed to be the only one truly mourning for Margie, weeping quietly while Cary tried to put his arm around her.

"You're married," Joan said as she pushed Cary's arm away.

"Just trying to be nice, what the hell?"

"Guess who I saw this morning?" Ruth asked.

"Who? You're a goddamned busy body, you know that?" Belle said loudly.

The rest of the congregation became quiet for a moment and Darla patted Belle's hand. Cary turned around and glared at Darla.

"Can't you keep her quiet?"

"She's your wife, you keep her quiet,"

"I told you we shouldn't have brought her." Cary began.

"Who the hell is he?" Belle asked Darla, but when she didn't get an answer she looked up at Ruth. "Who the hell is this man?"

"That's your husband, Belle, now shut up, this is good," Ruth said. "I saw Edwin Kranz today."

"Oh, God forbid," Darla said with a sigh. "I'd hoped that this was all a bad dream. I was hoping he'd denounced his citizenship and run off with some foreign woman."

"Utah. He met a woman in Utah and married her. They've got at least one child, a girl. I met her this morning. Her name is Ellie, short for Eleanor. Kind of like an Eleanor we knew," Ruth said while hooking her thumb toward the casket. Darla's mind began to race.

"I bet he thought she was one of them polygamists. That boy couldn't ever be happy with one girl, always talking like he was some prized bull or something," Belle blurted.

"Now, Belle," Darla said, "Let's keep our hearts and our minds pure here."

"Wagging that tongue," Belle repeated, "Licking in the air like he was some kind of Casanova. Pure evil is what he was."

"Belle, your grandson, Alton, was there. He talked to Edwin's daughter, too. He's supposed to take her out to the Eros place by the lake. I figured that's probably where Edwin was headed to."

"Probably looking for a place to open a goddamned whore house," Belle griped.

The organist looked at the group with a scowl as he took his seat. He began playing the obligatory death medley that they had become so accustomed to hearing, only louder than usual in his attempt to drown out their conversation.

"It's almost sinful to be talking about him and that place in here," Darla said. "What in the world is he planning to do with that place?"

"I don't know that he was actually out there, but I had hunch. Plus, Alton was trying to make contact with him. He said he's never met the man, they did the deal through mail and the internet."

"If I said it once I said it a thousand times. We should have burned it down years ago after it ruined this city and its people."

"It didn't ruin anybody but you," Ruth said to Darla. "You were tolerable until that place opened and then you got all high and mighty, going off worse than your daddy ever did. Let's talk about something else, I don't want to get you started on your pulpit."

"I don't have a pulpit and I've never acted high and mighty. Doesn't it seem odd to any of you that Edwin's here in town and he's not at Margie's funeral? I mean, you all know why I ask, don't you?"

"Well, Edwin would probably never step into a church, I'm afraid," Ruth said.

"Maybe," Darla replied and shifted her eyes to the others. "But that isn't exactly what I was talking about."

"Darla, don't start gossiping now," Joan said.

Darla put her hands to her chest and pretended to gasp. She feigned innocence, hoping that someone would take her bait.

"Well spit it out, for Christ's sake," Cary said as he spun

around to face them. "Anything to shut you up."

Darla gave him a cold stare and then leaned in toward the middle of their group. The rest of them moved to get closer.

"Edwin had a thing for Margie," she said and each of them looked briefly over at the silver hair sticking up over the end of the casket, the only part of her they could see from their vantage point. "I understand that they may have seen each other secretly for about three months."

"Her mother would've killed her," Ruth said.

"No, her mother wanted her to see him. She said it was therapy for her. He supposedly spent quite a few nights over there, from what I hear, and a few mornings after."

"Therapy? What kind of therapy could that boy—" Ruth began to ask but Belle cut her off.

"Therapy, hell! He was interested more with getting under her skirt."

"Belle!" the women said in a chorus as the organist increased the volume. Belle sat without remorse, her Alzheimer's making her oblivious to any shame for what she'd said.

"How do you know this?" Ruth asked. "I have a hard time believing it, and goodness knows I'm not calling you a liar."

"She told me herself the day she died. I suppose she just wanted to get it off of her chest and she needed someone to tell it to. I just happened to be there."

"What kind of therapy could seeing that son-of-a-bitch make any sense?" Cary asked.

"Keep your voice down, there's her sister," Ruth said, and all eyes shifted to the back as Karen Trimble pushed her mother, Norma, up the middle aisle and stopped in front of the casket.

Karen helped Norma stand so she could see her sister one last time. The rest of the congregation looked on in pity as Norma's scarred and disfigured face contorted as she wept. Pastor Carl Hauswirth joined them, providing comfort for a few moments and then helping them to their seats in the front row.

"Good morning, brethren," Pastor Carl said quietly as he looked over at the group around Darla and Belle. He stared at them the way a patient parent stares at a delinquent child. "We're gathered here to pay our final respects to Margaret Eleanor Thumpacker, a beautiful and loving woman..."

"I'll finish later," Darla said, and the group turned their attention to Pastor Carl. Hester made one final retching sound, then pulled her head back in the window while wiping her mouth and taking her seat. She nodded to Pastor Carl, who smiled at her with sympathy.

Pastor Carl performed brilliantly as expected, noting the good works, faithful heart, and generosity of a woman he'd never met, expanding on a few notes someone had handed to him at the last minute. Margie's regular preacher, Pastor Hugh, had only outlived her by a few days and his prepared speech was forever lost in his lifeless mind. But given the choice, everyone would have rather heard from Pastor Carl than Pastor Hugh, simply because Carl gave better odds of getting into heaven. Many of the women Carl said eulogies over had once been his baby-sitters which provided almost a familial bond between them. Darla, however, had a palpable animosity toward him. He was the competition, there to usurp her attempt to perform God's work in Fallon. Worse still was the fact that her old classmates and acquaintances seemed to prefer him over her for their spiritual needs. It wasn't like her to let those things go by unnoticed, nor was it like Pastor Carl to care what Darla thought or did.

The hornet's nest Darla had stirred up about Margie worked out better than she could have ever planned. She'd planted the seeds, was interrupted before the payoff, and had to leave halfway through the eulogy because of Belle's behavior. Belle became unruly and when Cary tried to take her out, she slapped him. Darla quickly obliged, leaving the rest of the group hanging by a thread of gossip. At the end of the service, each of them took just a little bit longer in viewing Margie, the woman they thought they knew, for the last time and in a different way.

While the others were watching Margie being carefully lowered into the ground, Darla and Belle crested the hill and looked down at an old building on the edge of the lake.

"I don't see him out here," Darla said.

"See who?"

"Edwin. Ruth thought he might've come out here, but I don't see him. There's a car down there, though, I wonder if it's his."

"Let's go down there and find out. It's hot in this car, let's go swimming in the lake."

"We're too old to swim, honey. And let's just wait here, see if somebody comes out. I'd know that man in a second if he showed his face. I don't think it's him. I think Ruth's full of it."

"Full of what?"

"Never mind. Look at it, Belle." Darla pointed at the building. "Beelzebub's playground. Do you know where you're at? Does this place look familiar?"

"Bubba's what?"

"Beelzebub. The devil?"

"Why do you have to make everything hard. You and that damn daddy of yours with all those names."

"Do you know where you are?"

"We're out at the lake. It's getting hot, let's go inside there. I need some water."

"This place is closed for business. And do you see all those machines over there?" Darla asked while pointing at the bulldozers and crane. "They were supposed to push all of the ashes of this place into a big pile and get rid of everything once and for all."

"Why would they do that?"

Darla looked at Belle with pity. She didn't understand much these days with her Alzheimer's starting to erode her memory. Six months ago she would have told anyone that was willing to hear what had gone on in the old retreat. But now her secrets were getting harder to discover and she showed little interest in anything.

"It's been sitting all these years inches from foreclosure and in the last second the son of Satan bought it up. We should be mixing the ashes with cow manure right now, but there it stands," Darla snarled, shaking her bony fist in the air.

"Why cow manure?"

"Because it…never mind. Let's just sit here and get one last look. I can see it now, that big old wrecking ball over there knocking it down room by room and inch by sinful inch into one big pile. I would have lit the match myself. I told them let's knock it down and then set it afire the next morning just before dawn. It'd be like Easter sunrise. We could have lit up the predawn skies with the sweet smell of God's vengeance on the carousers and fornicators."

"I just want a glass of water."

"I'll get you one, just give me a few minutes."

"A few goddamn minutes."

"Don't say that, Belle! You know using the Lord's name in vain insults me."

Belle stared at her blankly for a long time. The empty look in her eyes made Darla wonder if she was about to apologize or if she simply wasn't able to follow the conversation.

"You're a bitch," Belle said, and then closed her eyes and leaned her head against the window.

Chapter 3

"So, how far do we have to go to get to this place?" Ellie asked. They seemed to have been driving through the woods for miles.

"Not much further, it's right on the lake in an area that they planned to develop a long time ago," Alton replied.

"Planned? That doesn't sound good."

"It's quite a nice area and there's beginning to be some interest out here again. Every other adjoining property around the lake has either been developed or is gearing up that way."

"So, what is it about this property?"

"I don't know. Something about the retreat we're going to."

"It's really a retreat?" Ellie asked.

"Yeah. It was actually called Eros Retreat although it was only in business a few months. My understanding is that it was the place to be for big shots and those with money. Sort of a

Playboy mansion before they had Playboy mansions."

"Is it haunted?"

"No," he laughed, "Nothing like that. Not that I know of anyway. But something happened, some kind of scandal brought the place to its knees. It's been closed ever since but it's in remarkable condition. I've never seen anyone out here, but somebody's been taking care of it until recently. My guess is that someone died or something and whoever was overseeing it was going to let it go into foreclosure rather than keep paying taxes on it."

"How long has it been shut down?"

"Fifty years? Sixty, maybe?"

"Interesting."

The car topped a hill where the trees abruptly ended and below was a building sitting by itself on the edge of the lake. She could see the fencing for a tennis court, a large building to the back that extended over the edge of the lake, and a large parking lot. There were acres of well-manicured land around it and sidewalks surrounding the footprint of the property. The design of the building seemed more like that of a cottage than the three-story building it was, giving it the air of a home instead of a retreat or hotel.

"Wow," Ellie said in a whisper.

"Wow is right. It's a charmer to say the least. It's dated inside, though, and I think that's what scares people away. There's a lot to be done to update it and make it usable again."

"I wish you a lot of luck. I sure as hell couldn't afford this if that's why we're out here."

"No, not quite," Alton said with a smile.

"How much would it take to buy this thing?"

"Two point three million was the price with everything involved. That covered the building and the taxes."

"You're really fighting the odds trying to unload this place."

Alton refrained from telling her that her father had already purchased the place. He'd let the cat out of the bag the day it was supposed to be torn down against Edwin's wishes, but thought better about telling Ellie. He wasn't sure if she already knew but he wasn't going to take any chances at drawing the ire of Edwin.

"I've always been an optimist, much to the displeasure of that woman there," Alton said as they drove past a car. There were two women inside, the driver glaring at Alton and the passenger asleep.

"Who is that?"

"Someone who hoped the place wouldn't get sold. She hates this place and wants nothing more than for it to get bought by the city and razed. Her father was the Baptist preacher here in town for the longest time, a real fire-and-brimstone kind of man. She takes after him except she's a bit more vicious about it. At least that's what I've heard, but I've heard it from everyone. Anyway, you'd think sin was invented here if you talked to her. The other woman was my grandmother."

"Look down there, my dad's car. Now how did your aunt know he'd be here?"

"I'm sure we're about to find out. My aunt said he had some ties here a long time ago."

"That's odd. Dad's kind of a stuffy guy, I've never seen him be nostalgic about anything."

Alton pulled under the carport close to where Edwin was standing. Edwin had been staring at the car with contempt until he saw Ellie in the passenger seat and his face broke out into a big smile.

"Dad, what are you doing out here?"

"Looking the place over, I'm glad you made it out. How did you know I was here?"

"The lady at the front desk said you might be out here and she had her nephew bring me out."

"Who the hell is the lady at the front desk?" Edwin asked. His mood went from cheerful to cautious.

"Ruth Zingg, Mr. Kranz. She's my aunt. Do you remember her?"

"I do, so what?"

"She said she knew you and thought you'd be out here. I'm Alton Chandler."

"Did you say anything to Ellie about this?" Edwin asked.

"No, sir," Alton replied.

"Good, don't go anywhere. Ellie and I will be a while."

Edwin took Ellie by the arm and started leading her to the front door of the building when Alton called out to them.

"I've got a key for you if you'd like to see inside."

"We can get in, don't worry about it. The door is busted, you can walk right through."

"It wasn't like that yesterday when I was out here. I wonder how that happened?"

"I broke it, don't worry about it."

"But I have a key."

"Well, hold onto it. It might fit the other doors if you want to try. We'll be back in a bit. Don't go anywhere."

"Yes, sir," Alton said and then began mumbling to himself. "I've got a damn key right here, why would he bust down the door? The man is nuts."

Inside Edwin turned on his flashlight which revealed the ornate interior of the old building.

"Incredible," Ellie said. "They definitely catered to the upper crust. And in a gaudy way, too."

"What do you know about this place?"

"Alton said it was a not-so-nice place."

"I see. Well, that was in the past and this is your future."

"What?"

"Right here," Edwin said as he shined the light through a doorway, "A big kitchen. It needs updating, just like everything else. You can have anything you want to eat. This grand entrance here, all of the rooms and everything outside. You can decorate any way you like."

Ellie looked at him as if he had gone out of his mind.

"I don't get it."

"You told me over the phone last month that you were frustrated with your job. You said that no nursing home should be run like that and if you had your own it would be the best. Well, here it is."

"You're kidding? Dad you don't just open... I mean... wait a minute. Let me catch my breath."

"Take your time, it's not going anywhere."

"Dad, wait a minute. Do you know how much this place costs? And the taxes and—"

"Yes, I do. I have a budget for renovation and a contractor and everything. We just need your input."

Ellie opened and closed her mouth several times, trying to say something but not knowing where to start. She alternated putting her hands on her hips and turning, trying to see in different directions and then rubbing her head.

"So, I would up and move from Phoenix to do this. Have my own nursing home that used to be a bordello, for lack of a better term. I guess Larry should give up his business on a whim and come here, too?"

"Are you two still an item?"

"He's still my husband, yes."

"Then it would only be fitting for him to come here, too. You'll need a handyman and caretaker."

"I don't know what to say, this is just out of the blue."

"Why don't we look around and let's see what you think."

"Right now all I can think is how much money—"

"Forget about the money. I've got money, don't worry about it."

"How much do you have?"

"Enough for a few more lifetimes. Now quit stalling and let's look around."

Ellie took a closer look around the kitchen. Across the hall was a large room filled with tables and chairs, big enough for an activity room. From the back door she could see the outline of a pool that was filled in with dirt, and next to that what might have been a shuffleboard area. There was a disheveled dock and a boat house down by the water.

"We'd have to put in elevators," Ellie said.

"So, you're starting to put a checklist together? Good, but you can take elevators off the list. There's three."

"Three?"

"One right here across from the kitchen and dining area and one on each end of the building."

"Really? How long have you been checking this place out?"

"I've been here before."

"Before, as in this morning?"

"No, years ago."

"When it was a one of 'those places'? I don't think I want to know why."

"It isn't what you think."

"So, let's look at the rooms. Are they all the same?"

"Most of them, each floor has a few suites and each level has a large gathering area in the middle, just like the grand foyer right here at the entrance."

"There's some beautiful woodwork and detail here, I... wait a minute. Why are we even talking about this? Do you realize the work involved, the licensing, and all of that stuff? Who's going to supervise it? And what am I supposed to do for a living while all that's going on?"

"I have a contractor in mind. You tell him what you want, you can communicate through email. Come down here and inspect when you want, I'll pay for it. Keep working at your job for now and Gary—"

"Larry."

"Larry can slowly wind up what he's doing. Why don't you

call him now?"

"And tell him what? I can't just call out of the blue and ask him if he wants to turn his life upside down."

"Won't know until you've tried."

Ellie bit her bottom lip and looked around again. She began to envision different colors on the walls, fresh furniture and pictures. But most important, she saw an opportunity to do the job of caring for the elderly the way she thought it should be done and in a beautiful environment. She gave her father a menacing glance.

"This is such a big gamble."

"And you can't lose at this one. What's the worst that can happen, you have to go back to work for someone else?"

"Yeah."

"Just like you're going to do at the end of the week when our trip is over?"

"Look, don't try to make sense of this. Women don't operate that way. You're eighty, you should know better."

"You're my daughter, you should be thinking like me."

"That's scary. Give me a minute," she said as she pulled out her phone. "I need some privacy, I'll meet you outside in a minute. Or two. Give me a while."

"Tell Gary I said hello," Edwin said as he walked to the front door.

"It's Larry!"

"Whatever."

*****

The afternoon tea at Fallon Nursing Home was late due to the funeral. Darla had everything set up by the time Joan and Ruth arrived. Hester had excused herself after the service to catch up on cocktail hour and Cary was, as usual, nowhere to be seen. Eloise Laine pushed herself in her wheelchair into the Tea Room to join the others while Darla sat quietly fuming, dying for someone to ask her to finish her story.

"What do you remember about him, Eloise?" Ruth asked.

Eloise always had something interesting to say, and since she hadn't made it to the funeral the other ladies were anxious to talk to her.

"Oh, that's easy. It's been over sixty years since I last saw him but I'll never forget that night we went out. I told him 'Don't even think about putting my hand down there.' He pouted the rest of the night. Dropped me off at ten-thirty saying he had a job appointment the next morning. But I knew better, he just wanted someone to give him some lovin' and run off. Well, I let him have the runnin' off part!"

The other ladies laughed, some shaking their heads, others nodding from their own experiences. Eloise kept looking out of the corner of her eye at Darla to see if she could get a rise out of her, but Darla looked annoyed by something else.

"We're talking about sex, Darla, let us know if you need something explained. Anyway, that boy was up to no good as soon as he hatched. Used to come up to me and say he had a secret to tell me and then he'd stick his tongue in my ear."

"You're kidding!" Joan cried as she held her hands to her mouth.

"Not one bit. Nasty, I tell you! He didn't pass up any opportunity, used to come up behind me and hold my arms by my side to try and do that. He was constantly sticking his tongue out when I passed him in the hall and I'd cover my ears," she said and then lowered her voice. "Of course, I wasn't about to tell him I liked it."

"You little tramp!"

Darla had pulled her notepad from her purse and was writing, glancing up periodically to see if anyone was noticing.

"Hey," Eloise barked, "What are you writing over there? Hey, Darla, I said what are you writing?"

"Nothing. I'm just writing down some appointments I have, that's all."

"Well stop doing it. You'll be blabbing every word of this if you remember it. Why don't you go save somebody? Anyway, all he had to do was pretend that he liked me and I probably would have let him do what he wanted. I always wanted to see what he had down there."

They all giggled except for Darla, who breathed a sigh of relief. Eloise's bullseye had been taken off of her after she'd put her pad away, but Darla was still taking mental notes when Joan began to comment.

"I must admit, there were times that I envied the rest of you," Joan said. "I know he was crude, but I was so jealous that he never asked me out or tried anything with me. I just wanted that one chance to say 'No'."

"You weren't a challenge to him," Eloise said. "You were too insecure and he wanted a fighter and by God he got one with me!"

"Are you saying I would have been easy? I could have stood up to him, too."

"No, I'm not saying that. Hell, I was the one that was easy. Joan, stop taking everything so personal. He just didn't like meek girls."

"Or maybe he had you figured out before everyone else," Darla said, but with enough emphasis that it quieted the room.

"What? What do you mean?" Joan asked.

"He was quite intuitive, you know. Maybe he knew you might not have been interested in boys at all."

Joan turned red and her hands began to shake.

"Darla, mind your manners, you little shit. What do you know about men anyway?" Eloise asked.

"I know I prefer them over women."

"Ever been with one?"

"Doesn't matter. It's just that anything other than a man and a woman would be sinful. You probably have a different opinion on that, don't you Joan?"

There was a gasp throughout the room as Joan glared at Darla with red, teary eyes, her hands covering her mouth. Darla stared back at her, nodding her head up and down.

"Darla, stop it," Joan begged. "Why must you do these things? Why must you spread your hate for life to everyone else?"

"Because she's a frustrated, miserable woman who wants everyone else to suffer the way she does, that's why," Eloise said.

"I'm only speaking the truth. We should all come to terms with the past before we have to answer to a higher calling," Darla said.

"My God, you are dreadful. Who are you to tell me what I should do? And when are you going to face the facts that you're nothing more than a busybody gossip that hides behind that Bible of yours!" Joan screamed and then rushed out the door.

Darla stood still, defiant, with her chin raised in the air, but it was easy to see that she was shaken by Joan's words. The rest of the group looked at her, half in loathing and half in fear.

"Why can't you leave well enough alone, Darla? You've got plenty of money and you've got friends all around you if you'd just quit attacking us," Eloise said.

"I'm not attacking anyone. I'm helping people find their way to Heaven. Don't you think she'll feel better when she's not living under that cloud of deceit and sin?"

"No, I think she's embarrassed and hurt. What you did shouldn't be done in public and it ain't your calling to bring it out of her. She's right, you hide behind that Bible of yours to do your dirty work."

"No, I don't. I love each and every one of you like sisters. It would break my heart if I thought I ever hurt any of you maliciously. I truly hope you believe that."

"We don't. You're a conniving hussy that we can't get rid of. You're like a damn hemorrhoid that keeps popping out."

Darla looked hurt but still stood defiant in the face of the others, who seemed to gain strength in Eloise's words and now looked at Darla with reproach.

"Now, let's get this out in the open so we're not all taking off in different directions wondering what this is all about," Ruth said. "We know you're dying to tell us what Joan did, so tell us and get it over with."

"Well then, here's what I understand…" Darla began.

Darla recounted the story that Margie had told her, adding a bit of seasoning to ensure the proper emphasis was put where needed. When she finished, there were troubled looks on the faces of the others, but it was hard to determine whether it was because of the story or Darla's ability to uncover it.

"I guess we shouldn't be surprised," Eloise said, breaking the silence that had fallen over them. "We all probably thought we were normal in our time. I suppose we had to expect that things like this were happening. And so what? Keep this to yourselves, girls. Joan's none the worse for us knowing it in my opinion. She's a sweetheart and you all know it. Don't be blabbing this to anyone else, Darla."

"She's a sinner, she should repent," Darla countered, upset that nobody was as shocked as she wanted them to be.

"Ye who are without sin… you know what I'm talking about. I may be in a wheelchair but I'll bash your little head in with a rock if you don't keep this to yourself," Eloise warned again, but Darla was unswayed.

"You asked me to tell you, you're no better than me."

"I don't care, I'm not gonna use it against her, not like you did. Now let's tend to our other business."

"What business is that?" Ruth asked.

"Let's go wait for Edwin Kranz to show up at the motel."

Chapter 4

Edwin was annoyed and ready to take the first flight out of town. He'd let Alton take Ellie back to the motel while he drove around to cool off. The whole trip had been a ploy to get her down here to see the building and entice her to open a nursing home, but now that she'd turned him down he didn't feel like doing all the other things he'd promised.

Edwin had an affinity for the old building. His first and only visit there had been a cleansing of the soul, an unexpected gift to take his mind off a broken heart. Throughout the years the memories of the retreat had called to him, but it wasn't until now that he'd found his own use for it. He wanted it to be home but it was too big for him to live there himself. Plus, he feared that if he had another stroke there would be nobody to take care of him. That's where Ellie came in as a nurse and caregiver. She could take care of him if he became unable to do it himself and she would have a business to call her own.

Edwin drove through town looking for familiar places he'd known in his youth. Many of them were gone, having fallen to age and rot, and some had been razed to make way for newer buildings or parking lots. The old theater in the town square still stood but was in complete disrepair. The thought of buying and refurbishing it flashed through his mind. It wasn't the idea of making any money from it, the mega-theaters were too popular to do that, but it was the memories he wanted to recreate. That idea vanished when he saw a drunk vomiting on the sidewalk in front of its entrance.

Four hours had passed since he'd left Ellie at the retreat and he was getting hungry. Edwin drove back to the motel, and as he walked through the entrance, two women sitting in the lobby stood and one began to approach him.

"Edwin?" Ruth said. "Edwin Kranz?"

"Yes?" he replied hesitantly.

"Do you remember me? Ruth Zingg?"

"I do," Edwin replied. He smiled, but it was forced. He wanted to be polite, but he also wanted to run as quickly as he could.

"We were hoping we'd see you. You remember—"

"Darla McGee," she interrupted. She had a smug look on her face as she approached him. Ruth's smile seemed to disappear when Darla spoke.

"I'm not surprised."

"Why do you say that?" Darla asked.

Edwin dismissed her with a question of his own. "And who is that? Is she with you?" Edwin pointed to a woman who was almost hidden in the corner. Darla turned to look and saw Joan timidly start to walk toward them.

"Well that's—"

"I wasn't asking you," Edwin said as he turned to Joan. "Did you forget how to talk? Come over here."

"Joan Campanella, Edwin. Remember me?" she asked, but

shrank back into the corner when Darla leered at her.

"Yes, that's Joan. I'm guessing you know why she's happy to see you?"

"So, do you speak for all of them now?" he asked. Darla folded her arms in defiance but said nothing. "You haven't been waiting for me, have you?"

"We were at Margie Thumpacker's funeral, God rest her soul, and I mentioned that I'd seen you last night when you checked in," Ruth replied.

"Ruth said you were here in town and I thought that you might like to know that, seeing how you two were an item back then," Darla said.

"We weren't an item, just friends."

"You lived with them for a while, didn't you? Why else would you have been there?"

"I needed a place to stay; they opened their home to me. I think you'd be hard pressed to find any sin in that, but I wouldn't put it past you to try."

"They just up and said 'Edwin, you can stay here as long as you like', is that it?"

"My God, Darla, the man barely stepped in here and—" Ruth began but Darla flashed a look of anger.

"Actually, yes," Edwin said. "It was the Christian thing to do, don't you think? I'm guessing you're still into that."

"From what I hear it wasn't exactly—"

"It wasn't exactly any of your business, Darla. And since you weren't there, you shouldn't rely just on what you heard. You're still as self-righteous as ever, aren't you?"

"I call it devout," Darla said while reaching up and touching the cross hanging from her neck. "So, what brings you to Fallon? We're surprised you would ever show your face here again."

"Darla!" Ruth scolded, then turned her attention to Edwin. "Do you remember when you used to run up behind us in school and—"

"Don't encourage him! We don't need to hear about his old antics."

"Nor do you need Darla speaking for you anymore."

Edwin waved again at Joan to come over. He held his arms open and embraced her, kissing her forehead as she put her head against his chest. She began sobbing as she clutched the lapels of his jacket.

"Joan, it's good to see you."

"I'm so sad, Edwin. You know I always loved her."

"I know, you were a very special person to her. I didn't know she'd died."

Edwin looked up and saw that Ruth had gathered around him while Darla kept her distance, seething at the comfort he was providing. He gave Ruth and Joan a hug and stepped back.

"It's good to see the two of you."

"Eloise couldn't make it," Ruth said. "Her son showed up before we left but she wanted a full report."

"Eloise. Now there's someone I haven't thought of in a while. How is she?"

"Ladies," Darla said impatiently and both of them stepped away from Edwin. He was amazed at how they cowered to her voice alone. Darla stiffened her back and tried to speak more calmly. "Edwin, how long to you plan to be here?"

"Does it matter?"

Darla shrugged her shoulders, but Edwin was getting tired of her tone.

"I'm showing my daughter around, she's never been here."

"Your daughter? And where is she, I'd like to meet her?"

"I'm not sure at the moment. The last I saw of her she was out at the retreat."

"I heard that you bought the place. Is that true?"

"Yes."

"What business do you have with that place and why is your daughter out there? Haven't you told her about—"

"There's nothing to tell and it's my business, not yours," Edwin said as the front doors of the motel opened, drawing their attention the people coming in.

"Well there's Alton and can I take this to be your daughter?" Darla asked. Edwin nodded. "Well praise be to God, the daughter to Edwin Kranz."

"Praise who?" Ellie replied coolly.

"God, of course. You do believe in the Almighty, don't you?"

"Some, but I don't give him credit for every offspring that comes along. Do you?"

"I... well I—" Darla stammered.

Edwin stood silent, ready to jump in if necessary. But he was both amused and proud of the way Ellie was handling herself.

"Ellie Mintzer," Ellie said, offering her hand in a provoking manner. "And you are?"

"Darla McGee. I knew your father in high school. Has he told you about his shenanigans?"

"No, I'd like to think that we've all had our times and most of us outgrow them."

"Let's just say that we were all very surprised that he would come back at all, given some of the things he pulled," Darla said.

"What would he be coming back to, idle gossip and busybodies who had nothing else in life to do? I don't think you know him as well as you think," Ellie replied. Darla's reddening face was showing through her layers of makeup. The other women, however, seemed to be enjoying the banter. "I'm not inferring that that has happened, mind you."

"No, I suppose you aren't. But pray tell, Edwin," Darla said as she turned to him, "What business do you have out at the retreat? I would've thought you'd seen enough of that place."

"I told you before, it's none of your business. Regardless, I think there's still some use in that building."

"Well you certainly got your share of use from it, if memory serves me correctly."

"And you'd also remember that you were an employee there and part of everything that happened."

"I beg your pardon! I never—" Darla said in a loud voice, her veins bulging from her frail, thin neck.

"Let's talk about something else," Ruth said. "I think it's wonderful to have Edwin pay us a visit and Ellie, you're just the spitting image of your mother."

"You knew my mother?" Ellie asked.

"Well, no, but I'm guessing," Ruth replied nervously. "Edwin, I think it'd be wonderful for someone to do something with that old building. What have you got in mind?"

"I'm just putting some ideas together, we'll see."

"Mr. Money Bags comes in and buys the whole town," Darla said with a sneer.

"Not the whole town, but that building will suffice. Are you still interested, Dad?" Ellie asked.

Edwin almost lost his balance and wondered what might have changed Ellie's mind. But that passed in less than a second and he was ready to act.

"We just decided," Edwin said. "We're going to turn the retreat into a nursing home."

"Have we got a deal?" Ellie stuck out her hand with a bold look in her eye.

"You bet we do," Edwin said as he took her hand and kissed her on the forehead. Ellie was having difficulty containing herself in front of the others as she watched her father walk to the elevator.

Ellie smiled at Darla, who was furious. Ellie didn't know what was going on between Darla and her father, but the hostility was clearly between the two of them and not the others.

"I think your father may be in for a very big surprise," Darla snarled.

"I think there will be plenty of surprises to go around," Ellie replied. "Good day, ladies."

"Edwin," Joan called out before he could get in the elevator. Ellie winked at him as she passed by. Joan walked up and motioned to him to lean over. She cupped her hands and whispered, "Norma was there at the funeral and—"

"Don't say it. Thank you, but I don't need to know."

Joan looked hurt, but she nodded, understanding as Edwin made his way to the door for the stairs.

Ellie had waited until the elevator doors closed before she shut her eyes tightly and began pumping her fists in the air. She'd fallen in love with the retreat the moment she saw it but up until a few minutes ago hadn't felt the courage to go through with her father's idea.

For Ellie, this trip was supposed to fill in the gaps of the very few things she knew about her father and to build a connection they'd never had. He and her mother had divorced when Ellie was two and his infrequent visits only added to her desire to know him better. Edwin had always provided for her needs and she'd never wanted for anything but his love. During the rare times they did spend together, he was reserved, strict, and often critical of her passive yet spirited nature. For years she'd tried to emulate his character, learning that it put people off more than anything else. She'd hoped this trip would bring them together and put their relationship in perspective, and perhaps answer the question of why he was the way he was. He could be cold, demanding, and sometimes brutal in his desire to distance himself from others. Yet today he had displayed his trust and confidence in her with his offer and the sudden realization of that changed her mind. She felt it was his way to show his love and acceptance, which was all she had ever wanted from him. And she knew she'd made a connection with him that few others ever had.

For Edwin, being in Fallon again was beginning to feel like being on the edge of a black hole in space that was pulling him and all of his energy into it faster and faster. He wanted to be there, to die there, at the old retreat, but he hadn't given any thought about the people that he'd left so long ago. He thought most of them would have died by now or had moved on in life. But in some ways, it seemed that time stood still and that there were loose ends that the others needed to have tied up for them. There was a cry from those on the inside begging him to join them, protect them, but most important of all, give them hope as time and age made fewer things possible. He was a glimpse of what was, and for some of them who still had a penchant for fantasy, what could be.

*****

Even sitting in a booster seat, Jack Hartford could barely see over his father's shoulders as he drove. He loved looking through the front windshield, or what he could see of it, mimicking his father's turning of the steering wheel. He even pretended to put his arm out to caress the shoulder of a pretend girl, just like his father did to his mom, Valerie.

"Momma, when is Grandma coming back to see me?"

"She's only going to be gone for a few days, Jack. She's with Great-Grandpa Edwin, they're visiting a few places."

"Are they visiting his wife?"

"Whose wife?"

"Grandpa Edwin's."

"No, he doesn't have a wife. Remember I told you that he was married to my grandma once?"

"Yeah, but then he went to make oil or something."

"Yes, to drill oil."

"Where does he live?"

"In Tennessee, somewhere a long ways from here."

"Why does he live there?"

"I don't know, maybe he likes it there. He likes to hike and take his boat out, and —"

"He has a boat? I want to go see him," Jack said.

"Someday, sport," Tim replied. "If Daddy ever gets a job with a big school maybe we can afford to go on a vacation."

"You could be my teacher, Daddy. We like to color and sing and we're learning to count," Jack said.

"Daddy's a college teacher, Sport. I teach grownups."

"You could teach kids, too."

"Yeah, and I could hate myself a little more every day," Tim mumbled under his breath.

"It'd be nice if you got that job in Austin," Valerie said.

"I'd rather be in the northeast; it's too hot here in the south."

"I don't care where we wind up, it'd just be nice to have some insurance coverage."

"You worry too much."

Valerie looked at him with dismay. He never took things seriously and his outlook on life was a little too carefree and lofty for her comfort. It had been an attractive quality when they first met, but with Jack now in the picture she knew they had to be more responsible. She was beginning to see the wisdom of her parents and their frugal ways, especially since it was all she could do to keep the finances in order and food on the table. The best she could find was a part-time job and Tim only wanted to look for Ivy League positions. "Here, I'll give you something to think about instead," Tim said as he reached over and began to slide his fingers between the buttons of her shirt.

"Keep your hands on the wheel, Tim, and for God's sake stop tailgating," Valerie scolded.

"I'm not tailgating, we've got—" Tim began but slammed on the brakes.

"Shit," Valerie said. She didn't say it loudly and she didn't sound frightened, just resigned.

The truck in front of them had come to a sudden stop and within seconds their Mini Cooper would slide under the back of the trailer. Jack would spend the rest of his life trying to recall the events that happened between then and when he was pulled out by witnesses, just before the car burst into flames. All he could remember seeing was blood and hair on the headrests in front of him and then a blur of faces trying to comfort and shield him from the carnage before the ambulances arrived.

*****

Alton sat in the lobby feeling tense about meeting with Edwin. The last time he had seen him was at the retreat, storming off after Ellie had turned him down. It wasn't as if Edwin could back out of the transaction at this point, but Alton hated confrontation and hard feelings. He hadn't understood Edwin's intentions until this morning and still hadn't spent even a minute alone with him since the sale went through. The elevator doors opened and Edwin stepped out, smiling as he made eye contact with Alton. Alton took a long, cleansing breath and relaxed.

"Mr. Kranz, it's good to sit down alone with you after all of this."

"All of what? I bought a building, that's all."

"Well, it's a big building and, uh, I understand that you and Ellie are going to make a go of the nursing home project."

"I suppose. You still have that key you were talking about earlier?"

"Yes, sir," Alton said as he presented a folder full of papers to Edwin. "There's an envelope on top that has a key inside, and that's all the paperwork that's left."

"Thanks," Edwin said as he turned to walk away.

"Anytime. And by the way, my grandmother can't wait to see you. She hasn't been the same since I told her you were buying the old retreat."

"Do I know your grandmother?"

"I think so. Isabelle Chandler, or Belle as most people call her. She would have been Isabelle Bergen when you knew her." Alton saw Edwin take in a huge breath, his eyes growing wider and looking guarded. "Are you okay, Mr. Kranz?"

"Yes, I knew her."

"She definitely has a particular fondness for you."

"A fondness?"

"Oh yeah, but she didn't mention anything more. She's got Alzheimer's and sometimes things escape her. It's funny, she said that this place would be perfect for you and she appears to be right."

"Did she now?"

"Yeah," Alton said with a chuckle, "She also said that you owed her. That was really funny. In her mental state remembering so far back that you owed her something."

"Funny as hell," Edwin said, irritated.

The front doors of the motel opened and Alton's daughter ran to him and jumped in his lap. Alton's wife stopped at the front counter carrying a small child in her arms.

"The family," Alton said. "I've got a little girl of my own. She's like Ellie, she thinks she's the boss."

Ellie appeared from around the corner and Alton felt it was an opportune time to escape.

"Here's my little girl now. We're going to go out for dinner."

"I promised my wife a celebratory dinner tonight, but I wanted to say thanks," Alton said as he offered his hand. Edwin shook his hand but gave him a wary look. "Good night, Ellie, and congratulations."

"Thank you," Ellie replied.

As soon as Alton had left the building, Ellie sat down across from her father.

"You don't look happy."

"Don't worry about it. Are you ready for dinner?" Edwin asked.

"Come on, something's wrong."

"No, just something Alton mentioned."

"You still want to do this, right? I'm super excited now.

Nervous as hell, but super excited."

"Don't worry, I still want to do it. There's a few things I didn't take into account coming down here, but over time those things will take care of themselves."

"Over time? How much time?"

"Long enough for the other pains in the ass around here die off."

"Dad! That's mean."

"You don't think that Darla McGee wouldn't like to see me six feet under?"

"Well, those other women in here earlier seemed awfully happy to have you here," Ellie teased.

"Darla's trouble. Watch your back with her."

"I noticed. Did you stand her up a long time ago or something?"

"No, her daddy was a preacher and it rubbed off on her. But she's vicious about it, probably handles serpents for fun." Ellie laughed but he knew that she took his advice seriously. "I was proud of the way you stood up to her."

"Thanks. I'm hungry, how about you?"

"Same here."

"How about some Italian.... Wait a minute, my phone's vibrating. Caller ID says it's some sheriff's department. Did you kick in some other glass doors today?" Ellie teased.

She pushed the talk button on her phone and put it up to her ear.

"Hello?"

*****

There was a funeral, a gathering of friends and relatives at what was now Jack's apartment, and a decision to take him and all of his belongings to live with Ellie and her husband, Larry. Everything moved quickly, faster than he could comprehend, and the answers to his questions were just as vague as the faces that stood in front of him telling him how sweet he was and how someday everything would be all right. But while everyone else was busy creating their own solace, Jack kept a watch on the front door, truly expecting his parents to arrive from wherever it was they had suddenly disappeared to.

Chapter 5

Karen Trimble watched from across the desk as the social worker studied the notes on his computer screen. He looked to be in his early twenties, fresh out of college, and ready to change the world and all of its perceived injustices; just the kind of person that irritated Karen the most.

"So, you were displaced from work eight weeks ago?" he asked.

"I was fired, yes," Karen replied.

The social worker winced at her reply and Karen wasn't sure if it was from the word 'fired' or the abrupt way she'd said it.

"Very well. What have we been doing since then to find employment?"

"I've been putting out resumes and applications. I'm not sure what you've been doing about finding some help for my mother. I don't know if I mentioned it, but my Aunt Margie died recently and she used to help watch after her while I worked."

"I'm sorry to hear that."

"Yeah, well, I'm sorry, too."

"No success with the job hunting, huh? That surprises me, they seem to be begging for nurses out there."

"What can I tell you?" Karen asked as she shrugged her shoulders. "If they wanted me I wouldn't be in here."

"I see."

He wasn't sure but thought he was beginning to understand what the problem was. He leaned back in his chair for a moment, trying to think of a solution.

"So, I can still get my unemployment checks for now?" Karen asked.

"Yeah," he replied, "But I'd also like to suggest a workshop that might help."

"What kind of workshop? I'm a fucking nurse. Do you know how much training and experience I've got?"

"Oh, no, no, no! Not that kind of workshop, this is different. It's more designed to help with your interviewing skills and workplace relationships."

"No, forget it. I don't need a workshop, I need a place that doesn't have its head up its ass. Now, if you don't mind, can we find some kind of care for my mother so I can at least go out to find a job?"

The social worker sighed, looking as though all four years of his academic training and altruistic vision had been shredded into the pile of worthless inevitability that his parents had warned him about.

"I'll do my best," he replied.

*****

It had been a few months since Alton Chandler had spoken in person with Edwin and he wanted to leave a better impression than when he brought Ellie out to the retreat for the first time. He straightened his tie and tried to look as professional as he could before Edwin came through the door.

"Mr. Kranz, let me first say that I'm sorry for your loss."

"I appreciate that, let's get down to business. What did your guy say?"

"About three million."

"You're kidding? For that old building?"

"That's what he said. The building itself is a million and then to renovate it with new seating and and the lobby, not to mention all new projectors and a screen. It is in the town square, so that means a lot of traffic at a premium price."

"Shit. Alright, I'll think about it. You'd think restoring an old movie house wouldn't take that much. I'm lucky to have gotten the retreat."

"I'd like to have your luck. Do you mind me asking how you did it?"

"Did what?"

"How you made your money."

"I went to work in the oilfields. I met a man who was real slick and talked me into giving him about a third of everything I made as an investment. I did that for about eight years and then all of a sudden I stopped hearing from him. Lesson learned, but I kept working and saving my money."

"You didn't do all this by working in the oilfields?"

"No. When I was about sixty I got a phone call from that man. He'd invested it alright and he'd also found religion. He said he'd lost sight of what was right for a long time but saw the light and gave me my share. Turns out he was very successful, we were successful, and subsequently I became very wealthy."

"Religion is a good thing, sounds like."

"It's a tool that some people use. Sometimes it works for you, sometimes against you. It's mostly in your head."

*****

Hester Jorgensen was sad, and though that wasn't unusual, today was particularly difficult. She'd begun shaking by nine that morning and had felt the need for a gin and tonic before her lunch. Being both a diabetic and an alcoholic at her age was rare; at seventy-seven years old she should have been dead by now. Today was different and she was scared. Her feet were numb to the point she was afraid to walk and she needed to eat. She picked up the phone and dialed the number on the business card.

"Darla?" she asked into the phone.

"Yes, who is this?" Darla replied.

"It's Hester Jorgensen."

"Hester? Hester Jorgensen?"

"Yes, that's me."

"Yes, Hester. What can I do for you?"

"At the church. At the AA meeting that you organized. You said that if I ever needed anything to give you a call and I'm kind of in a rut right now."

"A rut? What kind of rut? Are you vomiting out of a church window again?" Darla asked.

Hester knew that Darla hated her being an alcoholic and never minded showing it. Still, she needed the help and swallowed her pride.

"If you remember, I'm a diabetic and I need to eat but I'm having difficulty walking right now."

"Don't you think you should call an ambulance?"

"Well, I suppose I could. I'm not having trouble with my sugars yet, it'd be a waste of their time but I can call."

"Okay, forget about that. What do you need me to do?"

"I was just wondering if I could ask you to come and help me get a sandwich," Hester said. There was a hesitation on the other end of the line and then an idea sprang into Hester's head. "I'm also wondering if it's a good time for me to be saved and accept the Holy Spirit into my life."

"I'll be right there," Darla said and quickly hung up. The excitement in her voice gave Hester a feeling of impending doom.

Hester looked around her apartment in shame. It was no secret that she liked to have an occasional drink, the more occasions the better. It had been a comfort to her while married to her first husband who, as far as she knew, was the only wife-beater in town. She had never told anyone; the bruises and scars were hidden beneath her clothes. Rodney had been careful that way and his Army medic training allowed him to stitch her up after slicing her skin for punishment. Nobody would've believed her anyway, she'd been known for telling outlandish lies as a teenager. But Rodney was dead now, along with husbands two, three, four, and five. Number six had left long ago and she had no idea where he was or if he still was. Now the beatings were of her own doing. She had a daily ritual of summoning the past, lamenting it, and then drinking it away. She would wake to the company of empty gin bottles and a Dean Martin tape replaying endlessly on her stereo. She reached for her purse and pulled out her compact to see if she looked as haggard as she felt.

"Sixty-some-odd years, Hester. Somebody you never got over comes back to town and look at you," she said while staring at the mirror. "He's probably in worse shape than you. Or I hope so. God I'd hate for him to see me like this."

Since hearing that Edwin might be coming back to town, things had gotten worse. It was the good memories that hurt, driving her to indulge more than usual. The only bad memories were the ones she created with her grand illusions of what could have been. Knowing what he and his daughter planned on doing in Fallon rekindled those imaginative fires. Twenty years ago the notion of being a patient in a nursing home owned by him would have sent her packing to another state, but now there wasn't time to be shy or embarrassed. She'd be lucky if she had two more years left before she could no longer walk, and who knows how fast she'd go after that? Why not spend her last days around someone she once dreamed about, maybe even have the opportunity to make him feel guilty for all these years of pain?

Hester's mind wandered, reminiscing about her brief encounter with Edwin and how it had changed her life. Her memories were exhilarating, sending tingles throughout her body.

The sudden squealing of brakes outside of her trailer home brought her back to her senses, and as Darla's car slid to a stop, Hester pushed her feet firmly against the floor. The sensations had returned and she knew she would be able to walk on her own again.

The doorbell rang over and over and Hester tried to ignore it until Darla began pounding on the door.

"I'm okay, Darla, you can go home now."

"What? Don't you want to pray with me?" Darla yelled. Not only had she grown impatient but now she was angry.

"Not right now. Uh, I'll call you soon, okay?"

Darla said nothing and Hester heard her slam her car door and screech her tires as she drove away. She sat back down, feeling that she should at least say a little prayer for recovering fast enough that she didn't need Darla after all. She looked up to the heavens through the roof of her trailer.

"Thank you, sweet Jesus, for freeing her up for someone else. I swear on my grave that I will not die an alcoholic," she promised herself. "One more drink, that's it."

Chapter 6

The death of Valerie and Tim had left Ellie feeling numb and empty, so much so that it had been hard for her to get excited about anything. The needs of Jack were understandably difficult to fill, but Ellie was doing her best. Ellie's time with Jack was helping her heal, his brown curly hair and inquisitive nature reminding Ellie of her daughter and son-in-law. It was time that they both needed but it made it difficult to focus on the vision of the nursing home.

For the last four months, Edwin had been calling her daily and sending emails to remind her of all the things he wanted in the renovations. Most of those had to do with his apartment, but sometimes he had endless questions about the rest of the work being done. Between his interruptions, the actual construction, and getting the license to open the nursing home, she had tried to have a normal life. Things came at such a rapid pace she started to question whether she wanted this to happen or not. Today, though, was an opportunity to relax. She, Larry, and Jack had flown to Houston and were on their way to the retreat to check the progress of the remodeling. Edwin was in Louisiana to attend a function with an old friend and Ellie hoped it would hold his attention for at least a few days. She looked down at the speedometer and saw she was driving well over the speed limit. She took her foot off the accelerator as much in an attempt to relax as well as to slow down.

Jack sat quietly in his booster seat and played with his action figures. He found ways of occupying his mind to keep from looking up when he went for car rides. Ellie watched him in the rear view mirror to see if he looked scared or nervous. She knew to watch her speed and the road more cautiously since sudden stops or jerky movements upset him, often eliciting the word "shit" from his lips.

"Jack?"

"What, Grandma?"

"Are you ready to see where we're going to live?"

"Yeah, is it a big house?"

"It's real big, and there's going to be a lot of people living there."

"Is my mom ever going to come visit?"

"No, buddy, we talked about that. She'll always be near you but she can't come to visit."

"Grandpa, are you going to live there, too?"

"Yep, and we're going to have lots of fun. But you gotta promise me one thing: Stay off of the dock unless somebody's with you."

"I promise."

"I can teach you how to swim, would you like that?" Larry asked.

"But I'll drown."

"You won't, not if you're with me. Who told you you'd

drown?" Larry asked.

"My dad told me. He said to never go in the water or I'd drown."

"Idiot," Larry mumbled.

"Larry!" Ellie said while reaching over and squeezing his hand for support.

Ellie knew Larry had never liked his son-in-law and blamed him for the accident and scarring Jack for life.

"Sorry," he replied. "Hey, Jack, I think what your dad meant was that if you went in the water before you learned to swim you would drown."

"He didn't say that, Grandpa."

"But I'm sure he meant it. He was a pretty good swimmer. Do you remember?"

"No."

"Well, he was."

Larry felt that his attempts to connect with Jack were falling well short. Ellie told him he was trying too hard, but it was the only way he knew. Larry turned around in his seat to face him.

"Hey, sport, how about some ice cream?"

"It's cold outside, Grandpa."

"So what? Who says we can't have ice cream in the cold?"

Larry saw a smile creep across Jack's face as he looked up. There was still some innocence left in his eyes that he'd expect from a five year old. Larry finally felt like he had accomplished something today.

"Yeah, so what?" Jack echoed.

"We'll get some right after we look around."

"Okay."

Ellie topped the hill and drove slowly down the road, trying to take in each step of the renovation in progress. She remembered the first time she'd seen it, and how the building had looked so inviting in its setting on the lake. Now it was surrounded by scaffolding, men, and contractor's trucks, with most of its siding pulled away.

"Look, Jack, there's your new home."

"Grandma, why are they tearing it down?" he asked.

"They're not, honey, they're just taking the old wood off so they can put new stuff on."

"Is this an apartment?" Jack asked.

"No, it's just one big house," Ellie replied.

"I liked our apartment. Dad said it was a bad place to live but Mom had a lot of friends there. There were lots of kids. I had a friend there, she was a girl though. Are lots of people gonna live here?"

"Well, eventually. I hope," Ellie replied.

"Are they your friends?"

"They will be. They'll be your friends, too."

"Will they have any kids?"

"Uh, not living with them, no."

"Oh. Who's all those people outside?"

"They're workers, Jack," Larry replied.

"No, those people," he said, pointing to the back of the building.

There was a gathering, mostly elderly women, looking at the work being done and pointing at different things.

"I don't know," Ellie replied.

"Maybe future residents?" Larry asked.

"I wouldn't want to count on that, but we certainly seem to be drawing some attention."

"Let's go talk to 'em," Larry said.

"Yeah, Grandma, let's go talk to 'em like Grandpa said."

"Okay."

There was hesitancy in Ellie's voice, but her expression was one of excitement. She pulled the car into the parking lot and as they got out, she could see Darla McGee talking to one of the construction workers, pointing to different things as if she were giving them instructions. Darla looked back when she saw the car doors close and returned to be with the rest of the group.

"Hello," Ellie said as they approached.

"Who are you?" Belle asked abruptly.

"Belle, mind your manners. Hello, I'm Darla McGee. Are you folks looking for a future home for your parents?"

"No, but I remember you. We met in the motel lobby the day my father decided to buy the place," Ellie said.

"Ah, yes, I recall."

"My parents are dead," Jack said.

"Oh, my word," Darla said. "I'm sorry to hear that."

"It's only been four months and we're still dealing with it. I'm Ellie Mintzer, this is my husband Larry, and our grandson Jack."

"We're all pleased to meet you," Darla replied, seeming to have a more cordial tone than at their previous meeting. "We're just looking the old place over, we thought it would have been torn down by now."

"We're hoping to have it open by spring, perhaps the first of May."

"Are you Edwin's daughter?" Belle asked loudly.

"Yes, I am. Do you know my father?"

"I know him better than anybody else here with that goddamn tongue waggin'—"

"Shush," Darla scolded as Cary Chandler put his hand over Belle's mouth. "She has a touch of Alzheimer's and you never know what she's going to say next."

Belle struggled against Cary's hand and, unable to push his hand away, bit him across the middle finger.

"Dammit, Belle! You drew blood, look at my finger."

"That's what you get. Don't you ever put your bastard hands on me again."

Darla attempted to shush her again and then turned back to Ellie.

"She's a handful, that one. Wants to be your first patient."

"Do tell."

"Oh, she won't be any trouble. There's probably ten people that we went to school with that'll be moving in as soon as you're open. Isn't that wonderful?"

"As long as they all behave," Ellie said and then saw a look of concern on Darla's face. "No, look, I'm being rude. Of course it's wonderful, I can't wait. And what is her name again?"

"Belle Chandler. They knew each other very well."

"I'll have to mention it to him."

"Will he be coming here?"

"Yes, he'll be living here with us."

"Is he here in town?"

"No, at the moment he's in New Orleans—" Ellie began but was cut short by Belle.

"An animal, living in sin on Bourbon Street I'll bet!"

Cary lightly smacked the back of Belle's head and she looked back at him in disgust.

"Be nice, Belle," Darla said. "I hope Edwin's health isn't too bad. He seemed to be doing okay when I saw him a few months back."

"Oh, no, not as a patient. He'll live on the third floor in an apartment. No, Dad is quite spry yet. He runs almost every morning, rides bicycles, you name it. I can't slow him down. You'll probably rarely see him."

"The third floor? You don't say," Darla said.

"Let's get the hell out of here, I'm cold," Cary said.

It was evident that the more they talked about Edwin, the more irritated Cary became. He was holding a handkerchief around his bloody finger and staring at Belle with contempt.

"I'm sure we'll be hearing about him for the next six months until this place opens up."

"What are you talking about now?" Belle asked. "Where are we?"

"Nowhere, just shut up. We're gonna go," Cary said as he tipped his hat to Ellie.

"Don't tell me to shut up, I'll—"

"It's probably a good time for us all to go, the wind off the lake gives this cold air a bite," Darla said. "We so look forward to seeing you again. Do you go to church?"

"No, not really," Larry replied.

"I guess that would make sense, Edwin never seemed to be the church type. It must run in the family."

"We're not your traditional family," Ellie said. "Pleased to see you again, Darla. I'm sorry what was your last name again?"

"Darla McGee. Tell your father I said hello, will you?"

"I will. Take care."

Ellie counted ten people in all as they headed for their cars, wondering what the fascination was.

"Sounds like you're off to a great start, sweetie," Larry said.

"I don't know. All of them were looking at me like vultures. They seemed nice enough, but I get the feeling something isn't quite right."

"They all know your father, so that should be a step in the right direction."

"I don't know, that's the part that bothers me. The one, Belle, God if she isn't going to be a handful. And was she talking about Dad when she talking about somebody wagging their tongue? That doesn't sound like Dad at all."

"I couldn't figure it out either. I think she's playing with a short deck."

"Maybe. Hey, where's Jack?" Ellie asked in a panic.

She looked around just in time to see him talking to Cary Chandler as he was putting Belle's wheelchair in his car. Jack was holding something in his hand that he quickly put in his pocket. Ellie called out to him and he ran back.

"Yes ma'am?" Jack said.

"Don't run off like that, honey, you worry Grandma when you do that."

"Okay. That nice man wanted me to tell Grandpa Edwin

something."

"What's that?" Larry asked.

"It's a secret."

Ellie eyed Jack suspiciously and began to speak but Larry put his hand on her shoulder and shook his head.

"Someday we might need him to keep a secret for us."

"I keep good secrets, Grandpa."

"I'm sure you do. Let's go inside and see how things are coming along." Jack nodded and grabbed one of Larry's hands. Larry grabbed Ellie's with his other. "It's going to be fine, what's the worst an old man is going to have a kid say?"

"That's true. Give me a minute, I want to talk to that guy over there."

"What for?"

"I want to find out what Darla was talking to him about."

"Okay."

Ellie introduced herself to the site supervisor and found out that Darla had wanted him to separate all of the demolition materials so she could go through them. The foreman said that he was only placating her when he agreed, but hadn't been complying with her demands. His workmen informed him that she'd been going through the rubble in the early mornings and after hours. Ellie instructed him to keep her off of the site and he agreed.

Ellie walked back over to Larry and Jack with an uneasy feeling. Both of her encounters with Darla had been negative and Darla had a disturbing air about her. Ellie was already feeling protective of the old building and what it's future held and she wasn't going to let someone else ruin it for her.

*****

Edwin drove down the muddy road, swearing every time he hit a pothole. He'd spent a lot of time finding a Jaguar to rent at the airport that was similar to his own and now it was covered with mud. The GPS navigator showed that he'd left the end of the road a quarter of a mile back and he was just now seeing lights far in front of him. By the time he reached the old trailer house on blocks he was more than annoyed.

"Get away from my damn car," Edwin yelled out while honking his horn, but Beau Vicnair's dogs continued to paw at the doors and windows. He could hear the men sitting out on the front porch yelling to the dogs but with little effect. The porch light came on and the front door opened to the silhouette of a man dressed in his Marine Corps blue uniform. He couldn't hear what was said, but the figure pointed to the car and the men immediately went to retrieve the dogs. Edwin knew it was Beau. His six feet and five inches on a skinny frame left little doubt about who was walking toward his car. The only thing different was the oxygen bottle on wheels he pulled through the mud.

"Look what your damn dogs did to the car," Edwin said, as Beau opened the door to get in.

"You ain't changed a goddam bit, have you, Edwin?" Beau grinned as he took a final drag from his cigarette and threw it in the yard, then put his oxygen tubing back into his nose. "A crabby son-of-a-bitch if they ever was one."

"And you're still a backward coonass," Edwin replied. The two men shook hands as Beau adjusted in the seat, putting the mud-caked oxygen cart between his legs on the floorboard.

"This ain't your car, is it?" Beau asked as he studied the mess he was making.

"Rental," Edwin replied.

"Guess it don't matter then. How you been, Edwin?"

"Okay, how about you? What's that thing?"

"A little somethin' for dem lungs. Bayou air eats up everybody's lungs at some time or 'nother."

"Couldn't have anything to do with the cigarettes, could it?"

"Nah, my momma smoked for seventy years, ain't never had

a problem."

"Yeah? What did she die from?"

"Bad heart. Nothin' to do with her lungs," Beau replied and Edwin just shook his head. "Where's your uniform?"

"I threw that away the day after I got out. It wouldn't fit me anymore, anyway. You of all people should know I was never all that wild about the Corps to start with."

"Mine still fits me like a glove." Beau looked proudly at the single chevron on the sleeve and smoothed down the front.

"It looks like your original. You can get replacement ribbons, you know," Edwin said while looking at Beau's faded and frazzled ribbons.

"You a damn walkin' insult, you know dat? Always was after your falling out with dat little girl. You never got over her did you? Whatever happened to you two?"

"You're going to start that shit again? Nothing ever happened, and there was nothing to get over. She went her way and I went mine."

"She went her way and you tucked your tail 'tween your legs is what you did. You was a happy bastard before you went off to meet her. You came back a beat man. You can't fool Beau."

"That was a long time ago. I just decided to grow up that week and you took it wrong."

"My ass. Dat little girl beat you up in da head. So, what'd you do when you got out?"

"I got married to the first idiot that would say yes, had a daughter, and we broke up not long after. Went to work in the oilfields until about fifteen years ago."

"You didn't marry dat little girl?"

"No, I didn't marry that little girl. Goddammit, can't you quit talking about her?"

"Still bothers you, don't it?"

"You're still annoying, you know that?"

"I guess neither one of us gonna change, is we?"

Edwin looked over at him and they both smiled.

"Were those your kids that were out there tonight?" Edwin asked, troubled by what they'd just left.

"Nah, dey's my nephews, second cousins, just family dat come by every night."

"Every night?"

"Yeah, dey good men. Never cause no trouble. Dey come over most every day with some fish and crawlers, maybe some vegetables. Dey help cook and den we sit out on the porch and drink beer. Sorry 'bout the dogs. Dem boys know better, but dey didn't mean no harm."

"Got any kids?"

"I got a boy, he lives close to your hometown."

"Fallon?"

"Yeah, right on dat lake. He was a cook at a fancy place here in N'Awlins before Katrina but it closed down. He moved with some of the others to Houston and settled down on dat lake."

"What does he do now?"

"He catches fish, hunts for crawfish, sells 'em to the marinas and the butcher shops 'round der."

"He could have done that here."

"He got an independent streak. Said he needed a fresh start, didn't want to live on the bayou no more."

"A cook, you said?"

"Damn good cook. He said he's cooked for lots of movie stars and once for the President."

"You don't say. That's interesting."

"So, what you up to dese days?"

"I'm starting a business with my daughter. She's going to run a nursing home and I'm going to help out."

"What da hell are you gonna do at a nursin' home?"

"I'm just the money man. I can probably help with odds and ends but more than anything I'm just there to help her get it off the ground."

"A nursing home, huh. Maybe someday you'll be taking care of dat little girl."

"You just can't leave it alone, can you?" Edwin asked, the irritation showing in his red face.

"Well if she still lives in dat area you can't help but wonder if she shows up at your door wit' a walker. You two would be sharin' the same roof finally."

Edwin looked over at Beau and his overgrown impish grin. He shook his head and continued to drive in silence until they got to the convention center. He pulled up to the front door, where men dressed in formal wear and uniforms rushed in with their dates to get out of the rain.

"You droppin' me off here?"

"Yeah, but I need something before you go," Edwin said while fishing out a pen and piece of paper from his pocket.

"What dat?"

"Give me your boy's number, I might call him."

"Just a minute," Beau replied as he reached for his wallet. "He ain't got a phone, but I get messages to him through a phone he uses at the marina. Here's the number."

Beau pulled out a scrap of paper and handed it to Edwin who quickly copied it. Edwin wrote down another number and tore it off, handing it to Beau.

"Here's mine. Tell him to give me a call."

"What you want his number for?"

"I might need a cook for my nursing home."

"You kiddin' me?"

"No, I love cajun food and if I can get a good cook it'll serve both of our needs."

"Well, I'll be damned."

"I gotta run. You think you can get a ride back home tonight?" Edwin asked.

"You spent all this money and time and now you ain't comin' to the Marine Corps Ball?" Beau asked. "It's a reunion."

"I know, but I don't give a shit."

"Got dat little girl on your mind again, don't you?"

"Get out of the car, coonass."

Beau got out, showing a toothless grin and very little concern about spreading mud across the passenger seat with the cart.

"You sure you can you get a ride?"

"Yeah, I can get a ride. I know all dem people. Hey, you know I was just givin' you a hard time?"

"Yeah, I know. Take care of yourself, Beau."

"See you in hell."

Beau closed the door and stepped up on the curb, watching the tail lights disappear down the road. He'd always missed Edwin over the years. Beau knew that nobody was going to hold Edwin down even for a moment, and if he got a mind to do something you could consider it done. By the same token, if he decided he was finished with something, he wasted no time going the other way. It was the certainty of knowing exactly where Edwin stood that appealed so much to Beau, and he envied Edwin's ability to make it look so easy.

Beau walked into the convention center and went directly to a lobby phone. Of all the people his son could ever meet, Beau thought that Edwin could be the most influential.

Edwin drove for an hour before finding a car wash open. He sat in the lobby waiting for it to finish. He thought he must have fallen asleep because he woke to a man shaking him by the shoulder, asking him if he felt okay.

"I'm fine," Edwin growled.

The man walked away mumbling something about a person drooling and falling asleep with his eyes open. Edwin wiped the dampness from his chin as the other customers stared at him. He stood and felt a little woozy but was able to make his way outside for fresh air. His car was finished and he left as quickly as possible.

"I'm tired. Tired of all this shit," he said to himself as he drove down the freeway, but then shook his head in self-admonishment. "No, you're just tired, Edwin. You're still as good as you've ever been and you've got life by the balls. You're just a little tired, that's all."

Chapter 7

Karen Trimble looked through the online ads hoping to find a job opening. All the nursing positions were either for less money than she could afford to make or with employers who'd already fired her. She wasn't panicking yet, but the increase in healthcare costs were beginning to eat into her savings. As she looked at her mother staring at the lights on the Christmas tree, she knew it was going to start costing a lot more soon.

"Mom," Karen said, but there was no answer. Norma Trimble was nodding her head ever so slightly up and down in rhythm and that worried Karen. "Mom," she called a little louder.

Norma stopped moving her head, but her body had become rigid and her gaze seemed fixed on the blinking lights in front of her. Karen rushed over and pulled the plug on the lights, then ran to the kitchen for Norma's medicine, mixed it in a small amount of applesauce, and took it to her.

"Hey, you've got to take this," she said. Norma moved her head away slightly. "No, you have to take this, stop fighting me." Karen grasped Norma's chin, forced her mouth open and shoved the food in. Norma stared at her blankly for a moment and with a deep breath blew the contents out of her mouth. Karen called for an ambulance.

Within an hour Karen was sitting in an exam room staring at Norma in anger. Karen wasn't pleased about being there and was still furious about the smatterings of applesauce she kept discovering on her blouse.

"You should just let me go," Norma said.

"You'll feel better in a few hours."

"I hate you."

"No, you don't. Your medicine hasn't fully kicked in yet. You've never hated anyone but my father."

"I hate both of you," Norma said, her face flushing with anger.

"I'm thrilled. Why don't you watch some television for a while?"

Before Norma could reply, the ER doctor and a nurse entered the room. Karen recognized the nurse as someone she'd worked with before but wasn't familiar with the doctor. He looked at them warily before he spoke.

"Mrs. Trimble, I'm Dr. Cassidy. How are you feeling?"

"Like shit."

"I apologize, she has a potty-mouth until she fully comes out of it," Karen said.

"Catatonia, correct?" he asked.

"Yes, schizophrenia induced. She's not always like this but it seems to be happening more often. I used to see it coming but now it's unexpected and more frequent."

"Looking at her chart, she's been in here seventeen times in the last two years. January 3rd, January 10th… this is the third time this month alone. Has she seen her doctor about adjusting her dosage?"

"Not lately."

"Does she have a doctor?"

"She does. I've been unemployed for a while so I've had some difficulty getting her in." The nurse looked away, visibly troubled by Karen's comment.

"I see. Well, I can only tell you that she needs to get in as soon as possible. You're a nurse, correct?"

"Yes, I understand what you're saying," Karen replied. "Look, I feel like a crappy daughter right now. I'll get her in somehow."

"You probably know I can't change her dosage, but we can give her a little more to get her out of trouble for today."

"That sounds great. Can you give me prescription to get me through two weeks?" Karen asked.

"I'm limited to one," the doctor replied.

"That'll do," Karen said. The nurse, showing a sense of relief, winked at Karen and Karen gave her a smile.

"Alright, let's watch her for another hour and if she seems to come out of it then I'll let you go."

"Thanks, doctor," Karen said.

The doctor left the room and the nurse stayed behind.

"I'm sorry, you're Penny...?"

"Penny Braxton, and you're Karen, right?"

"Yeah."

"Where were you working?"

"Fallon Nursing Home. The worst, don't ever take your family there."

"I've heard. How long have you been out of work?"

"Four months. I'm able to stay home and watch her now but I don't know how long I can keep it up financially."

"They have openings here. You're a good nurse, I do remember that. Have you worked with this system before?"

"Terminated three years ago."

"What happened?"

"Started a large bore IV in a patient that was a pain in the ass. They said it was excessive, borderline abuse."

"Large bore?"

"Fourteen gauge," Karen said with a frown.

"That's like a water hose," Penny grimaced, but then shook her head and smiled. "But, been there and done that. They terminated you for that?"

"There were other things, nothing safety related, but that one put me over the top."

"This is my second time with them, they may be willing to take you back. They're needing nurses yesterday."

"I'll think about it. You wouldn't consider—"

"Want to use me as a reference? I wouldn't mind at all."

"Thanks. That's the best news I've heard in a while."

"No problem. I'll get the meds for your mom."

"Thanks, Penny."

Karen sat back in her chair and stared at the ceiling. She and Penny were two of a kind, taking their jobs seriously and sometimes a little too extreme for management. Penny had a way of flying under the radar a bit better and always seemed to keep out of trouble. Their only difference was that Penny enjoyed the fast pace of the ER and dealing with the patients. Karen's talent was more in organizing and managing, but under the circumstances any job would be better than nothing.

"You hear that Mom, someone's trying to look out for me. We may have a job soon."

"See if you can keep this one and let me die at home in peace."

"Thanks for the uplifting support. If you don't stop talking like that I may strangle you when you're fully conscious."

Norma stared at Karen blankly for a moment and then went back to watching television. Karen wrote down Penny Braxton's name so she wouldn't forget it.

*****

Edwin sat by the fireplace with his feet up on the ottoman, glaring at the envelope in his lap. It had come in the mail earlier, unexpected and unwanted. It was from Joan Campanella and he had a pretty good idea what she'd sent him. He'd wanted to toss the letter into the fireplace unopened, but he knew the more wine he drank the less likely that was to happen. He raised the wine glass to his lips, swearing before taking another sip from his fourth glass.

"Kiss my ass," he said to the envelope. "You people are not going to suck me into all that shit again."

Edwin looked around him, knowing he had it made. A converted warehouse condo that was custom decorated with industrial-style furnishings, a luxury Jaguar in the private garage, and a thirty-five-foot yacht in the marina down below named after the person he loved to hate. He had gobs of money and time and, at the moment, reasonably good health.

The life he'd made for himself had advantages few could dream of, but there were disadvantages, too. There was an emptiness to his life in Tennessee, with nothing of real value to live for, nothing to achieve. He had always needed a sense of purpose and it just wasn't here. As he looked out the windows at the cold January sky, the warmth of being farther south beckoned him. Those were the surface things, the shallow agreements he was making with himself to justify his increased yearning to return to his roots.

But there were grumpy little truths roaming around in Edwin's head like noisy children stomping around on the floor in an upstairs room. He hadn't liked the way Darla browbeat the others, and seeing the old retreat turn into a time capsule instead of having a purpose had disturbed him as well. He wasn't interested in settling old scores but there were loose ends to be tied up, his relationship with Ellie being one of them. There was the one truth that seemed to be much louder than all the others and that was the one that bothered him the most: the truth of getting old. There had been two more incidents of lost time since the one at the car wash in New Orleans and now it worried him to be alone.

Edwin studied the wine glass he'd just refilled, knowing that if he drank it all it would probably make him sick. He looked down at the envelope and decided he was being silly. At his age there wasn't too much any one letter could say that would make much of a difference in his life. He opened the envelope and began to read:

> *"Dear Edwin,*
> *It was so good to see you on your last visit and I had to get in touch with you. I got your address from Alton because I felt it necessary to tell you about Norma—"*

Edwin stopped reading and crumpled the letter into a tight ball, throwing it with force into the fire. He took the envelope and tore it into small pieces in a rage and flung the scraps over his shoulder. And just to get even with Joan, he drank the rest of the glass of wine in one gulp.

Chapter 8

Ramy Vicnair led a simple life, mostly out of necessity, but it fit his gentle nature. He lived in a little pontoon cabin that stayed relatively hidden on an obscure inlet on the lake. He fished for the most part, trading or selling what he caught for life's necessities. It had been eleven years since he'd left New Orleans and he hadn't found a restaurant yet that would match his skills to their menu. His father Beau would say he was hard-headed, but Ramy knew what he wanted. Months ago, his dad had told him somebody might be calling about a job. It was the first sign of hope in years that he could get back to what he enjoyed doing, but the opportunity seemed less likely as the days went by.

Ramy walked into the back door of the marina pulling an old rusty wagon with three coolers stacked on it, each holding a variety of his daily catch. The stock room was empty except for the cases of bottled water and cans of sodas they sold by the tons each day. It was a good sign; nobody else had turned in any fish yet today and it was likely he'd be the only supplier until late in the evening. It was unseasonably hot for April and there weren't a lot of fish biting. Fortunately, nobody knew how to fish the way he did. Ramy pushed the button for the service bell.

"Coming," Loretta bellowed from behind the counter. She was a big woman, lumbering down the aisle toward the stock room in the back. She saw Ramy's face and broke out in a girlish grin. "I knew it was you. If anybody's gonna catch a fish today it's you."

"Sometimes Ramy just lucky."

"You ain't lucky, you know what you're doin'. Nobody else catchin' nothin' but their dicks in their zippers."

"Loretta, you got a heart o' gold but a mouth of venom."

"You're a sweet talkin' little coonass, ain't you?" Loretta had a twinkle in her eye that wasn't lost on Ramy and he knew how to make her swoon.

"Ramy know good people when Ramy see 'em and you ain't kiddin' nobody wit dem gutter words, you a sweet woman through and through."

"Shut up, boy, and let's see what you brought me."

Ramy sat the coolers down on the floor and opened the lids. One had catfish, another had a mix of crappie and bass, and the third had crawfish.

"You gonna find a surprise under dem catfish."

"I'm already surprised just by lookin' at all them crawfish. How'd you find them when we ain't had any rain in a while?"

"You flood the banks and ditches, dey start comin' out."

Loretta shook her head and smiled as she pulled the last catfish off the bottom of the cooler. Beneath it was a burlap bag with one end tied up with fishing line. She looked up at Ramy with a broad grin.

"Is that what I think it is?"

"With the skin on and everything. Probably 'bout four and a

half feet."

"Now how'd you find that?"

"Luck. Ramy don't lie. Ramy lucky not to get bit when he heard dat rattle go off, Ramy didn't even see 'em. Ramy introduced him to a shovel."

"That's gonna get you another hundred fifty."

"You gonna break your bank, Loretta. Just give Ramy seventy-five."

"You're a fisherman, boy, but you ain't no businessman. I'm makin' my money and as long as you're square with me, I'll be square with you."

"Ramy don't argue," he said as he put his hand lightly on her shoulder. "Ramy always trust Miss Loretta."

Loretta blushed again as the touch of his hand sent tingles through her body. But in the next moment, a feeling of sadness swept over her. They'd spoken before of his dreams and today she had some information to pass on to him.

"I got a call today, that man that knows your daddy. He left a number for you to call him, wants to get hold of you real bad."

Loretta handed the scrap of paper to him and Ramy stared at it longer than necessary, taking time to gather his thoughts.

"Dis is what Ramy done been waitin' for. You done knew dat."

"Yeah."

"Here's what Ramy gonna do. Ramy's cousin come out and take over. LeBlon a better fisher than Ramy, you never run out."

"Yeah, but he won't be Ramy."

"LeBlon likes to have fun though. He likes dem mean girls, he might like you," he said as he put an arm around her shoulder.

"You're a sweet talker, boy."

"Ramy just be on the t'other side of the lake, out in dat cove in dat big motel."

"I know, but you won't be comin' in here every day."

"It's Ramy's time to move on, though, do what Ramy do

best."

"I'll have to come over and try it sometime."

"You come try it, you'll know Ramy done what was right."
Loretta nodded and then put her head down to hide her tears. "Can
Ramy use Loretta's phone?"

"Yeah, go behind the counter."

Loretta watched him as he went to make his call. Ramy was
the only person she was really comfortable with, valuing his
honesty and easy-going spirit. She profited from his fishing skills,
but it was his charm that she'd miss most of all if everything went
right with this phone call. She listened intently as Ramy finished
dialing the number and began speaking on the phone.

"Dis is Ramy Vicnair. Is Mr. Edwin Kranz there?"

*****

Ellie topped the hill, marveling at her accomplishment. She'd
been waiting for this moment since the beginning of the
renovations and it had finally arrived. She drove a little way down
the road but not too close. She wanted the scenery to be perfect.

"Are you ready?" she asked.

"I've been ready," Edwin replied. Ellie could tell he was still
incensed at having a scarf used to cover his eyes. "What'd you
do, paint it pea-green?"

"No," she replied as she pulled the scarf from his eyes. "But I
did make some changes."

Edwin sat breathless as he took it all in. The building looked
as fresh as the day it was built, but with a few additions. The
pergola in the front and the courtyards to either side with
fountains springing water into the air, the lush green of the grass
and the backdrop of the lake made him think of heaven. He turned
to her with a grin.

"You did good. Very, very good."

"You think so?"

"I know so, it's remarkable."

"So, you're impressed?"

"Yes, yes, very much, Ellie," he said, patting her on the knee for reassurance.

"You haven't seen anything yet."

"It's fantastic, Ellie, I can't wait to see it all."

Ellie squealed with delight. She drove quickly the rest of the way to the circle drive under the carport.

"I owe it all to you, and guess what: I've got our first tenant lined up."

"That's wonderful."

"Yeah, she's local. She's got Alzheimer's but she still functions pretty well. She'll get here tomorrow."

"Dementia? How old is she?"

"Eighty, same age as you. You might know her."

"Could be, it's a small town."

"Isabelle Chandler. That name ring a bell? It's Alton's grandmother."

"I never met Alton's grandmother," Edwin said. "Maybe, I don't know. If it's who I think it is, she wouldn't have dementia already."

"Dad, at eighty a lot of people have dementia. You're not a teenager anymore," she and Edwin looked away. "Anyway, Alton says she goes by Belle. Belle Chandler. Said she was the mascot of the football team! Hard to believe it when you see her," Ellie giggled. Edwin crossed his legs and and folded his arms quickly, looking away in angst. "You do know her, don't you?"

"Don't know her. Heard the name, maybe, but I don't remember anything other than that. Long time ago, you know."

"I'm not buying it," she said, eyeing him warily. "Oh well, it doesn't matter. Are you ready to see the inside?"

"I'm ready to see the bathroom, actually. And my area, too. Third floor, right? Got the elevator fixed and running?"

"Yep, room 306 is the main entrance and they've opened up

all the walls in the two rooms on either side."

"Did they take the numbers off the doors other than 306?"

"Just like you wanted. And by the way, why is 306 significant? You promised you'd tell me."

"It really isn't that significant. I stayed in 306 one night after this place opened. Seems like I should have final dibs on it."

"No kidding? I've been looking all over for any records they may have kept, like a ledger or something like that. I'm sure I can find your name—"

"Oh, it probably won't be there, they didn't keep good records then."

"How do you know?"

"They didn't care about those things back then. Who knows, they probably fudged the records to make it look good. This place wasn't what you think, it was like Vegas; people came here to escape their own lives for a while."

Edwin was looking away, but glanced at her momentarily to see her reaction, and then looked away again.

"That is utterly preposterous, I don't believe a word of it. You're hiding something."

"Why would I hide anything? You know how things happen when a place just opens. They had a band out back and people were dancing and drinking, and the staff was going crazy. I just wouldn't expect the records to be that good for a newer business like that." Edwin's face was flushed, something quite out of the ordinary.

"You're hiding something," she repeated, but Edwin remained quiet and noticeably agitated. "Wait till you see the dock, it's right behind Kranz Gardens."

"Is that the name of this place? Sounds like a nursery, someplace you'd buy shrubs."

"Tough shit, I like it. I want people to think of a serene, natural place."

"To die."

"That happens anyway."

"What kind of staff do you have so far?"

"Not much. With only one resident, I'll be doing a lot of it myself. There's been a lot of interest in this place; the phones have been ringing off the hook. But I have a cleaning woman coming in every day for a few hours and two more assistants who are interested. Living on-site will allow me to be accessible and the cooking—"

"I can help with the cooking."

"Spaghetti and frozen pizza every night? Blueberry waffles every morning? Please."

"Worked for me."

"Yeah, well you're going to see that most folks your age aren't quite like you. These folks are gonna need a balanced diet and decent food. At some point I'll have a cook come in, but I can handle it for now."

Edwin looked at Ellie's profile. Her chin was high, her color was good, and he could see the determination in her eyes to make this work. He was proud of her and even happier that she was trying to make the best of this opportunity.

"Listen, don't stretch yourself out too thin. You love what you're doing but you have to find time to enjoy it, too. Don't be afraid to get what you need or who you need. There's no doubt in my mind that you're going to do fine and the money will come soon enough."

"I know, Dad, but I do feel guilty. I don't want to just blow your money, I want to earn this."

"You will, don't worry. I told you from the start to look at me like a bank. If you need it, borrow it. Pay me back as you can, and the only interest I charge is seeing that you do well. Okay?"

"I'll try."

"Good. Now we need to hire a cook. For me if nothing else. And we need one that knows cajun food—"

"She's not going to be your personal cook, and I don't think we'll be serving a lot of cajun food."

"I'll pay him extra for what I want."

"Him? What, you've got someone in mind already?"

"Yeah, the son of an old friend."

"I didn't think you had any friends."

"Just someone I ran into a while back. We were in the Corps together and he said his son is down in this area working."

"And he's a cook?"

"That's what he said. Worked in the French Quarter for a long time until Katrina came along. Now he lives around here. Let's give him a shot."

Ellie rolled her eyes. It seemed unlikely to work in the long run, but she had a hard time saying no to one of his requests. He was, after all, bankrolling the venture. With everything else on her plate, she felt it was too much to argue about and she could placate him for a short time until other arrangements could be made.

"We'll give him a try, but I'm not kidding. We have to have someone that understands nutrition and knows how to prepare food for these folks. This isn't a joke, Dad, I could get in lots of trouble if he doesn't."

"You're a good girl."

"You're incorrigible."

Chapter 9

"Are you here to take your mother home?" the nurse asked as she walked by.

"Not today," Patty Chandler-Dittmore replied. "I hope she's not being a pain."

Patty waited for an answer, but the nurse never turned around to respond. Patty was getting a cold reception at Fallon Nursing Home. Belle wasn't making matters any better with her sniping complaints and rabble-rousing with the other residents. When Patty got to Belle's room, she felt some of the same frustration the staff was experiencing. Her father was already there, sitting in the corner looking at his wife in disgust. Patty knew he would be no help since he was against her moving anyway.

"Mom, where are your sheets and pillows?"

"They're packed in the corner over there with my other belongings," Belle barked.

"What are you going to sleep on tonight?"

"I'm sleeping at your house. I can't sleep here tonight, they'll smother me with my pillow or cut my throat. They don't like me here."

"Well they certainly don't like you now," Cary said.

"Dad, that's not helping. Now come on, Mom, you know better."

"I'm not taking any chances. Why don't you take me home and we can get to Kranz's place early tomorrow. I've got a bone to pick with him."

"I can't take you home, we've got company and there's no place for you to sleep."

"I'll sleep on the couch, then."

"Already taken."

"How about the recliner?" Belle asked. Patty took a deep breath and looked over at her father for help. Like a child, he looked the other way.

"We don't have the recliner anymore."

"You don't have the recliner I gave you? What did you do, sell it to pay some bills? You kids live too high on the hog."

"Stop saying that, Belle, you don't know what the hell you're talking about," Cary said.

"Yes, I do, and look at you over there sulking. You've hated that man since I can remember and you've got nothing but revenge on your mind."

"Look who's talking," Cary shot back.

"What revenge are you two talking about?" Patty asked in frustration. "Look, can we just focus on getting you through one more night here? Just one more night, that's all I ask. Daddy, can you stay with her tonight so she doesn't worry about being stabbed to death in her sleep?"

"No."

"I don't trust him, anyway. He can't wait 'til I'm gone and then he'll be off chasing some skirt that uses a walker who can't defend herself. How much did you sell my chair for?"

"We didn't sell it, Mother, it was old and falling apart."

"I just gave it to you!"

"That was ten years ago. Look, you're staying here."

"I'll sleep on the floor or in the car."

"No, you have to stay here one more night and Daddy can stay with you."

"I don't want to," he whined.

"I don't care! You don't do a damn thing to help her. All you do is keep her blood pressure up by fighting all the time. It won't hurt you to do something for me for one night."

Patty saw Belle glaring at her in contempt. She'd become accustomed to it over the last few months, part of the pathology of her mother's Alzheimer's. Belle had wandered away three times while living with Patty, prompting her to place Belle somewhere where she could be watched around the clock.

"You just don't want me, do you?"

"I don't want you to get hurt. Sometimes you don't think clearly and I worry about you."

"Blah, blah, blah. Took my favorite chair and sold it off for grocery money."

"I'll get you another recliner. As soon as you get moved to Kranz Gardens I'll have it delivered."

"No, don't go in debt. I don't want my grandkids starving and you'd probably blame me for doing it."

"Shut up, Belle, her kids are all fat and grown. Obviously they ain't starving."

"Thanks, Dad," Patty said sarcastically, "Come on, let's get your bed made so you can get some sleep tonight."

"I ain't gonna sleep."

"Yes, you will, you're going to get tired later and you'll be dead to the world the rest of the night."

"I'll be dead, alright. These people can't wait to get back at me. They're gonna kill me before I can get into that Kranz place."

"Kranz Gardens."

"If I make it. You're probably in on it, too."

"In on what?"

"Letting them kill me."

"Whatever."

"I can't wait to see him," Belle said.

"Who?"

"Edwin Kranz."

"Will you stop talking about him? Jeez, you've never gotten over him after all these years," Cary said.

"Showing off, stickin' that tongue in my ear," Belle said with a whimsical, reminiscing smile.

"Stop it, now, we're sick of hearing it," Cary said.

Cary and Belle stared at each other with their own particular brand of hatred that had been fifty years in the making. It had gotten worse since Edwin's arrival, stirring new life from old memories and driving a wedge between them even further.

"May I interrupt? You know, he may not be there. He just bought the property. My understanding is that his daughter is running the place," Patty said.

"Well, sooner or later he'll show up, the bastard."

"Why do you say that? What've you got against him after all these years?"

"Never mind, help me make my bed."

"She's got plenty," Cary said, "Stick around and you'll hear every word of it over and over again."

"Shut up, old man. You should talk. You know, the way he wagged that tongue you would have thought that was all he had, but that boy was put together in that military suit and sonny, could he stand at attention."

"I'm going home."

"Dad, she doesn't know what she's saying, you know that."

"Yes, she does. I'm not kidding when I tell you about the things you're going to hear. That part of her crazy-ass brain is in high gear."

"Well, let's just leave it alone for now, I've heard all I want to hear."

"I'll be back in the morning."

Patty shook her head as he left.

"You shouldn't do things to drive Daddy up the wall, Mom. You're still going to need him to help you with things."

"He's the eunuch. He ain't even interested in me anymore, I don't need him. I'll tell you what, Edwin's going to be interested in me when I get through with him. You watch. That man can't turn me down."

"Do you have any idea what you're saying? You're eighty years old, what are you expecting to happen?"

Belle stuck her finger in her ear as she flicked her tongue out.

"Stop that, it looks disgusting."

"Lum lum lum…"

"Mother, stop that! That's trashy."

"He missed me, that's why he came back."

Patty bit her bottom lip, trying to make sense of the changes in her mother. On one hand it was refreshing to see her old feistiness, even it it was temporary and fleeting. And it was interesting to see her so focused on at least one topic when it seemed that lately her whole mindset had become random. At the same time it could be embarrassing and Patty was concerned with how she might behave once they moved her to Kranz Gardens. It was too late to change course now so she would have to play it by ear.

"Well, just remember you're still a married woman."

"Is he married?"

"I don't know, maybe."

"I doesn't matter. I'll chase her and your daddy off somewhere else."

"Sounds like a plan, now let's get you dressed for bed."

*****

With only a moment's notice, Ellie had picked an outfit worthy of the occasion. The last few weeks had taken a toll on her, causing her to shed ten pounds and now some of her clothes seemed a bit loose. The grand opening wasn't until tomorrow, but Alton Chandler had set up an interview with the local newspaper, giving her just the kind of publicity she needed. Everything seemed to be in order, at least what she would be willing to show to the reporter, and the rest would be finished in time for the opening.

The smell of cinnamon rolls was overwhelming, making her stomach growl. At first she thought someone had lit a candle for ambiance but Ramy had begun cooking early. She wasn't even aware there was food in the galley, having left all of the planning to Edwin; it was his idea to hire Ramy, she'd let him deal with the outcome. But the aroma of baked goods was getting stronger and at the moment she was glad Ramy was there. Larry came out of the dining room with two saucers, four cinnamon rolls on each one.

"You're gonna love these," he said.

"They're tiny, why does he make them so small?"

"I asked the same question. He said to save money and effort. Smaller rolls means less waste, people will only take what they want instead of getting a huge one and only eating half. He says he can make hundreds at a time and freeze 'em. Look at 'em, rolled up like those sushi things and the pastry is like wispy little crusts that aren't doughy at all."

"I like 'em doughy."

"You're just looking for something wrong with his cooking."

"I'm not, I just don't like the way this all came about, that's all."

"Well, don't blame that on him, he just took a job someone offered."

"Yeah, I know," she said and then took a bite of a roll. "That's interesting, it's flaky all the way through. Not enough glazing, though."

"For you or your patients?"

"That's true, they don't need it. But I do."

"Then just tell him to make some off to the side with more glazing. He'll do it. You really need to get to know him, he's a very interesting guy."

"I've got enough things going on, I don't need another friend and I'm not going to turn him into my personal chef."

"He is your personal chef, silly," Larry said with a smirk. "Fine, suffer with the ordinary rolls, I've got a little bit of painting to get done this morning." Larry began to turn away, but Ellie grabbed for the saucer he was holding that still had three rolls left. "Hey, gimme that back."

"I thought you brought this plate for me," she said as she popped another in her mouth.

"I can see how much you don't like them."

"Hate 'em, but I'll eat 'em."

"Asshole," Larry said as he kissed her on the cheek and then returned to the kitchen.

Ellie watched as an old sedan crested the hill and began winding its way down the road to the parking lot. A woman in her thirties got out of the car and walked quickly toward the front door, holding a notepad and thick folder. Ellie finished the last two rolls quickly and opened the door for her.

"Are you Ellie?"

"I am, are you from the Fallon Courier?"

"Yes," she said, extending her hand, "Adrienne Parker, so nice to meet you. I've heard Alton talk all about what you've done to the place and I hope we can look around a little bit."

"Absolutely. Have you had breakfast?"

"I did, but God doesn't something smell good?"

"You've got to try one of the cinnamon rolls here, they are to die for," Ellie said just as Larry came around the corner. He gave her a sideways glance and continued on his way. Ellie knew she would hear about this later. "This is the ground level foyer where the residents and their guests can lounge and visit. To the left is the front desk and there will always be someone there for visitors. You can see the dining area back to your left and the big room on the right side used to be a boathouse. We refurbished it as a craft room. If you look straight down that hallway running between the dining room and craft room is the door out to the patio and down to the dock."

"Very nice. It kinda has a four-star hotel feel to it."

"Thank you! I had hoped that others see it that way instead of your usual antiseptic-looking boarding house. Now to the left and right are the hallways that lead to the residents' rooms and there's an elevator here on the right by the craft room. This will make easy access for everyone with a central location. There are also elevators at each end of the hallways just in case."

"And the residents will be on all three floors?"

"The second floor will also have residents and the third floor is the living quarters for my family."

"The infamous third floor," Adrienne mused.

"Infamous?"

"Of course. The entire building had a very brief but scandalous history."

"Alton made mention of that, but he didn't go into a lot of detail."

"Oh, well, that's a different story for a different day. I can't wait to see the rest of the place."

The two walked into the dining room where there was a buffet table set up at the far end with a large bowl of juice containers and fruit on ice. Next to it was a serving tray with a clear plastic lid containing the cinnamon rolls and beside it was a large pastry box filled with even more. A note was written on the box with a marker: "For the Fallon Courier". Ellie smiled but something about it irritated her.

"Looks like these are for you to take back to the office," Ellie said.

"Oh, you're going to make my folks happy." Adrienne pointed to the serving tray. "May I?"

"Help yourself."

"Now these are unique. They melt as soon as they hit your tongue. Wonderful."

"I'll pass it on to Ramy, our cook. Let's sit down."

"Sounds good. And that's a good starting point, your cook's name is Ramy?"

"Yes, Ramy Vicnair. He was a cook for a restaurant in New Orleans before Katrina and he wound up in this area."

"Lucky find for you."

"We made it a point to find someone really good," Ellie said and then felt the presence of someone behind her.

"And is this Ramy?"

Ellie turned and looked up to see a man in cook's clothing standing behind her. He would have heard everything she said, but at the moment he was more focused on the reporter.

"Ramy Vicnair," he said as he accepted her hand. "Did you get a chance to try the rolls?"

"I did, they were fabulous. And thank you for the extras."

"Come by tomorrow and Ramy'll have lunch made at eleven, right Miss Ellie? Ramy's got a soup ya'll gonna like."

With that, Ramy walked away and disappeared into the kitchen. Adrienne looked across the table at Ellie.

"Third person?" Adrienne mused.

"Yes, uh…" Ellie replied, not exactly knowing what to say. Having never spoken to him, it was the first time she'd heard Ramy's quirk. "I don't know how one comes about that, but it seems odd."

"I think it's adorable. Like a little puppy that's only interested in doing things his way, not caring what others do."

"I suppose. You mentioned scandal earlier. What did you mean?"

"Nobody's told you?"

"Nothing specific, no."

"This place was a retreat for the filthy rich, or perhaps one could say the rich and filthy. Sort of a mixture of Vegas and Playboy mansion rolled up in one. They had gambling, booze, and orgies from what I hear, and God only knows what else. You had to be wealthy, very wealthy, to belong. Back then you had to go a long way not to be discovered if you were going to live that kind of lifestyle; wife swapping, drugs, gambling, or even being gay. It just didn't happen."

"I wouldn't guess so. Why did it close?"

"Poor management, things going a little too far. From what I understand they didn't screen the workers very well. One of the workers spilled the beans about everything when there was a huge fight between a man and his wife. The husband was a prominent attorney in Houston. He was in the shower when his wife came in the room in the wee hours and found an eighteen-year-old girl naked and passed out drunk on the bed. Made the papers the next day, all the smut and filth provided by a little Baptist preacher's daughter who wanted to save the world. I think she was sort of a hat-check girl. Anyway, they closed it down the next day. The property has been sitting here idle, but nobody can say why. I gotta tell you that you've done a remarkable job with it. I've been in here countless times trying to find anything left to write about but never came up with much."

"I've been hoping to find a ledger myself, but I haven't had time to look yet."

Ellie was lying; she'd spent more than a few hours looking for any piece of history left behind. At the moment, though, she didn't want to detract from why Adrienne was there.

"Good luck. Like I said, this was like Vegas and I don't think they kept records."

"How long was this place open?"

"Three months."

"Three? Barely enough time to even make sure all the lights worked."

"I hear that your father is a partner?"

"Yes, he is."

"Does he remember the place?"

"He does but he hasn't talked about it much."

"I can only imagine what a homecoming it might be for him turning this place from what it was into what it is now. Sort of the other end of the spectrum for its purpose."

"I don't know," Ellie replied. She found Adrienne's comment oddly amusing. "But you've given me some ammo to ask him about."

"And what about you, what was your motivation to do all of this?"

"I've always wanted to help people I suppose. I've worked in different nursing homes and they're so impersonal. I watched my grandmother and the way she was treated in a nursing home and I didn't want that to happen anywhere else. I thought that if I had my own place, I would run it the way I wanted to. I like the freedom of being my own boss and not having some corporation tell me how much time I can focus on one patient."

"Are you a nurse?"

"I am. I mainly like working with older folks and taking my time being with them."

"And you'll be managing as well as caretaking?"

"Yes. A bit daunting to think about but I can handle it."

"Impressive," Adrienne said as she took notes. "And your father?"

"He just wants to help me live out my dream."

"He's the talk of the town right now, did you know that?"

"No, I didn't. My dad? He's about as private and stuffy as you can be. I don't see others finding a lot to talk about with him."

"I think there are a lot of people excited to see him back," Adrienne said. Ellie seemed to get apprehensive when the subject of her father came up so she decided to leave it alone. "So, could you show me around the rest of the place, maybe see some of the changes?"

"I'd love to."

While Ellie showed Adrienne around, the urge to start searching for attic doors or crawl spaces began to creep into her mind again. The contractors had had explicit instructions to save anything that might be of interest but had found nothing, not even a beer can hidden behind the drywall of the rooms. Nonetheless, Ellie still felt an urge to look if she ever found time.

Chapter 10

"Grandpa!" Jack yelled, waving a painted picture over his head. "Grandpa, Grandpa!"

Larry looked around the schoolyard, pretending to search for Jack while hearing him call his name. Finally, he felt Jack's arms wrap around his leg and looked down.

"There you are. I've been looking all over for you."

"I'm right here, Grandpa. I was right here but you didn't hear me."

"Hmmm, that's because I was expecting to hear a little man's voice."

"You mean like this?" Jack said, trying to lower his pitch by putting his chin on his chest.

"Just like that! There's the little man I know."

Jack smiled broadly, something he'd been doing more often.

"Did Grandpa Edwin get his boat yet?"

"Not yet. Sometime tomorrow, I think."

"I painted a picture of it, look."

Jack held up a picture that looked more like a stick destroyer with sails than a ski boat. Larry was able to suppress his laugh.

"Looks good, Jack. Grandpa Edwin's gonna like it. Maybe we'll put it in a frame and give it to him."

"No, we have to give it to him when we get home before he dies."

"What makes you think he's gonna die?"

"Grandma said that all old people die like my Mom and Dad. I don't want Grandpa Edwin to die before I give him this picture."

"Got it. We'll find him as soon as we get home. But listen, I don't think he's going to die anytime soon, okay?"

"I hope not. He's funny and he promised to take me on his boat."

"I think you're right. Hey, we have to stop at a store first, I gotta get some stuff for Grandma before we go home."

"Is that our home now? That big motel?"

"Yep, that's it."

"That's where everyone's going to die, isn't it?"

"Well, that's where your grandma is going to help people live."

"That's nice. I just don't want all of us to die."

"It's okay, buddy, I promise."

"Okay," Jack said as he began walking pensively to the car. The spring in his step was gone and his little shoulders slumped.

"We'll get ice cream afterwards, whattaya say, sport?"

"Okay. You like ice cream, don't you, Grandpa?"

"I guess I do, don't you?"

"If you do. Can I have a sundae?"

"Yeah, you can have a sundae. Hey, Jack, look over there," Larry said, pointing to a pickup pulling a boat. "Maybe that's Grandpa Edwin's boat."

"No, Grandpa Edwin's boat goes in the water. That one

doesn't."

"Well, they have to take it to him."

"No, his boat is going to be bigger. It's gonna go fast, and he said he would take me fishing."

"I'm sure he will, sport. He always keeps his word, doesn't he?"

"Yeah," Jack replied. "Are we gonna live here forever, Grandpa?"

"Don't know. Maybe. If Grandma's business does okay, I'm sure we'll be here a long time."

"I hope so. I like it here. I like my teacher. She let me sit by her today."

"Sit by her? You mean at the desk?"

"Yeah, I tooted once and everybody laughed at me, and nobody wanted to sit by me. But she said she didn't mind, and if she didn't mind then nobody else should mind."

"Well, I'm glad she didn't make you feel bad. You didn't toot anymore, did you?"

"Two more times, but they were quiet. Her face was red, I think she was holding her breath."

"Could be, sport. You gotta try not to do that in class. You gotta excuse yourself and go to the bathroom."

"Dad always said it was natural and not to worry about it."

"I know, and he was right. But not everybody sees it that way. Sometimes we have to learn to get along with others in a different way."

"I want to do it my dad's way."

"Okay, but I think your dad was talking about at home. You wouldn't do it in a church would you?"

"No, that's a nice place. God would hate me."

"God would never hate you, buddy. He never hates us, but everyone else in church may not want to sit by you."

"Why, 'cause it stinks?" Jack giggled.

"Probably, and school is like a church. There's things you just don't do there."

"Okay. I'll just toot at home."

"Not at the table, though."

"I know, Grandma gets mad."

"Yeah. Okay, let's go get our stuff."

"Let's go get our ice cream first!"

*****

Edwin put his feet up on the handrail of the balcony outside of his third floor suite. The orange glow of the sunset was giving way to purple as the clear night took over. The building was as beautiful now as it had been back in his teens on the night that everything changed. It was all still very real in his mind and some of it had happened right in this very room.

There were some differences, things Ellie had done to make the building more functional. She'd converted what had been a patio and dance floor into an outdoor dining and gathering area filled with umbrella-shaded tables and chairs. She'd placed topiaries around the perimeter like pawns along the edges of a chessboard. To the right of the dining area was a wing of the main building that had once been an old boat house. Ellie had converted it into an indoor center where crafts could be created by day and movies or bingo offered at night. Beyond the dining patio was the path that led to the dock where Edwin was expecting his ski boat tomorrow.

"So damn long ago," Edwin mumbled to himself. "I stood right here on this balcony, a girl laying on the bed naked behind me. That was a good night."

Edwin looked down, remembering when there had been a pool with an attendant station before Ellie had filled it in to make shuffleboard courts and horseshoe pits. Guests could leave their belongings at the station and get a towel for the pool, or simply leave their drink on the bar as they enjoyed the company of others.

It had been a night very much like this one, warm with the soft glow on the horizon of the disappearing sun. Edwin remembered that Darla McGee had been working at the station, trying to hide her beautiful figure with oversized clothing that only her father found appropriate. A man had walked up to her and exchanged his room key for a voucher. She put the key in a cubby and gave him a numbered token for when he returned. Darla watched the man, seeing him look back to make sure his wife wasn't around. He quickly walked out to the dock, climbed aboard a teak cabin boat and went below deck as a woman pushed forward on the throttle and sped away.

"Sinners," Darla had mumbled in disgust.

The people in the pool wore little to nothing at all and Darla tried not to look at the naked breasts being fondled before her very eyes. Overt French kissing and rampant groping seemed to be the norm. One man was floating on a raft while another man rubbed his feet. Darla was ready to scream.

"Why are you giving that man the evil eye?"

Darla turned to see a tall figure in uniform staring at her with piercing eyes. Darla's face became flushed from being caught. She looked at him angrily, not immediately recognizing him.

"I beg your pardon?"

"I've heard of eyes like daggers, but yours are like swords."

"I was doing no such thing," she replied, her white skin glowing red even as the sky grew darker. It wasn't just the act of getting caught, but getting caught by a young man dressed in a green military uniform tailored to perfection to fit his lean physique. His dark eyes and strong bearing took her breath away. "If you'll excuse me, I—" she began, but then her mouth hung open when she recognized him. "—Edwin Kranz, I can't believe it's you. Look how much you've changed. Look at you in your uniform. Very sharp, very handsome."

Edwin's reaction was slight, shrugging with little interest to her compliment.

"So, what did that man do to warrant that Darla McGee glare?"

"Which one?"

"The one in the boat?"

"Well now, that would be gossiping."

"So what?"

"I guess you haven't changed after all, have you?"

"I don't see the point in changing," he replied as he walked closer and leaned on the counter, "You're only going to remember the bad parts anyway."

"What brings you here? Did you have a rich uncle that died or something?"

"No, I was invited by someone that saw me getting ready to leave at the bus station. He thinks everyone in a uniform is a hero. Anyway, I'm his guest."

"And who is 'he'?"

"The guy that just went for a moonlight spin around the lake with someone other than his wife. She's inside with some guy trying to put the moves on her. It seems to be working."

Darla looked away and shook her head but refocused as a pair of arms wrapped around Edwin's waist from behind. Belle's head popped around from his side with a grin at Darla.

"Look what I found, all dressed up and ready to go," Belle said. It was obvious that she was drunk as Edwin reached around and put his hand on her shoulder. Belle snuggled up to him, stroking his tie suggestively.

"Belle, you're drunk. Cary's going to be outraged."

"Only if you tell him. I'm certainly not going to say anything."

"This is crazy," Darla said, beginning to fume. "You two hated each other in school and now look at you."

"The key, please," Edwin said.

"What?"

"The key. I'm a guest and that's my key in pocket 306. I just saw you put it in there."

"That isn't your key, that's—" Darla protested, but Edwin wasn't going to let it deter him.

"The man who's gone off with another woman and whose wife has her tongue down another man's throat inside."

"You people are horrible."

"Darla, don't be such a prude, we're just going to make out. Jesus, we're out of high school. Some of us have even grown up," Belle said with a pout. Darla was furious, her face reddened and her hands shaking. "You know, someday you may find a man yourself. You might even enjoy it."

Darla spun around and grabbed the key and then threw it at Edwin, hitting him in the chest.

"Go on, sinners. Enjoy yourself, I hope you're ready to pay the price of eternal damnation!"

Her comments momentarily silenced the crowd around the pool before they began mocking and laughing at her.

An hour later, Edwin was looking over the balcony with blood trickling down his back from the scratches Belle had left. Someone was holding a large camera, filming all the goings on. He could see Darla still standing at the counter with a look of disgust. He guessed she was probably still seething about Belle going upstairs with him. Darla had always seemed to show a particular fondness for pointing out his shortcomings, but he also felt that she had a peculiar interest in him. He thought that if she had been the one in the bed behind him, he might have stayed for seconds. He looked back at Belle, who was sleeping, a combination of the booze and his handiwork, but being in there alone with her was risky. He walked back in the room, quietly put on his uniform, and left. That had been the first and last time that he'd set foot on the property before he bought it.

"So, what do you think?" Ellie called out from below.

Edwin sat up straight, smiling to himself over the memory of his youth. He looked over the rail to see Ellie staring up at him.

She had been busy lighting tiki torches on each corner of the patio and tea candles on the tables. They gave a warm glow through the umbrellas from his angle, eliciting the feel of a beach retreat instead of a nursing home.

"I think it looks great, cutie. Come look for yourself."

"Okay. Got any wine up there?"

"Red."

"You don't have any white?"

"No."

"Okay, red then. I'll be up in a minute."

Ellie moved quickly toward the rear entrance and disappeared as Edwin stood to go unlock the door. A feeling of dizziness overtook him and he grabbed the railing to get his balance. His next recollection was the sound of someone pounding on the door while he laid on the floor looking at the ceiling. He stood, feeling slightly numb in his left leg. The pounding on the door came again.

"I'm coming, just a minute."

"Are you okay in there?"

"Yeah," He said while opening the door. He shuffled his feet as he moved to let her in.

"What's wrong with your feet?"

"Muscle cramps. Too long of a run today. I'll be fine," he replied. Ellie looked at him from head to toe with concern but kept her thoughts to herself. "Come on in, I'll get your wine."

Edwin took a few steps and then felt a tingling in his leg as if the sensations were flowing back in. Seconds later he was fine.

"Do you have a corkscrew?"

"Looking for it now."

"I thought that would be the first thing you'd put away. Geez, Dad, what have you been doing all day, sitting on the balcony? You haven't unpacked a single box."

"What's the hurry?"

"No hurry, I guess. Hey, what's in the cooler over there?"

"Stuff for a picnic. I'm going out on the boat tomorrow and I've got some food packed and ready."

"What boat? You don't have a boat."

"It's being delivered tomorrow. Didn't Larry tell you?"

"No. I didn't know you were going to get a boat. You're going to put it here?"

"Yes, here. Why not here?"

"Because it's a distraction. Do you realize what you're going to do to these people when you saunter past them to go for a run or get on a boat and take off? Leaving them behind with nothing but agony—"

"Let's not get too dramatic, toots. They'll be all right. Half of them won't even remember what happened ten minutes after I take off."

"Yes, they will. You know, not everyone that will be here will have memory issues. A lot of 'em are just in poor health. Don't you think they still want to do things, like go out on a boat? Or just take a car ride to get themselves away from nurses and people bossing them around? They still have feelings."

Edwin closed his eyes and shook his head. It wasn't that she was wrong, quite the contrary. He knew she was right, but he didn't care; Edwin wanted to live his life his way and he wasn't going to get rid of the boat.

"You make some good points, although I think you're giving it a little more weight than it deserves."

"In other words, I'm right."

"Some, I suppose, but what did you think I was going to do with the boat dock, anyway?"

"I thought you were going to set up something so people could go out and be near the water."

"I named it Kranz Gardens, you know."

"Named what?"

"The boat."

"You don't name a boat after a business, you name it after a woman."

"I did that once, it didn't work out. Besides, it's good advertising."

"I don't want people getting the impression that we give boat rides to the residents."

"Why not? I'll get a pontoon boat and take the inmates out a couple of times a week."

"Don't call them inmates," Ellie scolded. "They are paying residents who need medical assistance. I don't want you calling them that."

"Okay, I'm not trying to make waves."

"Did you ever find the corkscrew?"

"No, I forgot I was looking for it," he replied. Ellie shook her head in frustration.

"It won't be long before you're downstairs in one of those rooms."

"You're mean and you're wrong."

"I know, I take after my father," she replied as she walked up and kissed him on the side of the cheek. "I gotta run, lots to do. I think I can find a corkscrew in my apartment."

"Okay. Big day tomorrow?"

"Yeah, and remember Belle Chandler is moving in and I understand from her daughter that she can't wait to see you."

Ellie stood in the doorway just long enough to see Edwin grimace before she walked away.

Chapter 11

It was five in the morning when Edwin pulled into the parking slot outside the courthouse. The building sat in the middle of the town square with a mix of quaint little shops and abandoned storefronts surrounding it on all sides. He remembered as a kid riding his bicycle up and down the sidewalks looking into the store windows. Some were familiar: the obligatory drug store with a soda fountain, a men's clothing store, an antique shop, and various offices for lawyers and real estate brokers. One block to the west was the fire station where he could hear the bells ring in the middle of the night. He'd lived close enough to sneak out through his bedroom window and follow the fire engines on his bike as far as he could until he either made it to the fire or failed to keep up. Those were the memories he enjoyed. Everything beyond that had been disappointment.

"You doing alright?" a voice said beside him. Edwin was

startled by a cop standing by his car door.

"I'm sorry?"

"Are you okay? You look a little confused."

"No, just being a bit nostalgic. I haven't been back here for a while. I'm going for a run this morning," Edwin said while getting out of the car. The cop backed away a few steps.

"Going for a run?"

"Yeah, I run most mornings, it keeps me young."

"Okay, I haven't seen you out here before. I'd park my car somewhere else if I were you."

"Why? I used to leave my bicycle leaning against that pole for hours at a time and nobody ever touched it."

"Those must have been the good ol' days, with all due respect. How long do you plan to be out here?"

"Maybe an hour."

"Why don't you park your car under the courthouse over here. There's a few spots marked for legal folks, but they won't be around until about seven. At least we'll have cameras on it if something happens. That's an awful nice car to leave out here in the dark."

"It's that bad around here?"

"Yeah, nobody has respect anymore."

"That's a shame. Okay, I'll take you up on your offer."

"And look, it ain't that safe to run around here, either. Just be careful.".

"Thanks, I will. Take care and stay safe."

"We're gonna try."

Edwin pulled his car around the south side entrance of the courthouse and parked. Little had changed to the place, even the door that led to the underbelly of the courthouse and jail looked as though the wrought iron protecting it was still the same. He'd only been brought there once and that had been enough. He got out of his car and stretched, noting that his leg still felt a bit sluggish from the night before. He started his run going south to see if he could find the house he'd once lived in when he was a kid, only to make it a few blocks before seeing a man lying face down on the sidewalk. He remembered a time when that wouldn't have scared him away, when he could have either fought his way past trouble or outran it. But those days were long gone and he knew it. He turned back and ran along the main road where there was a little traffic but plenty of light.

By seven, Edwin was pulling into the parking lot at Kranz Gardens and saw Ellie standing outside the front door with her hands on her hips. She was nervous about the grand opening and he knew why she was out there.

"You told me you'd be ready by eight," she said.

"That's an hour from now, Ellie. I'll be ready."

"You'd better be. I've got plenty of other things to do and I can't be worried about what everyone else should be doing."

"I'll be in the office so stop worrying."

"No, the reception desk."

"Office."

"Look—" Ellie began to protest, but Edwin was ready.

"Office or nothing."

"Fine. Whatever. Just be down here."

"I will. I'm going to grab some breakfast first."

"Dad, you don't have time."

"Just grabbing a biscuit, sweetheart, don't worry."

"Grandpa Edwin," Jack said.

"What do you want, boy?"

"I gotta tell you a secret."

"Tell me."

"Down here," Jack said while pulling on Edwin's running shorts. Edwin leaned down.

"That man wanted me to tell you something," Jack whispered.

"What man?"

"Mr. Chandler. His wife is in a wheelchair."

"Okay. What's his secret?"

"He said he's going to dump her here and never come back."

"Dump who? The woman in the wheelchair?"

"I don't know," Jack said with a shrug. "Is he going to be in trouble?"

"No, he's just having fun with us. I hope."

"Me, too. I'm going to school, want to take me?"

"No, he's got work to do." Ellie's tone left little doubt about her mood toward her father.

"She's mean, isn't she?" Edwin asked.

"No, she's my grandma!"

Edwin smiled as Jack ran to Ellie's side and hugged her around the waist. He looked up at Ellie, who wasn't amused. Edwin headed for the elevators.

"Fifty-three minutes, Dad."

*****

Belle had been flicking her tongue out into the wind every few minutes as Darla drove her to Kranz Gardens. Darla had a smile on her face and was laughing on the inside, not because of what Belle was doing, but because she knew what a handful she would be once she was living there.

"Are you going to do that the whole time we're checking in?"

"You know what it means. I'm gonna torture that man to hell, you watch. You know exactly how he was, him and that 'gift' of his," Belle replied.

"No, I don't know what you mean. I never received that 'gift' you keep talking about, Belle."

"You may lie to everyone else, but I've known you too long. That boy was sniffing your butt every time you walked by, don't tell me you didn't have a weak moment. Not me, Darla, I've known you all my life. We've all—"

"No, don't say all. Just you, you old tramp."

"I'm not a tramp! I wasn't then and never was. I had fun when

I wanted to, not just when the boys wanted to. I knew what I wanted, and if you missed out on the fun, then tough, little missy. You're just bitter for not kicking up your own heels."

"So, you were in control all along?"

"Yes, ma'am, all along. Every one of 'em."

"Even Edwin Kranz?"

Belle glared at Darla for a moment and then turned her head away.

"Old biddy," Belle said quietly while shaking her head. They rode in silence for another mile and then Belle flicked her tongue out again while staring at Darla. Darla began to laugh. "See, you know what it means. Don't lie to me!"

"I'm not lying to you, Belle, you told me all about it. At least a million times."

"You're teasing me."

"No, I'm not. I love you more than my sister, but you're acting like floozy."

Darla and Belle took the long way from Fallon Nursing Home to Kranz Gardens, driving through town as they often had in their youth. Sometimes they drove around on special occasions when Darla would take time away from her ministering to anyone who would put up with her. They would reminisce as they drove by the old buildings, efforts to either recapture or retain old memories and feelings. Today it seemed especially appropriate since Belle's mind was a bit sharper than usual.

Belle and Darla weren't the only ones rehashing their past. As Edwin leaned against the counter in his apartment, eating the biscuit he'd gotten from Ramy, he wanted to be anywhere but downstairs. Edwin was troubled by his memories here in Fallon, the scenes from his youth that replayed in his mind as he ran past familiar sights on his morning run. The distance he'd put between this town and himself had served as a buffer against bitter feelings of the past. He'd had months to prepare for this day but now it didn't seem long enough. He wanted his freedom, or at least a little latitude in how much he was willing to be exposed to his youth again. The hardest part was keeping it all to himself.

*****

Ellie was on fire, running from room to room and trying to remember everything that needed to be ready. She wanted no stone left unturned. Larry wasn't back from taking Jack to school and picking up the extra cleaning supplies. The man could be a nuisance when he had nothing to do, but at the moment it would have been a comfort to have him available if she needed something done quickly. He's a pain in the ass, Ellie thought, but he always keeps his word and he did, after all, agree to do this with me.

Ellie's stomach growled as the aroma of food drifted down the hallway, though she couldn't quite put her finger on what it was she was smelling. She'd given Edwin explicit directions to have Ramy vent his cooking so that the smell didn't permeate the building the way it seemed to be doing now. It did make her curious, giving her an excuse to both introduce herself to Ramy and to see what was being cooked. She walked in while he was pouring spices in his hand to measure, watching him toss them into a pot that was boiling.

"That doesn't look sterile to me, Ramy. And how do you know you aren't putting too much—"

"Experience," Ramy said. He had a smile on his face as he stirred the ingredients without looking up at her.

"Well, it would be nice if you had a recipe—" she began, but Ramy stopped her by pulling out a printout from his pocket and holding it out for her to take.

"It's all right here, ma'am. Ramy can't tell you everything dat goes in his hand is exact, but it's all on dat paper. Ramy's probably within a quarter of a teaspoon."

Ellie looked at the handwritten menu and recipes for the lunch and dinner entrees. The names of the meals were the standard, bland, easy-on-the-stomach items but she had to admit the blackened chicken and vegetable soup smelled heavenly. The effects on her stomach made it difficult for her to be critical at the moment.

"Well, it certainly smells good in here. Is there anything else you need for the kitchen?"

"Just one somethin', ma'am, one of dem computers would be nice in the kitchen."

"A computer?"

"Yes, ma'am. To do inventory, keep Ramy's stock up to date, dat kind of thing."

"I see."

"Anythin' wrong, Miss Ellie?"

"No, I'm just, uh, never mind. I'll check the budget."

"Ramy's good on computers, ma'am. Ramy knows how to keep from running out of food at the last minute. Ramy can show you how to figure your taxes, too, if'n you get the right software."

"I'll keep that in mind, thank you."

Ramy looked up at her and noticed her staring at the pot of soup.

"Missus could use a small bowl of soup right now, couldn't she?"

"Thanks, Ramy, but I really don't have time—"

No sooner had the words left her mouth than he'd pushed a bowl in front of her.

"You work too hard on a empty stomach, you'll just be another patient here."

"I'll take it with me. And thank you," she said as she headed out the kitchen door. "Lunch will be ready at eleven?"

"Eleven to one, ma'am."

"Good," she said as she took her first spoonful. "My God, that's wonderful. And by the way, I don't think I thanked you for having the rolls ready yesterday morning. They made quite an impression."

"Thank you, Miss Ellie. They's plenty more of dat soup if'n you want more."

Ellie waved as she walked through the door, unable to speak with her mouth full. She stopped just short of the lobby to savor the rest of the bowl before getting back to work. Quietly, she had wanted Ramy to fail because he didn't fit the vision she'd had for a cook. And though referring to himself in the third person was particularly annoying, it wasn't enough to justify letting him go. She knew her frustration was with the fact that Ramy had been Edwin's decision instead of hers.

"You've got to be more assertive, Ellie," she mumbled to herself. She stiffened her back with her new resolve, putting the bowl of soup to her mouth and pouring the rest down in a single motion. As the spices continued to dance on her tongue, she felt relieved that at least the cooking was one less thing she had to worry about. Ellie rounded the corner and saw Edwin sitting at the reception desk, staring out at the entrance. "So far, so good?"

"Yes," Edwin said absently.

"I thought you were going to sit in the office?"

"Changed my mind."

"Dad?"

"Yes?"

"You okay?"

Edwin turned his head toward her, but his eyes seemed to be decades away.

"Yes, cutie, I'm fine. Just thinking."

"Okay, I gotta hand it to you, I think that Ramy is gonna work out great if he keeps cooking like this. Have you had his soup yet?"

"No, not really a soup fan."

"Anyway, just wanted to say thanks for finding him. I actually think he's going to be a breath of fresh air around here."

"Yes, he certainly seems to know what he's doing."

"Dad?"

"What?"

"Something's up. What's wrong with you? Are you angry that I want you to help me?"

Edwin turned back to look at her and this time she knew she had his attention.

"Everything's fine, Ellie. Lots of old memories around me and it's just got me to thinking. That's all."

"Thinking about what?"

Edwin looked outside for a second and then back at her.

"Why don't you let me hire a staff of nurses and helpers so that—"

"Dad, no! You already think I'm failing, don't you?"

Edwin realized he'd made a mistake. She was under a lot of pressure and it hadn't occurred to him how she might react to his comment.

"No, not at all, Ellie. Look, this more about me than you. I was just looking to make it easier so that I wouldn't have to do anything."

"Dad, we talked about this. I want to make the decisions. I don't want to have to rely on you."

"You aren't relying on me, Ellie, but you're going to be too busy to do all this by yourself. Don't be like me, don't be so stubborn. Think of me as your vice president that carries out your vision of what you see the company being. Now what's wrong with that?"

"Because my vision is for things to happen when they're necessary, not at your whims. C'mon, Dad. Dammit, I feel like you don't have any confidence in me."

"I've been watching you work and I have plenty of confidence in you, and I'm certainly not trying to hurt your feelings. I just don't want you to be short on help when you can least afford it."

Ellie walked around the desk and leaned over to be eye level with him.

"I'm not overwhelmed, Dad. Not hurting, not overworked, not anything else. I've got things in order and we're about to launch this business, good or bad, into something that I can be proud of. And you know what? I'm trying awful hard to do this right so that you'll be proud of me."

"But I am proud of you."

"No, you haven't seen what I can do yet. You haven't seen how hard I can work and how much I can tolerate to be a success. Please give me that chance. Mom never did, and to hell with her."

"Ellie, don't say that about your mother."

"No, to hell with her. I never got anything but lectures from her, but somehow I always knew that you loved me. It would've been nice if you were a little more expressive at times. But you have to let me do this my way. Please."

"Okay, but I'm not going to let you go underwater before throwing out a raft, got it?"

"Dad, I have one resident, I think I can manage that for the moment."

"One?" he asked as he pointed to the entrance doors. "You better look again."

Ellie walked to the door and saw a line of cars each with their trunks open and luggage and boxes stacked on the sidewalk.

"Holy shit. It can't be, I've only heard from one person."

"Yes," Edwin said as he walked up and put an arm around her shoulders, "And that one person knows everyone in town. You're going to be so busy you won't know which way is up."

"I don't even know which rooms to assign these people."

"Put 'em in the dining room for breakfast while you figure it out."

"I don't know if there's enough food."

"There is, Ramy knew about this."

"How would he know?"

"I told him," Edwin said with a grin, but Ellie seemed more frustrated than before. "It was just a hunch."

Ellie stood dumbfounded as she watched everyone congregate on the sidewalk, talking and laughing as if it were a planned reunion. To Ellie, it was like a horror show. She wasn't ready to deal with all of these people and now she felt terribly ill-equipped to handle her new role. She felt a hand on her shoulder and turned to see Larry walking by with a valet cart.

"Open the door and let's go bring in our guests before they die without paying," he said with a smile.

Ellie opened the door, speechless as Larry stepped through and announced to the crowd: "Welcome to Kranz Gardens."

Chapter 12

Hester stood looking in the mirror, knowing it was her vanity that was causing her to dress up for Edwin. The thought of seeing him again today was overwhelming, and visions of what he might look like made her feel giddy. She wanted him to remember her, wanted to see if anything from their past had left an indelible impression on him. She looked at her picture in her high school yearbook and then back in the mirror and shook her head. It was likely he wouldn't recognize her, but she hoped that he'd remember their brief time together as teens. She looked over at the bottle of rum, wondering if it would help to show up with that in her hand. The thought of it made her thirsty.

"Hester, honey, there's no telling what he looks like or if he's still married," she said to her reflection, "And what have you got that he wants?"

"Everything," she replied to herself, fantasizing as she often did. "I want your lips pressed against mine, your arms around my neck, and your body firmly pressed against me."

"You can't have me, Edwin. Not in a million years. You left me, alone and cold, in a shameful state. I couldn't face my parents for a month. I threw myself at you and you forced me onto the path of destruction that's made me into what I am today."

"No! You know it didn't happen that way. I loved you, but you were too young. What else was I to do? I was confused, I didn't want to hurt you, but I was torn and had to let you go."

"Do you mean it? You loved me?"

"Yes, from the moment I laid eyes on you. You knew what you were doing to me, toying with me and making me weak with your beauty and charm."

"But you resisted! Why?"

"Because I wasn't good enough for you."

"You were!"

"No, I wasn't."

"Yes, you just needed reassurance. I was the one who needed you, as I still do."

"To this day?"

"Forever!"

"Be mine, sweet Hester. Fulfill my lifelong dream and stand at my side like the prize, the perfection that you are."

"I will, Edwin, take me as your queen."

"Indeed. But—" her alter ego began to say, and Hester looked into the mirror knowing how she would finish the fantasy as tears began to flow from her eyes. "—you must stop drinking."

"I can't," she said in despair. "I guess it just wasn't meant to be."

Hester sat down in the chair in front of her vanity and put her head down onto her folded arms. She'd cried about her alcoholism many times over the years, painfully at times. Yet this time was different. There was no wailing, no yelling at herself or throwing things about the house in frustration and self-hate. It was a cry of sorrow that only one who has let their life slip by one drink at a time can understand. After a few minutes she raised her head and looked sadly in the mirror.

"We're all too old to worry about little things anymore, aren't we, Hester? We are what we are and who knows, maybe Edwin hasn't missed a beat either, maybe he still enjoys a little bit of good times now and then. It isn't like you're going to marry him or anything. We can still have some fun."

Hester tipped her head back, opened her mouth wide, and pressed the opening of a gin bottle up against the roof of her mouth as if it were the barrel of a gun.

"It's the same result," she mumbled into the bottle, "It just takes a lot longer."

*****

Ellie forced a smile as she held the front door open for the people coming in. Not all of them would be residents, and the way they ignored her as they filed in made her feel more like she was hosting a garage sale than a grand opening. She chalked it up to her own anxiety as she continued to put on a good face.

"Welcome to Kranz..." Ellie began, echoing Larry's words from a moment ago.

"Where is he?" Belle demanded as she pushed her walker through the doorway.

"Belle, show some manners," Darla scolded.

"Are you Mrs. Chandler?" Ellie asked.

"Yes, this is Isabelle Chandler. She goes by Belle, unless she's being difficult, and then we make up names for her depending on her disposition."

"Well, who are you?" Belle asked, disregarding Darla's comment.

"I'm Ellie Mintzer and this is our home."

"Whose home? Does Edwin Kranz live here?" Belle began

flicking her tongue in and out repeatedly with a wicked grin. Ellie looked horrified.

"It's our home: mine, yours, and the others that will live here. I like to think of it as a home with a large family," Ellie replied. She'd been practicing saying it, but the words seemed to fall flat with her new tenant.

"Where's Edwin? My grandson said he was staying here, too."

"Yes, well, he was going to run an errand and—" she began, but Belle began flicking her tongue again. "Are you thirsty?"

"No, why do you ask? What have you got to drink here?"

"I just wondered if maybe your mouth was dry or something?"

"She's just being a pain in the backside," Darla replied.

"Are you related to her?"

"Might as well be, but no, we're old friends and I try to keep her out of trouble."

"I see. So, I guess we should get you settled into your room. You're probably tired."

"No, I'm not. Where's Edwin? Where's 'The Tongue'?"

"The who?"

"She has this fixation with Edwin, something that goes back to our teens," Darla said. "I'll tell you about it later."

"Sounds interesting. Edwin is my father and I'd love to hear about his early years."

Belle stared at Ellie, an evil smile forming on her face while Darla's looked troubled.

"So, you're the daughter of Margie and Edwin?"

"Wait, who is Margie?"

"Never mind," Darla said in a rebuke to Belle. "This isn't the time, this is his daughter for heaven's sake."

"She looks old enough to know what—"

"Shut up, Isabelle," Darla said while covering Belle's mouth.

"Now what could be so bad that you couldn't tell me?"

"We should probably just get Belle to her room."

Ellie grabbed the folder that she had prepared with Belle's information and began walking when Alton Chandler came through the front door along with another elderly man, both carrying boxes of Isabelle's belongings.

"Ellie, this is my grandfather, Cary."

"Hello, good to meet you," Ellie said.

"Same to you, Miss Kranz."

"Mintzer. My name is Ellie Mintzer, but my father is Edwin Kranz."

"Is he here?"

"Somewhere," Ellie replied. Everyone's fixation him was beginning to get irritating. "Do you know him?"

"Oh, yeah, who didn't?"

"Hmmm, my father seems to have been a popular guy—"

"He was an asshole, but I won't hold that against you."

"Grandpa!"

"I can only guess there's a story there," Ellie said.

"Does he still walk around boastin' about everything all the time? Trying to make time with all the women?"

"I think you may have him confused with someone else."

"Grandpa, you definitely have the wrong Mr. Kranz; he's quite reserved."

"That's an understatement," Ellie echoed.

"Y'all must have neutered him," Cary muttered as he began to shuffle along down the hallway. "Hope you sewed his damn lips together, too."

Ellie looked at Alton as Cary continued to talk to himself, knowing that he could be heard.

"I apologize, Ellie, I know there's some history here with my family and your dad."

"It's okay. I'm sure we'll hear about it in due course."

"Unfortunately, I'm pretty sure you will. I'd tell you myself if I felt comfortable about it, but I don't think I can."

"It can't be that bad, can it?" Ellie asked. She was trying to reassure herself, but she was beginning to worry.

Alton was barely able to make eye contact with her, shifting his weight from one foot to the other and squirming with the boxes in his arms.

"These are getting kind of heavy and I've got to get the rest of the stuff that's still in the pickup."

"Okay, Alton. Use the valet cart in the corner and I'll go down to get her settled in."

"Ellie?"

"Yeah?"

"She's not in her right mind, please don't take it the wrong way."

"Don't worry, I've been dealing with elderly patients for a long time."

Alton nodded but appeared to be developing indigestion. Ellie began walking down the hall and could hear Cary getting angry with Belle.

"We know, Belle, now keep your damn tongue in your mouth. Darla, for the love, shut her up. Shit! She goes on and on," he said as he came out of the room and passed Ellie. "I knew this was a bad idea. Shoulda told that man to stay wherever the hell he was before he came back here, and now the whole town's gonna be in an uproar."

Ellie stopped short of the door and listened to see if she could get an inkling of what was going on. But the only thing she could hear was Cary continuing to complain from down the hallway. Ellie walked in to see Darla about a foot away from Belle's face with her finger pushing on her nose.

"Stop it!" Darla said. Belle stuck her tongue out and then back in quickly, laughing at Darla like a child. "Behave, Isabelle, dammit."

"Hey," Ellie said while touching Darla on the shoulder. "Can I talk to you in the hallway for a moment?"

"Yes, just a minute." Belle stuck out her tongue again and

Darla glared at her. "Stay here and keep your yap shut."

Darla started for the door and Ellie followed. They stopped just outside the doorway so they could listen for Belle, who was fidgeting with the buttons on her blouse.

"She seems to have a tic or something, is that part of the progression of her disease?"

"A what? I'm not sure what you mean."

"A tic, a nervous habit or uncontrollable movement. That thing she does with her tongue. Has she done that for long?"

"Oh, that's not a habit. That's pure meanness. She's got a score to settle and this is just a teaser."

"I don't think we're on the same page here, I'm talking about her tongue control, or lack of it."

"She's mocking Edwin when she does it. Look, I'm going to be brutally honest with you, Miss, uh, what was your name again?"

"Ellie Mintzer, but call me Ellie."

"Ellie, your father was a very crude little scoundrel when we were kids. If there was a prank afoot, he was behind it. If something smelled in the lunchroom so bad that you couldn't eat, you'd want to know what he was up to."

"I'm sorry, this certainly isn't the man I know. Perhaps there's more than one Edwin Kranz."

"Oh no, there's just one. One that just happened to pick this retreat to buy."

"Okay, look, maybe he had some wild oats to sow, but what does it matter now?"

"To Belle? Lots. This place has a hell of a meaning for her, and I'm one of the few people that know the truth about it. And of all the things she remembers, your father and this place are stuck fresh in her brain."

"Let me guess, he took advantage of her here?"

"That's not all of it."

"This place is like a college dorm when everybody's moving

in," Belle said to herself.

Darla and Ellie looked around the corner to see what she was up to.

"You never went to college, Belle."

"No, but I spent a lot of time in the dorm rooms!" Belle cackled. Darla just shook her head.

Ellie looked at her watch and noticed that she was losing time and hadn't even begun to care for Belle or anyone else.

"Darla, for the sake of time can you tell me what is wrong with her tongue?"

"She's pretending to be your dad, that's what's wrong with her tongue. He used to walk around boasting about how long his tongue was, and how wide it was. He would go around flicking it in and out, flaring it like a cobra or something. It was impressive come to think of it."

"A cobra? So what, so he had a weird trick?"

Darla's gaze came to a clear focus and her hand came to rest between her breasts as if she were catching her breath.

"He used to tell the girls how good he was with his tongue, how he could make us all slaves."

"Oh, I don't believe all that," Ellie protested, her face becoming flushed. "Dad would never—"

"Yes, he did. I can march a dozen girls in front of you tomorrow that would say the same thing."

"I don't believe it. Mind you, I'm not calling you a liar, but I have a hard time believing it."

"I'm sorry, there's no other explanation for it. We lived it."

"She's got dementia. They pretend, conjure up stories. They, well—," Ellie began to say but then realized the futility of her argument. "Okay, it doesn't matter. What's in the past doesn't matter and we'll just have to get through it. Let's just make sure she's comfortable and get the rest of her stuff moved in."

"Ms. Mintzer, for your sake, I hope Belle can overcome this. But ever since she heard he was in town, she hasn't let up one ounce."

"We'll deal with it, I'm sure. Do you know where her daughter is? She was supposed to meet with me this morning to complete the paperwork."

"She had to close with the other facility Belle was in. She should be here within the hour."

"Good. And ma'am?"

"Call me Darla, you're going to be seeing a lot of me. I'm her best friend."

"Great. I'll be up at the front desk if you—" she started and then heard Cary come up behind her pulling a wheeled suitcase and carrying a box.

"Coming through. Hey, Belle, I just saw 'The Tongue' out in the lobby."

Ellie clutched the file folder to her breasts and stormed off to find Edwin. Behind her she could hear Cary and Darla trying to keep Belle from leaving her room, and in front of her she could see Edwin's eyes barely peeking over the counter of the front desk.

"I need a word with you," Ellie said, pointing an accusatory finger at Edwin, who in turn pointed his finger at the front door. A man with a walker shuffled through the doorway, followed by an entourage of what Ellie assumed was children, grandchildren, nieces, nephews, and their pets. Ellie looked back at Edwin with contempt. "Later," she said with a glare. "Hello, welcome to Kranz Gardens. Can I help you?"

"We're—" one of them began to say but was silenced by the man with the walker.

"I want to move here. I heard that Belle Chandler was moving in today."

"Yes, she did. Just minutes ago. Can I show you around and tell you about Kranz Gardens?"

"No, just give me a room key and I'll find my way."

"Well, we need to discuss at least a few things. Maybe—"

"Over coffee?" Ramy said as he leaned against the wall just beyond the desk. "Or, Ramy'll bet a man like you likes a good bowl of soup."

"Is that what I smell in here? Smells good. That other place smells like death and shitty diapers. We'll have the soup," he said.

"We?" Ellie stammered, watching the entire family nod their heads.

"Y'all come on into the dining room and Ramy's gonna feed you. You won't eat no better than here at Kranz Gardens," Ramy said, and then turned to look at Ellie with a wink. "And they's plenty to go 'round."

Ellie stood frozen in the lobby, watching as they disappeared through the doorway of the dining room.

"Have I just lost all control here?" she asked herself aloud. She turned to look at Edwin, who had conveniently disappeared. "Dammit. Dammit! Where did he go?"

"What's up, doll?" Larry asked.

"Grandma, look what I got. A picture of Grandpa Edwin's boat and Grandpa got a frame." Ellie looked at the two, trying her best not to scream. "Did Grandpa Edwin's boat get here yet?"

"I don't know. You might check out on the dock."

"There it is," Larry said while looking out the front entrance. "I'll be damned, I'd swear it's the same one that Jack saw yesterday."

"Grandpa, that's Grandpa Edwin's boat, isn't it!"

"It looks that way, Jack."

"I'll be damned!" Jack said, prompting a gentle scolding from Larry.

Ellie waved her hand quickly, shooing them out the door to settle the boat issue. As they walked out, another woman walked in. She only took one step in the doorway and then scanned the foyer, even straining her neck to look behind the front desk. She had a sweet, pleasant manner and was dressed very nicely. Something about her demeanor put Ellie at ease.

"Welcome to Kranz Gardens, my name is Ellie. Can I help you?"

"I'm Hester Jorgensen, nice to meet you," the woman said while offering Ellie her hand. Her eyes never stopped moving, as if she were looking for something in particular. Her breath also had an aroma of mint and alcohol.

"Good to meet you. Is there something I can help you find?"

"I'm looking for Edwin Kranz, I haven't seen him in years."

"You know my father?"

"You're his daughter? What a lovely woman you are, I should have guessed. He was such a handsome man, such a gentleman."

"Ah, so you did know him?"

"Oh, yes. He was quite the charmer. We only went out on one date, but he is forever planted in my heart."

"How sweet! I'm sure he'd love to see you. I bet he's got a lot of fond memories."

"Maybe," she said wistfully, but then a frown came across her face. "Oh, what am I saying. He probably doesn't even remember me. Too busy with the other girls, wagging his tongue here and there, and the rumors I used to hear. Oh, I'm sorry, honey. You don't need to hear all of that."

"It's okay, I'm getting used to it."

"Listen, don't believe everything you hear. For all of his talk, he was a gentleman in his own way. He made sure I got home safe one time when I wasn't quite feeling well, you know."

"Really?"

"Yes. Of course, my father didn't see it that way at all and carried a knife with him just in case he saw Edwin out where he shouldn't be."

"He wanted to stab my father?"

"Oh, yes. It was quite sweet. He wanted to avenge my honor for what he thought your father had done. I never could bring myself to tell him nothing had happened. It was bad of me, I know, but it was also thrilling. And the other girls! They were beside themselves thinking I had made time with an upperclassman, one with such skills."

"Okay, thank you Miss, or is it Mrs.?"

"Miss, I think. After you've been married six times, does it really matter?"

"I suppose not, Miss Jorgensen. I hate to cut this short but—"

"Is he in?"

Before she could answer, she saw Edwin out at the boat dock with Larry and Jack.

"There," Ellie said pointing, "He's the tall one with the green shirt getting on the boat. You may be just missing him."

"Yes, the one that looks more my age, I'm afraid."

Hester was noticeably delighted, already walking to the back door. She smoothed her hair and dress as she walked.

"Would you like me to—"

"No, I'm fine, I'll just pop out there and wait on the patio. We'll see if he recognizes me."

Ellie felt Hester either had the innocence of a child or the anguish of an ax murderer. She worried that Hester was a little too eager to see her father and might be carrying a knife of her own around.

"Did he know you were coming?"

"I suspect that he's always known I would be waiting."

Ellie nodded with a nervous smile as she watched Hester walk with an unsteady gait to the back door.

"Good God, what have I gotten myself into?"

"I beg your pardon?" a woman said from behind her. Ellie jumped from surprise, not knowing how long the woman had been standing there.

"I was reflecting—"

"My goodness, what a beautiful job you've done with this retreat," she said, looking around from one angle to another. "I never stayed here, but I would come and help my mother work sometimes, and it was such a spectacular place. It looks much different now, but still just as beautiful. That must sound odd, doesn't it?"

"It's about par for the course today," Ellie said. She was becoming fatigued with the new faces and stories. "But thank you for the compliment, it's been a pleasure bringing it back to life. You say your mother worked here?"

"Yes, she worked here in the kitchen on the weekends as a cook. She loved to cook and it gave her extra income. She worked at the high school, too. All the kids knew her and she loved them all. All except one, I remember."

"I can only guess who that could be."

"You probably wouldn't know her so I guess there's no harm in telling you. She complained constantly that the spaghetti sauce was too thin. Spaghetti was hardly served at all in schools then but mother did her best. She would come home beside herself, swearing about how rude this girl had been."

"I'm sure that was frustrating," Ellie replied, relieved the story did not involve Edwin.

"It was, and mother never forgot her name in all those years: Hester Jorgensen."

Ellie looked quickly out to the patio to ensure that Hester was still out there.

"I can just imagine. Listen, how would you like to see the kitchen?"

"I'd love to, but I don't have the time. I needed to ask you if you had any vacancies?"

"Many, as a matter of fact. Are you looking for nursing care or just assisted living?"

"Nursing care; for my mother that is."

"She's still, uh, with us?" Ellie asked before thinking.

"Oh, yes, and just as active as ever."

"That's fantastic, and yes we do have vacancies. Sit down here and we can talk about her needs and what arrangements can be made."

"That would be wonderful, and what is your name, by the way?"

"I'm sorry, I should have introduced myself earlier. Ellie Mintzer, and yours?"

"Dorothy Cardenas, and my mother's name is Annette, although everyone called her Nettie."

"What a pretty name. I think we can make your mother very happy."

"I hope so, because she can be such a crabby woman when she's upset."

Ellie smiled but wondered if everyone who moved in would either have a romantic connection to her father or some less desirable quirk. It didn't matter at the moment because she needed the business, but it suddenly occurred to her that she was going to need more help. That would require admitting her father was right and that wasn't something she was ready to do.

Chapter 13

Edwin was only out on the water for a few minutes, wanting to get the feel of the boat. He'd seen the sad look on Jack's face back at the dock when he left without him and hoped he would still be there when he got back. Jack stood alone at the end of the dock while Larry was talking to someone closer to the patio when Edwin returned. Jack's life jacket was almost as large as he was and he waved excitedly as Edwin returned. Edwin motioned to Larry to show that he was taking Jack with him.

"Never been on a boat, huh?" Edwin asked.

"Never, Grandpa."

"You're not going to get seasick, are you?"

"Never. I don't get sick on boats."

"Right. Should we wait for Grandpa Larry?"

"No, I have a question to ask you. It's just for you, I don't want Grandpa Larry to hear it."

"Okay, then it's just me and you."

Edwin helped Jack into the boat and made sure his life jacket was snuggly fastened. He began to back the boat out just as Ellie appeared at the back door waving her arms. Edwin pretended not to notice, put the boat in drive and escaped quickly amid shrieks of laughter from Jack.

"Where do you want to go?" Edwin asked.

"I want to go over there," Jack replied, pointing at a spot on the horizon.

"Where all those boats are?"

"Yeah."

"Why?"

"Because I want to see if their boats are as big as ours."

"Well, I'm sure some of them are. How is school going?"

"It's fun. Today we got to write our names and make a necklace."

"A necklace? That's for girls."

"No, it's not, Grandpa Edwin, it had our names on 'em."

"How do you know it was your name?"

"I don't know, my teacher told me. Can I just call you Edwin?"

"Why?"

"Because it's too hard to say Grandpa Edwin."

"That makes sense. How about if you call me Gramps?"

"Gramps? Why Gramps?"

"Because it'll drive your Grandma crazy."

"No," Jack said with a smile, "Grandma's a nice lady. That's mean. Gramps sounds like a stomach-ache."

"Have you ever been fishing?"

"No."

"Do you want to try?"

"Not anymore."

"Why not?"

"Because they bite."

"Not regular fish," Edwin said, "Just sharks and they don't live in this lake."

"Ramy said this morning that the fish bite all day if you go to the right place. I don't want them to bite me."

Edwin was amused at the misunderstanding.

"Ramy was just saying that the fish were biting the bait. You see, you put worms or minnows on a hook and the fish bite them."

"With their teeth?"

"No, they don't have any teeth. So, they can't bite you."

"Then how come people say they're biting?"

"I don't know."

He smiled at Jack, noticing not only the physical resemblance he had to his father but also the never-ending questioning that his father had thought was so clever. Edwin had only met Tim a few times but had never been impressed with his smugness.

"Hey, do you want to drive?"

"No."

"Okay. Why not?"

"I don't want to crash."

"What if I help you?"

"I don't know."

"Does it scare you?"

"Yeah."

"Make you think of something?"

"Yeah."

"Alright then."

Edwin wanted to give Jack the opportunity to talk but didn't want to force him. They made it halfway across the lake when Jack got up from his seat and held his hand out to Edwin for balance. He got in Edwin's lap and stared out over the bow of the boat.

"Grandpa Edwin?"

"What, buddy?"

"Why do people have to die?"

"I don't know, Jack. Things just don't seem fair, do they?"

"No. I asked Grandma for something."

"What's that?"

"I asked her if she could bring Mommy and Daddy back. She said no."

"That's right, Jack, nobody can."

"You can't either?"

"Nope, nobody. Is that the question you wanted to ask me?"

Jack nodded and sat still for a moment, then slid from Edwin's lap to the floor and made his way back to the passenger seat. Edwin saw the dismay in his eyes and within a few seconds saw the tears begin to trickle down his cheeks. Edwin slowed the boat down and turned off the engine, stepped over to Jack and wrapped his arms around him.

"If you can't do it then nobody can."

"I know, Jack, I'm sorry."

"It's okay."

Edwin was uncomfortable with the role he had in Jack's life. Jack had obviously made his own connections with Edwin in some way and Edwin realized he was now going to have to be a role model instead of just a fun old man who would take him places and buy him things. Edwin had never experienced this with anyone else. It wasn't that he didn't want the responsibility, he just didn't want to mess it up.

"Hey, I want you to call me Gramps."

"No, it sounds stupid."

"Okay, we'll just stick with Grandpa Edwin. How's that?"

Jack nodded in agreement.

*****

There were two things missing from Kranz Gardens: Edwin at the front desk and his new boat from the dock. Ellie had seen him leave with no indication of when he would return.

She stood by the door in a trance; the noise coming from the hallway and dining area was mind-numbing. She'd lost control the moment Belle Chandler had walked through the door. While she'd done her best to get Belle settled in without losing her own mind, others had taken it upon themselves to find rooms to their liking and had moved in. As she made her way back to the front desk, Ellie could see that half of the first floor was filled with people mingling in the hallway, hanging personal items on their doors as if they'd been there for years. Ellie felt powerless and decided to square it all later.

By noon, Ellie couldn't be sure how many rooms remained on the first floor and she was afraid to look upstairs at the second or third. She was sure that the surviving members of Edwin's graduating class were all having lunch in the dining room judging by the way everyone had congregated in one area. She had never set out silverware, napkins, or even provided a menu; somebody had taken on that task without her. It should have been a comfort, yet it was a reminder that she hadn't been able to think of everything. Ellie was in a stupor, wanting to take a vacation already when someone began tapping on her shoulder.

"Ellie, I've got a question for you," Cary said.

"What is it, Mr. Chandler?"

"You got that room over there, the craft room, and I was wondering if you'd be kind enough to let us have it for a few hours every Tuesday. We want to kind of reserve it, you know what I mean?"

"What do you want to do with it?"

Cary squirmed a bit and looked around before answering. He seemed to be on his best behavior and spoke softly, completely out of his normal character.

"Me and the guys, we wanted to have a weekly prayer meeting. It's for those of us that don't feel comfortable going to church. I think you get the idea, right? I mean, you don't go to church either, right?"

"No, I don't. Uh, let me think this over and I'll get back to you."

"Yeah, I don't want to rush you, but today's Monday and tomorrow's Tuesday and we can't meet over at the other place because Belle doesn't live there no more. Like I said, I don't want to rush you, but I'll be around for a few hours."

"Okay, look, I don't have anything planned for tomorrow in there so I guess it wouldn't hurt for this week. We'll see how it goes or if it interferes with anything else. How does that sound?"

"I knew you would be a reasonable woman. Unlike your dad, but I ain't gonna hold that against you. Much obliged."

"What times are you looking for, Mr. Chandler?"

"You can call me Cary, and we were thinking about ten in the morning until one in the afternoon. Give or take."

"Three-hour prayer meeting? That seems like a lot."

"We're old, we have a lot of issues to deal with."

"I'm sorry, I'm not judging you. Sure, go ahead."

"Thanks again," Cary said as he turned and hurried down the hall.

"God bless," Ellie called out, and Cary simply waved to her.

Ellie put her hands to her face and closed her eyes, wondering when the madness of the day would end. There was nothing wrong with Cary's request, although something about it seemed suspect. The truth of the matter was that it was just one more thing she hadn't planned on dealing with today. She had envisioned one patient, maybe two, moving in and having plenty of time to spend to get them settled. She'd also fantasized about people coming in and inquiring about the kind of care offered that they couldn't get anywhere else and getting the opportunity to show people around. What she had gotten instead was a walker stampede of senior citizens taking over as if they owned the place. Ellie rubbed her eyes, hoping that when she opened them again everything would look crystal clear, only to find a bright young face looking at her.

"Hello?" the young woman said timidly.

"Hello," Ellie replied, "Welcome Kranz Gardens, or Kranz Mayhem at the moment."

"Opening day, how exciting! Can you tell me where I might find the manager?"

"That would be me, what can I do for you?"

"I'm Jenna Pack. I'm a CNA and I was hoping to get an application."

"To work here?"

"Yes," she nodded. Jenna looked barely old enough to be out of high school but appeared to have both the eagerness and attitude Ellie would have wanted in an employee.

"Do you have experience?" Ellie asked, but then interrupted herself. "No, wait. I don't care."

"Yes, ma'am. Lots of experience. Three years worth, anyway. Some people say that's a lot."

"When can you start?"

"I can help out the rest of the day, if you like, but I have to give two weeks' notice."

Ellie stared at Jenna for a moment, her mind focused on Edwin who was halfway across the lake. Edwin's decision to abandon her there at the busiest time was the inspiration for her to take his advice and spend some of his money. Maybe lots of it.

Although Jenna knew nothing about Ellie, she felt afraid to move or say anything to the wild-eyed creature in front of her. Before she could make a dash for safety, a look of clarity came to Ellie's eyes. It was a defiant look, that of a person who had come to the conclusion that getting even was in order.

"If you'll start tomorrow, I'll cover your two weeks at the other place," Ellie said with a menacing smile.

"Uh, sure!"

"Hours are seven to five, is that okay?"

"Perfect, may I ask how much?"

"Two bucks more per hour than you're making now."

"Well, I make—"

"I don't care what you make now, we'll talk about that tomorrow. Right now, I need someone who can organize this mess."

"Can do. And I'm sorry, I didn't get your name."

"Ellie Mintzer, I'm the owner of Kranz Gardens."

"So, your father is Edwin Kranz?" Jenna asked with a look of surprise.

"You know him, too? Good God, this is phenomenal."

"I'm sorry, I've heard so many things about him from one of your patients. I took care of Belle Chandler at Fallon Nursing Home. She is so adorable."

Ellie smiled and put her arm on Jenna's shoulder.

"She's all yours. In fact, she's exclusively yours, you can take her home with you when you leave in the afternoons if you like."

"She's easy. They're all easy if you keep them together. Most of them moved out today together. I hope they found rooms close to each other."

"Oh, they picked their rooms alright. Just go down the hallway to your right and see how many you recognize. I have to run, I have no idea who half of these people are in the dining area."

"I'll find my way around. Thanks, Mrs. Mintzer."

"Ellie. Call me Ellie."

"I like that name. Thanks, Ellie."

Ellie watched as she walked down the hallway. Jenna stopped at the door of the first room on the right and Ellie heard people cheer. Jenna smiled and waved at them, turned back to wave at Ellie, and continued down the hall to the delight of the rest of the new residents. Ellie felt a bit of a burden had been lifted off of her shoulders.

Beyond the madness and confusion, Ellie felt a degree of satisfaction that she'd never experienced before. It came as a surprise because for all of the years she'd longed for her father's love and approval, and all of the years she'd wanted a normal family with that pride of belonging, she'd also wanted some sort of revenge for not having it. It was more of a need to vent, once and for all, the frustration and sadness she felt should never be thrust upon a child. It was therapeutic, she thought, and like a drug she craved it even more. The hiring of Jenna Pack might be just the beginning.

Chapter 14

Edwin wiped the crumbs of the potato chips from the seat of the boat, leftovers from Jack's first ride. Jack seemed more relaxed on returning to Kranz Gardens and Edwin was relieved to see that his longing for his parents had subsided, for the moment at least. It would be up to all of them to be supportive and patient with him.

"Hey, Edwin, somebody's looking for you," Larry said with a grin.

"Is it Ellie? Ready to shoot me or something?"

"Nope, it ain't Ellie. Some lady named Hester. I forget her last name."

"Jorgensen?"

"That sounds right. I told her you might be out here, but she wanted to wait inside, too hot for her out here. I think she's sweet on you."

"You may be right. That girl caused me more trouble than you can imagine."

"Tell me, I want to hear about it," Larry said as he stepped aboard the boat and sat in the captain's chair.

"Her brother was a friend of mine, played on the football team when we were seniors. She was a sophomore and couldn't get to the game on her own, so he asked me if I'd take her. I said sure and we left a few hours after school let out. The game was about thirty miles away."

"What did she look like then?"

"Cute, very cute. Dark hair, trim body, the perfect girl next door. But I was never into younger girls and she was Eric's sister, so I minded my manners."

"So, where did the trouble begin?"

"I always kept a bottle of rum under the seat of my car. They didn't have open container laws then and you could have a beer or two and not worry too much. I was old enough by then and I felt safe. Anyway, I bought us a couple of sodas for the trip, drank down about a quarter of mine, and topped it off with rum."

"Oh shit, here we go."

"Yeah, well, she asked if she could have a sip, said she'd never had alcohol before. I thought why not, it was just a sip."

"Famous last words."

"She liked it. Took to it like water. She drank her soda down a bit and I poured a little rum in hers. Again, I figured one drink wouldn't kill anyone. We had about four hours before she'd be getting back home so I thought she'd have time to burn it off. By the time we got to the game she was tipsy, but not too bad. She asked if I minded if she sat with her friends on the other end of the bleachers and that sounded fine to me. I didn't want my friends seeing me out with a sophomore. By the time I found her at the end of the game, she was plastered. Somebody had given her booze and she could hardly stand, and I still had to get her home."

"Is this where you tried to take advantage of her?"

"No, that never happened. But she did accuse me of it."

"No kidding?"

"Yeah. We knew her parents were out and I thought I could drop her off without any fuss, but she'd forgotten her house key. So, we drove back to the high school parking lot to wait for the team bus. Her brother would have a key and I could get it from him. I was so pissed at this point. She kept yammering about how much trouble she was going to be in and that it was my fault. That's when she said I got her drunk just so I could take advantage of her."

"What did you say?"

"I didn't have time to say anything, she threw up all over me and the dashboard of my car. I was cleaning vomit out of my blower vents for weeks. Every time I turned on the defroster it stank and little dried chunks of food would come out. I had to take out the heater core and clean it before the smell would go away. Shit was stuck to it like a magnet and it reeked."

Larry was bent over laughing and Edwin couldn't help but laugh a little.

"It is funny, isn't it?"

"It isn't just the story, it's you. None of this sounds like something you would've been caught up in. That's what's funny. I would've loved to have been there. How did you get her home?"

"Her brother finally showed up at school on the team bus and I got the key from him. I told him what had happened and he got this worried look on his face. At first, I thought that maybe he was suspicious of me, but then he asked me if there was somewhere she could stay to get cleaned up and sober. I didn't know of any place so I just took her home."

"What happened?"

"Her parent's car was in the drive when we got there. I had her get out and when I saw her open the front door, I stepped on the gas."

"That was close."

"That wasn't the end of it. I didn't realize they lived on a cul-de-sac and I was boxed in. The end of the road was about a quarter of a mile down, plenty of time for the old man to be waiting for me in the middle of the road with a baseball bat. I had to drive through five yards and over a mailbox to get past him."

"Did you ever hear from him again?"

"Not really, but a few months later I was in a store and Eric ran up to me saying his dad had spotted me and was headed over. I got out of there quick and that was the end of it."

"And now she's back to rekindle the flames."

"Maybe. Is she still here?"

"No, she had to leave. She seemed a little antsy, I think she waited for about an hour. I didn't know when you were going to get back."

"She'll probably show up again," Edwin said.

The sound of a motor coming up from behind caused them to turn and look. A bass boat approached quickly, the motor turned off just in time to slow the boat as it pulled to the other side of the dock. The two men looked at each other and Edwin stood, irritated that someone was coming to his dock. Before he could make another move, a stocky, mean-looking woman got out of the boat carrying a large cooler.

"Where's Ramy?" the woman demanded, her cigarette jogging up and down between her lips as she spoke.

Both men pointed to the back door. The woman grunted and continued up to the building.

"What the hell?" Edwin asked in a whisper.

"Girlfriend?" Larry countered.

"God, I hope not."

The back door opened and Jenna walked out just in time to hold the door for the woman with the cooler.

"Mr. Kranz?" Jenna yelled.

"Yes?"

"Ellie wanted to see you as soon as you got back."

"Shit, I thought I could sneak in without being noticed," Edwin said to Larry and then looked back over to Jenna. "I'll be right there."

"She's been watching for you ever since you left."

"Should've known. By the way, who the hell was that?"

"The big woman?"

"No, the little tart that just stuck her head out the door."

"Jenna, a CNA. Ellie hired her not long after you left."

"What's a CNA?"

"Certified Nursing Assistant. Ellie said she had to have her."

"Did she? I should take off more often, maybe she'll start hiring the help she needs."

"I think it's starting to eat her lunch already."

"She'll be fine, she just needs a little dose of reality for a while."

*****

Joan Campenella sat in the dining room alone, watching Edwin and Jack take off in the boat. She wanted Edwin to take her for a ride so she could talk to him without anyone interrupting. He'd kept her sexuality a secret and even enabled it when they were young, so he was the one person she could completely open up to. She recalled him shielding her and Ruth from Darla the day they waited for him at the motel back in September. She'd gained a new level of respect for him, as well as a newfound attraction. Most important, though, Joan felt a duty to tell Edwin about Norma Trimble.

Joan knew that Edwin was avoiding her and she was certain she knew why. Finding a way to endear herself to him was the trick, and the best way to do that would be an attack on a mutual enemy: Darla McGee.

The words spoken by Eloise after Margie's death still

bothered her. Eloise had said Joan wouldn't have been a challenge to Edwin; Joan saw that as a challenge in itself.

"Eloise would say I'm too timid, that I don't have what it takes to pull something like that off. She just doesn't know me well enough. I could do it. What's the worst that could happen? They wouldn't put a little old lady in prison," she mused.

Joan rushed back to her room to write down a few ideas before she forgot them, hiding them in her desk until she was sure her plan would work.

*****

After two weeks only a few rooms were vacant on the first floor, with one being across the hall from Belle. The workload on everyone grew as confusion and disarray ruled each day. Ellie appeared to be making strides, but it was evident she wasn't keeping pace with her compounding duties.

Edwin walked down the stairs to the lobby feeling frustrated. Looking out of the back door, he could see the bass boat of the large woman leaving the dock while his own boat sat tied like a caged animal. Within moments, the water was calm again and the warm breeze blew through Edwin's hair. He knew there wasn't a sliver of a chance that he would get out on the boat today. Ramy stepped out of the kitchen, drying his hands on a towel and looking out the back door as well.

"It's going to be a beautiful day to be stuck in this place," Edwin said.

"Ramy knows you're right, Mr. Kranz. Ramy look out yonder and see dat water and dat sun and wonder 'bout all dem crawfish out dere waitin' on someone to scoop 'em up. It rained hard last night, they's some pools out in dem shallows and dey full of crawfish. And dem catfish be out there yellin' for a worm or two. Ramy miss it. Mr. Kranz missing something dis morning, too."

"Freedom. I didn't sign on to work all the time, I did enough of that on the oil rigs. We're going to have to find some help here pretty soon. Ellie's going crazy with all this."

"She's busy for sure. She tries to do it all. Can't nobody tell her nothing, she won't hear it. She must take after her mother."

"No, I guess I have to own that one. I was always hard-headed and wanted to do things my way. Life had to wear me down to the point that I had to ask for help."

"You doin' a good thin' here. Dis place shines compared to some other places Ramy's seen. Miss Ellie is proud of dis here place, dat's the truth."

"I know she is. How about you, do you have enough help?" Edwin asked. No sooner had the words left his lips than Nettie slowly rolled past him in her wheelchair. She only used her hands to steer, letting her feet pull her along for momentum.

"Yes, sir, Ramy got plenty of help right here," he said while looking down at Nettie. "Ramy got your work set up for you, Miss Nettie."

Nettie smiled as she continued into the kitchen. Edwin looked at him, perplexed.

"Nettie Cardenas?" Edwin asked.

"Yeah, she told Ramy she worked here when it was open. Said she worked at school, too."

"Shit! I remember her when I was in school. She's got to be a hundred and fifty years old," Edwin said. "What do you have her doing?"

"She likes to think she's helping out, but Ramy don't make her do no work. Most of the food gets prepped at night and Ramy cook it the next day. Ramy don't need no help."

"Good, good. By the way, who the hell is that woman that's been coming here in her boat with an ice chest?"

"Dat Miss Loretta. She run the marina across the lake. Ramy used to sell her fish and crawlers, now she brings Ramy fish to cook."

"She's a scary woman."

"Miss Loretta's a good woman, make somebody a good wife. Not Ramy, dat's for sure. But somebody."

Edwin laughed, thinking about how he would have pictured a woman like Loretta being from bayou country in Louisiana where Ramy was from. It also made him think of Ramy's father, Beau.

"How's your daddy doing?"

"Not good. He don't know how to quit dem cigarettes and dey killin' him. Ramy got a good family but dey don't know how to take care of him."

"Does he need to go into a nursing home?"

"Probably, but he won't want to. Too stubborn. Ramy don't know if he can afford it."

Edwin looked out the back door again, his mind racing. Ramy thought he might be reflecting on how old age was catching up with all of them and decided to leave Edwin alone.

"Ramy gonna get back to cookin'. Mr. Kranz ready for some breakfast?"

"Call him, Ramy. Tell him he can stay here. Won't cost him anything and he can smoke out on the dock by the water. I'll take him fishing or we'll just go for rides," Edwin said. The words seem to gush from his mouth, leaving both he and Ramy stunned. "Can you get hold of him?"

"Ramy can. Can't make no promises, but Ramy sure appreciate your offer. He likes being on dat water and he likes dat fishin'. Ramy gonna call dis mornin'."

"Good. Let me know as soon as you talk to him. I'll talk to him, too, if you think that'll help."

"Will do, Mr. Kranz. Ramy thanks you."

"I'm going for a run. Can you make me an omelet and put it aside?"

"The usual?"

"Yeah."

"Ramy knows. Ramy knows you're a good man, too."

"Go tell that to that batty bitch down the hall," Edwin said.

"You talkin' 'bout Miss Belle? Only person in Kranz Gardens dat scares Ramy," he said as he smiled and returned to the kitchen.

Edwin smiled back, surprised at the statement. Ramy rarely had a harsh word for anyone.

Edwin looked out the front door and saw a woman in a wheelchair being pushed to the door by a large man followed by another woman carrying suitcases. Edwin had become more sensitive about every person who walked through the door, never sure if they were connected to his past. This woman, however, he recognized instantly and rushed to open the door for them.

"Eloise Laine," he said with a smile.

"Oh, for heaven's sake," she exclaimed, "I didn't even know if you'd recognize me. My God if you don't look handsome as ever."

"Are you kidding? I'd recognize you anywhere. You're looking wonderful yourself."

"You always were the biggest liar in town. Come here and give me a hug."

Edwin bent down and wrapped his arms around her and she returned the hug.

"I may have stretched the truth now and again."

"You're a bastard, Edwin. You know I was ready to light into you as soon as I saw you and now here you are, your same old charming self."

"Charming? I didn't know you ever used that word for me."

"Well, I wasn't going to let you know, it would have gone to your head. It didn't need to get any bigger."

"So, what's with the wheelchair? You look fit enough to me."

"Bad hips. Too many kids came out of 'em."

"How many is too many?"

"Just this one," she said, pointing at the man behind her. He was obviously embarrassed by her words, but he was also a very large man. The young woman with him was trying not to laugh. "I was in labor with him so long he reached puberty before he delivered."

Edwin remembered Eloise as someone who was always bold and spoke her mind. It was nice to see she hadn't mellowed like the rest and wasn't wasting time wondering how long she had to live.

"You've made my day, Eloise, I don't think I could put it any other way. So, what do you want? Have you come to torture me or are we finally going to sleep under the same roof?"

"Oh my God," the young woman gasped and then began to laugh. "Eloise, I think you've finally met your match."

"I can't believe what I'm hearing," her son said.

"Don't mind him. At six foot seven, he's still afraid of heights. This is my son Champ, by the way, and his wife Liza."

"Good to meet you," Edwin said while shaking their hands.

"You got any rooms?"

"Yeah, we've got rooms. There's twenty rooms to a floor, the second floor only has a few rooms taken right now. I've got one room left down this end—"

"I want Glamour Hall," Eloise said.

"Glamour what?"

"I heard they have all of our class in one hall and they call it Glamour Hall, just like they did in high school. Don't you remember? The upperclassmen called us Glamour Dolls because of the way Belle and Ruth dressed and they called the wing that our classes were in 'Glamour Hall.'"

"Didn't know that, but then again I don't think I would have been considered glamorous. Let's see, down this way is Belle Chandler and a few others from that class that I never met. There's some other people, too. I think there's a room across from Belle's."

"I want that one, give me a key."

"Well, on the other end there's Joan Campanella—"

"No, she's boring. Too damned needy, always talking about what she should have done. I want Glamour Hall because I am, after all, glamorous."

"Yes, you are," Edwin said with a smile. "Alright. Now listen, I need you to check in with my daughter or she'll be kicking my butt for not doing all the paperwork right. She keeps telling me this isn't a motel."

"She's right, this our home. An old folks home for the others, a playground to have fun and swap stories for people like you and me."

"I like the way you're thinking. You like to go boating?"

"Yeah, if you can get me onboard with this thing," she replied while banging her hands on the wheelchair.

"We'll get a pontoon boat, that'll make it easier."

"Well, hurry up and do it then before we both die. You won't see much of them, I sure as hell don't," Eloise said as she pointed over her shoulder to her son and daughter-in-law.

"We visit twice a week," Champ said. "It's about all we can take of her."

"Lightweights, both of 'em."

"Alright," Edwin said, "Room seven down the right hallway. I'll check on you in a little while. Have you eaten?"

"No, I heard the food is good here. Point the way."

"Right through those glass doors on the left is the dining room and you'll see the buffet line. I think Ramy's got some food left."

"God, if it isn't good to see you again, Edwin," Eloise said in a softer voice. She reached out and grabbed his hand and he took it, wrapping both of his around hers.

"Like I said, you've made my day."

By noon, Edwin had checked in two people who had heard more about the accommodations of Kranz Gardens than they had about him. It was a good sign because he knew at some point all of his classmates would die off and the business would have to rely on service. Judging by the way Ellie was running around crazy and barking at half the people, that part wasn't going very well.

Before he had a chance to sneak away from the desk, a tall man in slacks and a sport coat entered just as Belle yelled out, "Where the hell is he?". The man smiled broadly, brought his bible to his chest and bowed his head for a brief moment.

"Are you here visiting or for last rites?" Edwin asked.

"I don't do last rites, I'm afraid. I think someone else has been filling in from what I hear," he replied. He stuck out his hand and Edwin shook it. "Carl Hauswirth, but most people call me Pastor Carl."

"The Odds Maker," Edwin said.

"What?"

"The Odds Maker is what some of 'em call you. My understanding is that you give better odds of someone getting into heaven. Did you say Hauswirth?"

"Yes, Pastor and roulette wheel spinner at Pine Tree Evangelical Church. Are you a spiritual man, Mr... I didn't get your name?"

"Edwin Kranz, good to meet you. You must be related to Gerry Hauswirth."

"My father, did you know him?"

"One of my best friends in high school. He was truly one of a kind back then. How is he?"

"Gone. He died when he was forty-two of a stroke. I was sixteen."

"I'm sorry to hear that. I never really kept in touch with anyone around here when I left, but he would've been one I'd like to have seen again."

"He was quite the character from what I understand. These people around here never forget anything so they've filled in a lot of the blanks for me."

"You weren't close to him?"

"Nobody was. He was difficult. Not to me or my sisters, but with everyone else. He never quite found that niche in life, always worried about doing something with himself."

"I think we all know that feeling. A stroke? That's awful young."

"Yeah, but I guess he didn't exactly live a healthy lifestyle. I don't know, we seldom saw him. He was always on the road working many jobs trying to make ends meet."

"He was a hard worker, I never could keep up with him. So, who is your mother, is she from around here?"

"Yeah, Connie Britton was her maiden name. A few years younger than Dad."

"Doesn't ring a bell."

"Well, your name sure as hell does. Ever since you got here it's been all the buzz. Have you had any trouble with Belle yet?"

"No, I haven't even seen her, I avoid her. I've heard her big mouth but that's about it."

"I'd give anything to see her reaction if she saw you."

"So, how did you come to be in the business?" Edwin asked, changing the subject quickly. "Your father wasn't religious, at least not when I knew him."

"I was looking for something that everyone else wasn't doing. I was good in debate classes, speeches, research. Put it all together with a bit of begging and you can have a pretty decent life."

"Better you than me."

"I heard you're a runner, is that correct?"

"Yeah, but I'm pretty slow."

"Mind if I run with you sometime?"

"You're not going to try to save me or anything, are you?"

"Nah, I've never been into winning hearts and minds, just wallets."

"You're not the typical preacher."

"It's a sin to lie," Carl replied with smile. "I do a good job, if that's what you're wondering. I know my business inside and out and I give good guidance and support. I'm like a doctor who smokes, drinks, chases women, and sneaks off to Vegas once in a while. Of course, you're the only one that knows these things."

"Why are you telling me all of this?"

"I gotta tell someone, don't I? Plus, I'd like to hear more about my father when you've got time."

"I can certainly do that. I like to run at five-thirty in the morning, leaving from the parking lot out there. How about tomorrow?"

"If I'm not tending to someone I'll be here."

"Sounds good."

"Carl!" a voice called from the back door. Darla made her way to the front desk and held her arms out for a hug. Carl obliged. "I haven't seen you since Margaret's funeral."

"Well, if you came to my church once in a while you'd see a lot more of me, Ms. McGee."

"You know you're too lukewarm for me, I like the fire and brimstone."

"You like scaring the hell out of people."

"It works. Just so you know," she said while hooking a thumb at Edwin, "You're wasting your time with this one."

"I wouldn't say that, he just gave me a confession a few moments ago."

"You're both lying, he'd never confess to anything. Did he tell you why this place closed down?"

"I had nothing to do with it, Darla."

"I've heard rumors," Carl said. "My understanding is that a privacy issue came up and that people were afraid to come here anymore for whatever it was they were doing."

"They were sinning left and right. You couldn't look anywhere—"

"There's sinning everywhere, Ms. McGee, we can't shut the whole town down. And that would include a fair number of churches in this town."

"Certainly not mine!"

"Certainly not yours, no. Not the place that shames people mercilessly and encourages them to expose their guilt in front of the world for all to see and then wants a large piece of their wallets."

"It's called confessing and it's meant to cleanse the soul. Something Edwin should be doing for all the trouble he's caused. Surely you've heard some of the rumors about him by now."

Carl smiled and shook his head.

"Not a word. Just so you know, the folks that migrate from your church to mine come with a lot of guilt that we have to work on, so I don't know how effective you are at cleansing."

"Well, it isn't the church's fault that what they do makes them feel guilty."

"No, but you don't have to feed off of that guilt, either. I've got to tend to my flock," Carl said as he looked over at Edwin. "Come with me to see Belle."

"I'll pass."

"She's been dying to see you."

"Not fast enough."

"That's okay," Darla said, "I need to talk to Edwin anyway. I want to start a weekly prayer meeting for everyone so that they know they can reach out if they're in despair."

"Don't ask me, ask my daughter. She runs the place, it's hers. I think you're just looking for trouble myself. Plus, we've already got a men's prayer group."

"You're kidding?" She said and then looked angrily at Carl. "Is that you're doing?"

"No, it isn't him. It's somebody else."

"This I've got to see," Darla said.

"It's a men's prayer group, you're not invited."

"Do you go to it?"

"Hell no." Edwin replied.

Carl laughed, catching Edwin by surprise; it sounded exactly the way Carl's father had laughed and Edwin felt a sense of loss for his old friend. Darla chewed on her lip for a moment, giving up on the argument and trying to think of something to say.

"You know you're going to run into Belle sometime in here," Carl said.

"Probably, but not today."

"So, five-thirty?"

"I'll be right out front."

Carl nodded and walked down the hallway toward Belle's room.

"Why are you always trying to undermine me?" Darla asked.

"How do you mean?"

"Taking his side against me. For all the things that I do around here, and for Belle—"

"Darla, you haven't changed a bit. You've always wanted to get people to confess their sins to you, dragging them kicking and screaming if you had to. And then you hold it over their heads. You use religion as a weapon. And how do we benefit from your being here?"

"I give people hope and counsel. And I'll have you know that I get along with everyone else, just not you," Darla said.

"They only tolerate you because they're afraid to fight back. I'm not."

"You've got your skeletons, mister, and I know about some of them."

"Go for it, blab 'em out to everyone. I really don't have anything to hide at this point. What are you going to tell anyone here that they don't already suspect? And I'll bet they'd believe me over you anyway, whether I lied or not."

"We'll see. I'm not going to let you run wild over these people again, not over my dead body."

"You don't like the competition? You're a damn hypocrite. You know, you should've picked drama instead of religion, you would've been a lot more believable."

Darla was angry that she couldn't get a rise from him. He stayed calm and seemed to be disinterested in everything she said. Of all the people she knew, he was the only one she didn't care whether she saved or not. Her goal was to get the better of him, she just didn't know how.

*****

That evening, Edwin stood out on the balcony of his room feeling sorry that he'd ever talked Ellie into creating the nursing home, but for reasons he hadn't considered before. There was his past, which garnered some attention from those who refused to let him live it down. He actually found some of it amusing, antics he'd forgotten all about. What troubled him most was seeing the fate of those he'd long left behind. The term "ignorance is bliss" seemed to resonate clearly with him now, and every day something new reminded him how little time they all had left to live.

At the end of the hall, Ellie opened the door to her apartment. Larry stood inside the door wearing a party hat and holding a cake with a single candle. Jack held balloons in one hand and a small bouquet of flowers in the other. Ellie looked distraught, wondering if she'd missed an important event.

"What's this?" Ellie asked.

"Happy Anniversary! We've been open one whole month today," Larry said.

Jack began jumping up and down until he saw Ellie cover her face to hide her tears as she ran to her room.

Chapter 15

There was a sharp series of knocks on the craft room door, and a few seconds later a banging. Cary made his way to the door room to see who it was.

"Turn off the damn television already," Cary said.

"I'm trying, the remote ain't working," Al Cartwright replied.

"Put some new batteries in it, that's one of your problems. You're a goddamned idiot is the other."

After Al pushed the button several more times the screen went dark and Cary turned up the dimmed lights. The room was crammed full of men, most gathered around the screen with racing forms, others sitting at tables in the back playing poker. Only a few were residents and the rest were a variety ages and backgrounds, and all of them looked nervously at the door as Cary opened it. Another man walked in with hors d'oeuvres, laughing and shaking his head.

"You're late!" Cary complained. "We're right in the middle of a race and you're beating on the damn door. Al, turn that damn thing back on and let's see who wins."

"Better get out there, Cary. Your wife is making a scene."

"Now what?" Cary grumbled as he walked out into the hall.

"Cary, come here," Belle said.

She was dressed only in panties and had walked down the hall to the dining room to find him. Her hair was combed on one side and she'd put her lipstick on unevenly, but she felt pretty.

"Holy— get back to your room!" Cary yelled. He rushed to her side to herd her back down the hallway. "Look at you, parading down the hall half naked. Who left your door unlocked and what the hell are you doing?"

"I need you to come to the room, I have a question for you."

Belle was smiling and rubbing his arm as they walked. The commotion gained the attention everyone in the hall.

"Well, get a good look," Cary said. "Look at the crowd you've got going here, Belle. An hour ago, you didn't even know my name and now you gotta do something like this. What's the matter with you?"

"Just come into the room, I have a question for you."

"I'm coming, already." The two went through the door to her room and she closed it behind them. "What is it?"

"Come sit down on the bed."

"No. What did you want to ask?"

Belle gently took his arm with both hands and tried to pull him toward the bed, smiling and batting her eyes at him.

"Come sit down."

"Are you crazy?"

"I want you to love me. Do that thing, you know, lum lum lum—"

"That wasn't me, that was that bastard, Edwin. For Pete's sake, Belle." Cary's frustration gave him an idea. "Look, we can't. I've got a disease. I got the clap, so we can't."

"How did you get that?"

"You gave it to me."

"When?"

"Doesn't matter. It means we can't do that anymore, you ruined me for life."

"I see. Do you want to lay down by me then?"

"No, I want to go finish my game, the guys are waiting on me."

"Okay, I want to take a nap then, I'm not feeling so good."

"Alright, you take your nap. I'll tell the nurse you aren't feeling good."

"But I feel fine."

"Okay, I'll tell her that, too."

"If you see that little boy, tell him to come here. He's a sweet boy."

"Just a peach, now go lay down."

"Okay."

Cary walked out of the room, shaking his head and closing the door behind him. He had never once had a guilty conscience and the little lies he told her now he felt sure she wouldn't remember tomorrow. As he got close to the lobby, Jack came around the corner on his tricycle as if he were on a mission.

"Hey, kid, do you know how to count?"

"A little."

"Do you know what an eight looks like?"

"A snowman!" Jack exclaimed.

"Look, go down there and when you see a snowman on the door, go inside. There's a woman in there that wants to talk to you."

"Grandma said I'm not supposed to go in the rooms."

"Here," Cary said, fishing out two one-dollar bills from his wallet. "I won't tell if you won't."

"Okay," Jack said, taking the money and wadding it up so it would fit in his cargo pocket.

"Now don't forget where you put that."

"No, sir, I won't. Thanks!"

"Hey, one more thing, kid. When you get done, come back to the craft room. I've got a job for you."

"Yes, sir!"

Jack headed down the hall to Belle's room with more money than he'd started out with that morning. Moments earlier, Joan had finalized her plan, written it down in a note, and was paying Jack to deliver it to Belle. Cary wouldn't have known that and Jack wasn't going to tell him.

Cary headed back to the craft room to rejoin the other men but saw a familiar face standing in the middle of the hall, turning her head back and forth as if she were looking for someone specific.

"Hester?"

"Edwin?" she replied and then squinted to look at Cary a little better. "No, you're not Edwin."

"What do you need Edwin for when you could have me?"

"I'm looking for Edwin, you had your chance a long time ago."

"Things were different then. And I'm almost a single man now."

"Yes, and things are different now and I'm looking for Edwin. I have to go."

Hester's speech was a little slurred and she didn't seem steady. Cary followed her to the dining room where Edwin sat at a table alone working on his computer.

"To hell with this," Cary mumbled to himself, but Hester heard it and turned around to give Cary a smug look. She continued into the dining room as Cary gave the secret knock and was let back into the craft room.

Hester tripped on the hem of her flowing green formal gown that would only be fitting for a high school prom. She felt dazzling and romantic, and maybe a little too tipsy for the occasion but it helped her be a bit more bold. She knew that the handsome-looking gentleman seated at the table was Edwin.

"Can I share this table with you, Edwin?"

Edwin looked up at her, puzzled at first, and then, while trying to suppress a laugh, stood and pulled a chair out for her.

"I think so. And what is your name?"

"Hester Jorgensen," she replied with a sultry tone. "Don't you remember me?"

"Like it was yesterday." He was trying to match her face and features with his memory of her and the only thing that was close was her short frame. "How have you been?"

"Good. Well, good enough anyway. Age claws away at us, I'm afraid, but our memories keep us young, don't they?" Her jet-black hair was recently dyed and her glazed eyes told him she needed a nap more than anything. She began digging in her large purse, glancing up at him every few seconds with a grin, finally pulling out a small flask. "Look, I brought something for us. Something for you to remember me by."

"Now what do you have in there?"

"A bit of rum! Remember that night out? That was so much fun, and I have to admit that I was smitten with you forever after that."

"I remember you got sick."

"Did I? I don't recall. Oh well, it doesn't really matter does it? What do you think about having a toast to those memories? Do you have something to go with this?"

Edwin looked at his watch. It wouldn't be long before people began gathering for lunch and he didn't want to be seen having drinks in the dining area, nor did he want a lot of attention on him being with Hester.

"How about some fresh air?"

"Okay, but let's take something to mix this with, too."

"Alright. Give me a minute."

Edwin walked into the galley area to grab some styrofoam cups and ice and pulled a two liter bottle of Coke from the refrigerator. It had been a long time since he'd had rum and he wanted to keep it at a minimum, remembering the predicament it had brought on years ago. He felt a tap on his shoulder and turned around. Joan had followed him into the galley.

"Edwin, do you have some time?"

"Not right now. In a little while?"

Joan turned to see Hester at the back door, swaying from either a song in her head or from alcohol-induced imbalance.

"I see. Never mind."

"Joan, it's just bad timing."

"The story of my life," Joan replied as she walked away.

Edwin felt guilty for hurting Joan's feelings and knew that at some point he wouldn't be able to avoid her anymore. But for now, he was willing to be amused by Hester. He walked up to her and allowed her to take his arm as they walked out the back door and toward the dock.

"How would you like to go for a boat ride?" Edwin asked Hester.

"I haven't been on a boat in years, that would be fun."

"Good. A little fresh air and the water rushing by is always relaxing."

"And a few drinks along the way?"

"We'll see."

Edwin carefully got Hester aboard and got them on their way just as Joan got back to her room. Minutes later Jack knocked on her door.

"Did you give the message to her?" Joan asked as she smiled sweetly at Jack.

"She was asleep, but I left it in her hand."

"That'll do. Thank you so much, and here's an extra dollar for being such a hard little worker," Joan said. She was a little discouraged but knew the results would come soon enough.

"Thank you!"

"And you check in with me every day, I may have some other

jobs for you to do sometime."

"Yes, ma'am!"

$$*****$$

Edwin pulled into the cove that had become his favorite spot when taking the others out on the boat. It always felt significantly cooler there beneath the canopy of the trees on shore and there were few waves from the passing boats. After tying the boat to a tree, he looked back to see Hester crying while clutching the flask of rum to her bosom.

"What's the matter?" Edwin asked as he walked to the back of the boat and sat beside her.

"Look at me, Edwin. I'm a mess. How in God's name did I pick this dress to come out here?"

"Looks okay to me. Wear what you want to wear."

"Don't be patronizing, Edwin, I wore it to impress you. I swear that I've done everything possible to screw up my life."

"You think you're the only one, Hester? Don't you think that everyone around you has made some poor decision at some point?"

"But all of mine were. If it was just here or there, I could take it. I wouldn't let it beat me down. But it's been everything, and it all started with this." Hester held the flask out in front of her, glaring at it as if it were a demon. "It's a damn cycle. A vicious, horrid cycle. I drink for a while until one day I feel like I've beaten the pain back enough to stop. If nothing's bothering me, why do I need to drink? And a day after I quit, the pain comes back. And then the drinking. After fifty years you'd think I could have driven all of that baggage out of my head, but it's still in there. You're still in there. You were the first man that was nice to me, other than dropping me off that night."

"Yeah, I didn't handle it well. I apologize, and I mean that. I shouldn't have left you the way I did. I didn't do anything wrong, but I figured your father would have thought I did."

"He was jealous."

"What?"

"Jealous. He was jealous that you'd had me."

"I think he thought I had been with you, but I don't see where that would make him jealous."

"If the person you were sleeping with had sex with someone else, wouldn't you be jealous?"

"Yeah, but don't—" Edwin began, but then it occurred to him what she was getting at.

"No, nobody thought about that. Or maybe they just didn't care. I don't know.

Hester took the cap off the flask and looked out over the water as she took a long swig. Edwin watched as she swallowed without even a hint of a wince from the burn of the alcohol, but that was still less shocking than what he'd just heard.

"Your father was molesting you."

"He was raping me, don't try to make it sound like something else. He raped me that night and then beat me. He called me a whore and told me I deserved everything that a man could dish out. He had me believing that I'd be lucky to find anyone that would put up with such a slut. I proved him wrong. I married someone just like him. I married a man who stormed into my dad's house the day after we eloped and told him that if he ever touched me again, he'd kill him. My dad cowered in a corner and stayed there until we left. I felt so relieved, so vindicated. And then my husband took me home and guess what he did?"

"I don't know."

"He tied me up, beat me, and raped me. I now belonged to him."

"Hester, I'm sorry. I don't know how anyone could ever do something like that to another."

"It's easy. You let them know that you'll do anything to make them happy and worship at their feet. And from then on, you take whatever they give."

"How long did that go on?"

"Twelve years. He divorced me and took off after someone else. He's dead now."

"So, where do you live now? Got any kids, any family?"

"Nobody, never had kids. I was always afraid of how they'd turn out or what they'd think of me. I knew what I was and where I was headed."

"It's a shame."

"I don't feel shame. I don't feel anything."

"No, I meant it's a shame that things didn't work out for you. You know, you were a very cute girl. Had I not been such a skittish upperclassman, I might have gone for you." Edwin had a grin on his face, trying to cheer her up.

"Haven't you been listening?" Hester said, looking at him with reproach. "Nobody was going to have Daddy's girl."

"You're right, I'm sorry."

"So, are you going to help me drink this or not?"

Edwin reached over to the cooler and got out the Coke and a cup. He felt a little odd having to mix his drink after watching her drink the rum straight, but she was in much better practice than he was.

"I don't see how I can refuse."

*****

Cary had almost finished watching the second race before it occurred to him that Belle had been undressed when he sent Jack in to see her. He opened the craft room door to go down and check, but Jack was standing outside the door ready to knock.

"Everything okay, kid?"

"Yes, sir. She was asleep."

"Alright. How would you like a little backpack?" Cary said, dangling a small red backpack that had a cartoon character on it.

"Really?"

"Yeah. And look, go up to room two-ten and he's gonna give you something to bring to me. Here, I'll draw the number out on paper for you. Bring it back and I'll give you fifty cents for every time you do it. Okay?"

"Yes, sir!"

"Now don't tell anybody and me and you can make lots of money off this. How does that sound?"

"I won't tell anybody," Jack replied as he grabbed the backpack and put it on his back.

"Now one more thing: Open this zipper on the back of your backpack and see all of those papers back there?"

"Yes, sir."

"Give one to everybody you see except your grandma and grandpa, and that bas—, and your Grandpa Edwin. Don't put it under their doors, you put it right in their hands. You got me?"

"I will, I promise."

Cary drew the number out on a piece of paper and handed it to Jack.

"Don't be telling anybody else about this and don't tell 'em they came from me. Now hurry up and take this one to room 210 on the second floor and then come right back. You can work on the rest of it later."

Jack took off on his tricycle for the elevator. Cary walked by the dining room and noticed that Edwin and Hester were gone. The early lunch crowd began to gather, either looking for someone to talk to or fearing there would be nothing left if they came down later. He looked at his watch, knowing that the next race was coming up, and went back into the craft room and watched through a slit in the curtains for Jack to return.

*****

Darla pulled into the parking lot in a rush. She knew Belle

became fidgety when the smell of food wafted down the hallway and nobody was around to take her to eat. Darla passed Ellie on her way to Belle's room, noticing that she seemed oblivious to everything around her.

"Good morning, Ellie," Darla said.

"I'll be there in just a minute, give me a chance," Ellie replied without stopping.

Darla shook her head and found Belle putting her panty hose on over her slippers. She got the hose away from her and helped her dress without seeing the note that had dropped from Belle's hand next to the bed.

"Come on, let's go have some lunch."

"I already ate," Belle said.

"Really? When?"

"This morning, we had birthday cake."

"Okay," Darla said as she smiled. "Let's go have some lunch anyway."

Darla pushed Belle in the wheelchair to the table where Eloise and Ruth sat.

"I just passed Ellie in the hallway. She hardly even noticed me. Said good morning to her and she ranted some gibberish back to me. Didn't even make sense."

"She needs to hire more help," Eloise said.

"Why do you say that?" Darla asked. "Did Edwin tell you while you were out on the boat doing whatever?"

"No, you nosy busy-body, he didn't. I've been watching to see when Ellie was going to hire somebody; she's going crazy around here."

"I agree, she's burning the candle at both ends," Ruth said.

"Eloise called you a busy-body, did you know that?" Belle asked Darla. Belle glared at Eloise, who seemed to be amused by it all.

"It's okay, Belle, she didn't mean it," Darla said while stroking Belle's hair.

"I might stab Darla with a knife later," Eloise said.

"Don't tell her that! You're just stirring up trouble."

"You're a bitch!" Belle yelled, causing Eloise and Ruth to burst out in laughter.

"Stop it, both of you."

Belle looked over her shoulder, angry but not exactly sure why or what to do about it.

"I remembered something funny this morning. Do you remember the time that we all played strip poker—" Ruth began.

"No. Let's talk about something else."

"Not you, of course," Ruth continued, "But Eloise and I were playing with Belle, Cary, Charlie Marks, and that European guy that was visiting Charlie."

"Oh heavens, I forgot all about that," Eloise replied.

"I don't know if I want to hear it," Darla said.

"Where's Cary?" Belle asked.

"He's out grocery shopping or something, Belle, he'll be back."

"You know, Charlie could speak German, but his friend didn't speak a word of English."

Ramy came out of the kitchen and sat down next to them. Every few minutes another resident came into the dining room and soon most of the first floor was there sitting at tables ready to eat.

"Do sit in on this, Ramy, it's so funny. Anyway, after every hand someone had to take off a piece of clothing, but Charlie's friend didn't know why. He didn't understand the game and Charlie thought it was funny to watch the look on his face whenever one of us girls took off our clothes."

"Ya'll talkin' 'bout strip poker?" Ramy asked.

"Yes, it was something we did when we were young."

"Ramy's played it, too. It's still a good game."

"Anyway, we pretended to lose until us girls had our bras off and we could see that he was more than a little enthused!"

"I remember the look on his face and I swear I thought his little schnitzel was going to pop through his pants at any time," Eloise said with a laugh.

"This is disgusting. I had no idea you were doing this stuff when we were kids."

"We know, Darla, now zip it," Eloise said.

"So, when we had our tops off, he whispered to Charlie to find out what was going on and Charlie told him that it was customary for everyone to take off a little bit of clothing at a time. He told him that he didn't have to if he didn't want to but us girls thought he was scared of us."

"He lied to him about that?" Darla asked. Ruth and Eloise rolled their eyes.

"Charlie told him to go in the bathroom and take off all his clothes and come out naked. And when he came out," Ruth said, trying to contain her laughter, "We'd all put our clothes back on and he was standing there buck naked!"

"Buck naked!" Belle yelled.

"And built like a horse!" Eloise added.

Ellie had been eavesdropping at the door during the last part of the story and stormed into the dining room.

"Don't you have anything better to do?" she said in tears. "So, he made some mistakes! So, what if he had a little fun but goddammit do you have to keep going on and on about what my father did?"

"What makes you think we were talking about your father?" Eloise asked. "Heavens, if you aren't just like him, always thinking everything revolves around you."

"You weren't talking about my father?"

"No, some other crude boy from the past," Darla replied.

"Miss Ellie, you need some bayou coffee," Ramy said while pointing to the kitchen.

"Maybe, uh, maybe I do. I'm sorry, everyone. I'm just a little tired of my dad at the moment."

"Well, we all know that feeling, don't we girls?" Eloise said

"She called her a busy-body," Belle said while pointing at Eloise. "She's gonna stab Darla."

"Don't mind her," Darla said.

Ellie turned away and followed Ramy into the kitchen. More than anything, she wanted to get away from the others, but when Ramy added the shot of whiskey into the coffee she was glad she'd followed him.

"I think she needs a man. She's a bit high-strung these days," Eloise said.

"She's a married woman and that's none of our business," Darla replied.

"She's tuckered out, I'm afraid. Remodeling this place, running back and forth from Arizona every month. Do you know they stripped every wall in this place?"

"Every wall," Darla said with a hint of relief.

"All but the laundry room. Somehow that got missed, one wall of it anyway. But still, can you imagine how much that cost and how much of a headache that was for her. Now she's putting up with all of us!"

"You said the laundry room?" Darla asked.

"Yeah, why do you care?"

"I don't, just curious."

"I always wondered what Edwin was like," Ruth said.

"You mean in the sack?" Eloise asked.

"No, all men are the same in the sack."

"Not all of 'em."

"I just wondered how he was, you know, built?"

"Ask her," Eloise said, pointing to Belle.

"Don't get her started!" Darla scolded.

"Hey, Belle, how did Edwin look naked?"

"He was handsome. All lean and muscles," Belle said and began licking the air over and over.

"See what you've done? Are you happy now?"

"Must not have been much down there," Eloise said, and Ruth began to laugh.

"I would've thought you'd know by now going out on that boat with him," Darla sniped.

"That isn't what's going on when we go out on the boat with him."

"We? You mean both of you have gone out with him?"

"The more the merrier, Darla. You should come out with us."

Darla stood and grabbed the handles of Belle's wheelchair and turned her away toward the door.

"Sinners, both of you. You don't have a lot of time left, you could go any minute. Repent is all I have to say to you. We'll come back when there's better company."

"Big muscles and a big pecker," Belle yelled as Darla pushed her down the hall. Ruth and Eloise gasped in surprise and laughed.

Ruth noticed Jack going down the hallway. She grabbed her purse and excused herself for a moment while she rushed to catch him. Moments later she returned with a smile on her face.

"What are you all smiles about?" Eloise asked.

"Nothing. Just a cute little arrangement, that's all."

"Up to no good, that's what it is."

"Maybe, but I'm too old to get in trouble."

*****

It was almost one in the afternoon when Edwin pulled the boat back into its slip at the dock. Once Hester had had a few drinks out in the cove, she'd stopped talking about the bad things that happened in life and had shared some of her better memories with Edwin. Edwin enticed her to go back to Kranz Gardens so she could eat on time. They made it as far as the bench on the dock before she had to sit down and rest and both of them were oblivious to the attention they'd garnered from the windows in the dining room.

Edwin sat watching the fish occasionally break the surface of the water for a bug as Hester took one sip after another and talked about how much better she felt after exposing her past. Edwin patted her hand as she leaned closer and closer to him while stroking his arm. Before long he felt her head lean against his shoulder and she began snoring. He put his arm around her and lay her head down in his lap so she could sleep. He looked out at the lake again with a big smile on his face while shaking his head.

"Some things never change, do they, Hester?" he said while stroking her hair.

He felt sad for her and reached over to pull her legs up onto the bench. The stench of alcohol and perfume mixed together made him thankful that he'd only drank half of what was in his cup. Any more and it might have made him sick. Besides sad, though, Edwin felt somewhat responsible for the way Hester was. It was likely that if it hadn't been him that had introduced her to alcohol, someone else surely would have. But it was just one more thing that he'd been able to put out of his mind for so many years and now it was front and center, needing to be dealt with in a way he wasn't yet sure of.

"I'll take care of you, Hester. We'll make sure you're happy for the very short time you probably have left."

Hester moved around a bit and Edwin wasn't sure if she'd heard him or if she was just trying to get comfortable.

As Hester squirmed outside, Ellie was still enjoying the effects of the bayou coffee from earlier. As she passed through the front lobby, she could see that the people in the dining room were gathered at the window talking quietly and smiling, some laughing. The craft room was open, meaning the men had finished their bible study. That room, too, was crowded with gawkers paying close attention to something outside the windows. There was no rhyme or reason for their being there and Ellie didn't want to embarrass herself in front of everyone again. She walked to the back door and saw Edwin sitting on the bench with his back to them, staring out at the lake. The residents had grins, some were shaking their heads and it made her feel uneasy. She'd come to the point where she didn't trust them anymore.

A feeling of sadness swept over Ellie as she watched Edwin sitting still, staring out at the lake. From where she stood, he looked lonely. There had been a strain in their relationship since Kranz Gardens had opened and seeing him out there made her feel guilty. Ellie thought he was avoiding her and she didn't want that.

"What's out there, Grandma?" Jack asked as he came up behind her.

"Grandpa Edwin's sitting out there by himself. Why don't you go sneak up on him and scare him?"

No sooner had the words left her lips than Jack ran out the door toward the dock. He turned to look back at Ellie, who put her finger up to her mouth to get him to go quietly. Jack slowed down and began sneaking across the planks of the dock. At the same time, there was an elevation of excitement coming from the craft room, but Ellie wasn't paying attention to it. She smiled as Jack got to the end of the dock, but was concerned when Jack squatted with his hands on his knees, looking curiously at Edwin. He stood back up and then yelled out.

"Grandpa Edwin, who is that?"

The shrill voice of Jack startled Hester and she began to lift herself from Edwin's lap. Ellie saw her head rise above the back of the bench but then Hester leaned over and vomited all over Edwin's lap. Edwin stood with his hands out at his sides, looking down at the mess on his shorts and began laughing. Jack looked confused, Hester looked dazed, and Ellie looked like a mass murderer.

There was a roar from inside with clapping and the thumping of canes on the floor. Ellie bit her bottom lip and balled her fist up as she prepared to confront her father.

"I've had enough," Ellie mumbled to herself. "He's out, I'm throwing his ass out of here tonight. There's no room for this shit here. I can't operate with this man trying to hump everyone in the building."

"That's a good man to have, right there," a voice beside her said.

"Who—?"

"You're a young fool. You don't know how to have fun anymore," the woman replied with a smile and kept walking.

Jack walked back slowly, glancing over his shoulder every few steps while trying to process what he'd just seen. Ellie met him halfway.

"Go on up to your room and play, Jack. Grandma will be up there pretty soon."

"Grandma, am I in trouble?"

"No, honey, but Grandpa Edwin is."

"She got sick, what was she doing?"

"Nothing, honey, go up to your room."

"Okay," Jack replied, still looking puzzled.

As soon as Jack was inside, Ellie charged down the dock. Hester turned to look at her with embarrassment and fear.

"It's not what you think."

"Oh please!" Ellie cried. "What kind of fool do you take me for? Act your goddamned age! Shit!"

Ellie paced back and forth and stomped on the planks of the dock while Edwin stood quietly looking out over the lake. He was biting his lips, trying to keep from smiling.

"You're trying to make me a laughingstock, aren't you? Do you realize how disrespectful all these people are to me? Because of you?"

"I'm sorry, Ellie, we thought we were alone. It was just an accident that Jack—"

"Do you know that half of the people here were watching you two from the windows of the craft room? The other half are in the dining room eating popcorn and acting like they're at a peep show."

"They're perverts, they always have been."

"Them? You think they're perverts? What about you?"

"What the hell is it that you think we were doing. She passed out in my lap, Jack surprised both of us, and she threw up on me. That's twice now, how many times does it have to happen before I get a little sympathy?"

"I'm sorry, Edwin," Hester said as she tried to stand. Edwin grabbed her arm so she could get her balance.

"We're two old fools getting drunk by the lake, Ellie, that's all."

"Fine, but could you do it somewhere else? You've got a damn boat."

"We took the boat out, now we're back. I did what I could."

Ellie put her hand to her head, trying to come up with words to argue with. She sat on the bench, exhausted from the confrontation, and buried her face in her hands.

"Why, Dad? Why are you doing this?"

"I'm just trying to live my life, Ellie. I'm sorry, I had no idea this was going to happen."

"Dad, you're an intelligent man but you're not thinking."

"She showed up, Ellie, looking for some companionship. Right, Hester?" Hester nodded but was beginning to look a bit pale.

"I'm not feeling too good again."

Edwin sat her down next to Ellie, but Ellie stood to stay out of range.

"I've come to realize something, Ellie. If we're lucky, we get time to put things to rest. And that's all we're doing. Me, Hester, all of those people watching out the windows. We're trying to make sure the ending is right, or at least right for us. I'm sorry for putting you on the spot. We're just trying to enjoy the time we have left."

"Can you do me a favor, Dad? Just one favor?"

"I can't change who I am, Ellie, or what any of these people think. Consider that before you ask that favor."

Ellie looked at him, feeling brow-beaten and defeated. She knew she had every right to be upset and every right to demand he change how he conducted himself. But she didn't have it in her to stand up to him, to be firm and cold like he could be so effortlessly. She could never emulate him, no matter how much she wanted to, it wasn't in her. She threw her hands up and sighed.

"Can you at least get her back inside and clean yourselves up? Do that for me, will you?"

"Yeah," Edwin said. He could see the dejection in her face and felt guilty. "And I'm sorry."

"Sorry doesn't—" she began to say, but an unfamiliar sound began blaring from the back of the building. It was steady and piercing and it made Ellie's heart sink. The fire alarm was ringing.

*****

Two hours later the fire trucks were leaving. The chief had done a quick inspection of the building for any safety issues and the cause of the alarm was now known. The only thing left was for Ellie to get to the bottom of what was going on. After she made sure everyone was back in their rooms, she passed by the front desk where Edwin should have been sitting and then made her way to Belle's room.

"Okay, Belle, where did you get the note?" Ellie asked.

"What note? I didn't have any note," Belle responded.

"The one that told you to pull the fire alarm."

"I didn't pull a fire alarm. It was probably that bastard Edwin."

"Belle, you were standing in the hall with the lever in your hand."

"Where's Darla?"

"I'm hoping she'll be here soon," Ellie replied. "Did somebody come into your room today?"

"No."

"You don't remember anybody coming into your room?"

"Nobody came in. Hey, there's my grandson!" Belle said as Jack walked past the door. He sped up, walking quickly down the hall to the dining room while looking over his shoulder. "He's such a sweet boy. He comes to see me every day."

"Does he now?" Ellie asked rhetorically. She was annoyed she couldn't get the information she wanted, much less keep Belle's attention. "Well, let's wait until Darla gets here, we'll see if she knows anything about this note."

"Let me see it."

"Oh no. Not again. We've had enough trouble for one day." Ellie looked Belle over to make sure she was okay and noticed that she appeared to have lost some weight. "Are you getting enough to eat?"

"When?"

"When you eat. Are you eating enough?"

"Where is Darla?"

"Forget it, I gotta go. Why don't you take a nap until Darla gets here?"

"I'm not sleepy."

"Yes, you are."

"You're a bitch."

"I feel like it sometimes. I'll be back pretty soon."

"Okay."

Ellie stood outside the door and wondered why anyone would write:

Pull the fire alarm to see if it works. Darla

Ellie didn't think Darla wrote the note and she was certain Belle hadn't. She saw Jenna coming out of a room and got her attention.

"Jenna, where the hell have you been?"

"Upstairs, mostly, getting the rooms ready like you asked me."

"You're right. Sorry, it's been crazy. Did you see anyone go in or out of Belle's room?"

"No. Well, Darla came by, but that was earlier. I heard Belle had a note?"

"Yes, right here."

Ellie handed the note to Jenna who shook her head after reading it.

"That's odd. That certainly isn't Belle's writing. I'll keep a lookout, sometimes they leave out letters and envelopes and I can look for handwriting that matches."

"I appreciate it. I don't even know if it's somebody here. The only people who come here to see her are Darla and—" Ellie said with a pause, "Pastor Carl."

"Oh, wouldn't that be funny. A pastor causing mischief. Especially when he and Darla don't see eye to eye. Oh, you don't think—"

"How should I know? He certainly isn't your typical preacher from what I hear and like you said, they certainly don't get along."

"I've got an idea. The other place I worked at kept a visitors log at the front desk. Maybe if you put one out there we can find out if he's doing this."

"That's not a bad idea. It might take few days but we could find out for sure."

"We'd have to find something in common with this note and Pastor Carl's handwriting."

"That shouldn't be hard to do at all. I've got this note and all I need is a signature from him," Ellie said.

"This is so exciting, I've never done anything like this before."

"Well, hopefully we won't have to do it again. I gotta grab my father before he ducks out on me for the second time today. And, hey, sorry for getting crabby."

"It's okay. These folks can keep you on your toes sometimes."

Ellie looked up and down the hallway for any sign of Edwin but didn't see him. She thought about going up to his apartment until she saw him step out of the elevator.

"Stop right there," Ellie barked as he started to get back in.

"Now what?"

"You know, you could've helped when all the commotion was going on."

"Welcome to management. If you want something done you need to either find a way to do it or delegate it."

"I'm stretched a bit thin right now and I can't count on finding you when I need you."

"I'm not going to sit around waiting for you to put me to work."

"Fine. Since you're already here I need your help at the front desk."

"For how long?" Edwin whined.

"From now on. After this afternoon, you owe me. Big time."

"Ellie, come on."

"Don't 'Ellie' me, I need help and you're the one who has to do it."

"Why me, why not Larry, or—"

"Or who, Jack? Frankly I'd probably be better off with Jack, but then you wouldn't get what you deserve."

"What? What do you mean?"

"Here," she said grabbing a piece of paper and a pen, "Write your name."

"What are you going to do, copy it and have me committed?"

"I should. Just write."

Edwin signed his name and slid it across the desk to her. She compared it with the note that she fished out of her pocket. She looked at him and sighed; the writing didn't match.

"Satisfied?"

"I've got a damn zoo here because of you. A crazy woman that can't keep her tongue in her mouth because you couldn't control yours a long time ago. I've got a cook that I couldn't get rid of if I wanted to who feeds everyone in town like it's a soup kitchen. Drunken women who want to visit, people having prayer meetings that don't even live here, and a grandson who's bound to start picking up bad habits if he hangs around you too long."

"That's not fair; Jack is not my fault."

At that moment, Jack wheeled past them on his way down the hall and Ellie heard him say "Pecos Pete to win in ten". She looked at Edwin, puzzled.

"What the hell was that about?" she asked.

"You're asking me? I don't know."

"Never mind. You know, I should tie you to that desk and poke you with a cattle prod once an hour. I've got too much going on here and I need your help. Just give me three hours and I'll find someone to take your place. Deal?"

"Alright, but you need to hire some help. You can't keep trying to do everything yourself."

"Dad, until I'm comfortable with the finances I don't want to take on any more debt."

"It didn't bother you when you hired Jenna. We had fewer receivables then than we do now."

"I was pissed off when I hired Jenna. She showed up at the right time, I don't know. Besides, what happens if you die tomorrow? Is there going to be enough money for me to keep running this place?"

"Absolutely."

"How am I to know that for sure?"

"Because I don't have any reason to lie about it, you know that."

"Fine, but I have to know how to run a business, one detail at a time, and I'm not going to learn anything if you keep making decisions over my head and doing all this other shit."

"Shit, shit, shit!" a voice repeated from the end of the hall. Belle's voice made Ellie cringe. Ellie began to speak but Edwin held up his hand.

"Ellie, you don't even have time to catch your breath, how are you going to figure out the business? You need help."

"I'll manage. I've got Jenna now, she's a gift from above. I'll let you know when I need help, and that'll be when I'm comfortable doing so, not you. Right now isn't that time." Edwin shook his head. "Look, if you really want to help me, get a handle on the rumors around here."

"What rumors?"

"That every time you go out on the boat you take a woman with you for some love tryst. I can't even trust you on the dock, for crying out loud."

"That's not true—"

"I'm warning you, Dad, you're going to get us in trouble. You took Eloise out the other day without telling anyone and she missed her medications."

"No, she didn't, I looked in her file and took them with us. She got them on time."

"You're kidding?"

"No, ask her."

"You cannot administer meds to these people! You're not licensed."

"It's a prescription, what can go wrong?"

"I give up. Look, don't do it again and quit inviting people here to eat lunch for free. It's blowing my budget."

"We're investing in the future, Ellie."

"Give me a break! What kind of investment do you call—"

"Doesn't everyone worry about their parents and grandparents eating well? Isn't the word of mouth getting out about how good the food is?"

"How do you know the word is getting out?"

"You've seen how many people show up to sample the soup or one of the entrees. We're not running a soup kitchen."

"Damn near it," Ellie said.

"Damn near it, damn near it, damn near it!" Belle shouted.

"Not even close, Ellie. A cup of soup here, an eclair there—"

"Eclairs? He's never given me an eclair! This is bullshit!"

"Bullshit, bullshit, bullshit!" echoed Belle.

"Shut up, Belle!" Ellie yelled while stamping her foot. "You see what you've done?"

"I didn't do anything."

"My ass. You've turned me against the people I'm trying to care for. I don't even have time to sit and talk to them for five minutes because they're all more interested in what you're doing."

"Should be ashamed of yourself, Edwin," Eloise said with a grin as she pushed her wheelchair past them.

"You," Ellie said, glaring at Edwin and pointing her finger at his nose, "You sit in that reception chair and don't move. That's all the help I need for the moment. And put on some khakis and a dress shirt for your shift." Ellie spun around and headed to the kitchen.

Edwin looked down at his Bermuda shorts and flip-flops and decided that's where he would draw his line. He took his seat at the reception desk and searched the computer for the Fallon Courier newspaper to place an ad.

Chapter 16

By mid-month, the lower level of Kranz Gardens was full and there were reservations coming in for the rooms remaining on the second floor. It had been agreed early on that the upper level would be the resident quarters for the family with, perhaps, some exceptions. Ramy, too, had a room up there and Edwin had some ideas for the remaining empty space. Revenue was coming in at a steady rate, but the accounting was a mess. Ellie was trying to oversee the residents, the books, and the staff while Larry was trying to keep up with the maintenance, cleaning, and laundry. Jack was busy running from room to room, bonding with many of the residents and their visitors like a family. It was therapeutic for Jack and gave the residents an opportunity to fawn over a child.

As eager as everyone was to move in, there now seemed to be an undertone of unrest that Ellie couldn't put her finger on. She didn't think someone was sabotaging her efforts, not directly, but the effects were beginning to mount, doubling her workload and frustrations.

"Ellie," Eloise asked, "Didn't you just come from Belle's room?"

"I did."

"How is she?"

"About the same."

"Nothing new with her? I mean, is she getting that problem treated?"

"Well, we're caring for her if that's what you mean. You know, Alzheimer's isn't a treatable disease really. There's some new drugs but—"

"No, I meant the other thing. And would you mind washing your hands one more time?"

"What other thing? I did wash my hands when I came in, Eloise. I always wash them when I come in."

"I know you do, but I'm just worried about getting that disease. God, if anybody were to find out I had what Belle had, why it would be the scandal of town."

"You can't catch Alzheimer's, Eloise, you know that."

"No, I'm talking about the clap."

"What?"

"Don't tell me you don't know what it is?"

"Yes, I know what it is. Who told you she had the clap, I mean gonorrhea?"

"Well, I just heard. She had it and gave it to Cary and now he's got it."

"Are you kidding?"

"No, I heard through the grapevine that she got it somehow and gave it to Cary. I didn't know they were still doing that, especially with her condition and all. You know how you catch it don't you?"

"Yes, I— Look, she doesn't have gonorrhea. I'm almost

certain or she would have said something," Ellie replied.

"Almost certain? I think she needs to see a doctor so the rest of us don't get it."

"You're not going to get it, you can't. Or you won't. What the hell am I saying? Listen, I'll check up on it. But you have to have sexual contact to get it."

"Or if you're cleaning her up down there. You do that sometimes don't you?"

Ellie began rubbing her head, looking for a way to end the conversation. She had enough experience as a nurse to know that spreading the disease through casual contact would be a very rare event, yet she couldn't prove it hadn't happened any more than she could prove that Belle hadn't given Cary the disease.

"I'll check with Cary and her daughter and see what they say. If need be, we'll get her into the doctor. Until then I really want you to know that I do my best to clean my hands and keep everyone healthy, I really do."

"I know you do, honey, it's just that we all see you working so hard and we wonder if you forget sometimes."

"I can appreciate that. Now are you ready for your medicine?"

"Yes, but, uh," Eloise said while pointing at the sink and rubbing her hands together, "Can you just wash 'em one more time?"

Ellie closed her eyes and nodded, giving up on the issue.

"Sure."

By the end of the rounds it was obvious that Ellie would have to get Belle to the doctor to allay the fears of the rest of the patients, even those who didn't know her. An underground network of communication had developed in the facility and rumors seemed to spread like wildfire. She'd talked to Cary, who completely denied having gonorrhea and denied any knowledge of what Belle was talking about. A visit to the doctor by Belle the following day confirmed she was disease-free. Someone had called the health department and a visit by one of their agents was nerve-wracking in itself. That evening she knocked on Edwin's apartment door. He opened it up just a crack, revealing the lights low and soft music in the background.

"Hi, sweetheart, what is it?"

"I need help."

"Now? I'm a little busy."

"No, I mean another nurse. Can we afford it?"

"I put an ad in the paper yesterday."

"Thank God. Do you have any wine?"

"White?"

"Yeah, or whatever you've got," Ellie replied.

"Just a minute," Edwin said and closed the door. Moments later he opened it just enough to stick the bottle through to Ellie.

"Is your apartment that dirty that you won't let me in?"

"I have a guest at the moment."

"A guest? You don't mean a lady guest?"

"Yes."

"A woman? Oh my God, not one of the residents?"

"No, hardly one of the residents."

Ellie put her hands over her ears as if trying to protect herself from anything else that could happen that day. She turned and began walking away.

"Goodnight, Dad,"

"Goodnight," he replied with a smile and closed the door. He turned to look at Adrienne Parker, relaxing on his couch with a joint. "So, what can we do that would be worth writing about in the Fallon Courier?"

*****

Edwin turned the handle of the craft room door, surprised that it was unlocked this time. It was supposed to remain open but the last few times he couldn't get in. He put his feet up on the table, and the aroma of glue, paints, and crayons made him reminisce about his days in elementary school art class. There was also the smell of stale cigars that he hadn't noticed before. The door opened and Ruth Zingg entered.

"Edwin, what are you dreaming up now?"

"Not much, just thinking."

"Are you going to make something for us in here? Little valentines? Stick figures out of pipe cleaners?"

"Nah, nothing like that. I just like coming in here, reminds me of art class."

"It does, doesn't it? I would sit in here for hours if I could, but I don't live here."

"Doesn't matter. Come in here all you want, I don't care. Why do you come out here, anyway? Who are you taking care of?"

"Nobody and everybody, I guess. Being around the girls keeps me young. They remind me of our time growing up together."

"I guess I don't see it that way. Being around the same people every day drives me nuts, makes me feel old."

"You left, everything is new to you and it's easy to walk away from. Not for us. We've spent our whole lives together. For better or worse, they've all become like family. Didn't you keep up with anyone after you left?"

"No. Nothing and nobody. There was nothing here for me. Whatever I thought there might be just turned out to be a big disappointment."

The door opened again and Eloise came in pushed by Joan.

"Never thought I'd see you two alone in the same room. Edwin, go get us some mixers," Eloise said and then pulled a bottle of scotch from a pouch on her wheelchair. Edwin smiled and shook his head.

"You know there's no drinking in the craft room."

"You made that up. What makes this damn room so special? And what the hell is that smell? I thought there wasn't supposed to be any smoking here?"

"I don't know. Maybe it's left over from the old building. Anyway, I'm not sure Ellie would be wild about me letting you ladies drink in here."

"Shove it. Go get me something to mix this stuff with and some plastic cups. And pull those drapes so nobody can see in here. All we need is Darla to show up and ruin everything. If Ellie gets in a tizzy, I'll handle it."

"Alright, give me a minute," Edwin replied. He opened the door and saw Al Cartwright reaching for the door with some men behind him that he'd never seen about to come in.

"Are you part of the group now, Edwin?" Al asked suspiciously.

"What group?" Edwin asked. Al looked into the room and saw the women sitting at the table.

"Uh, nothing," Al said, suddenly looking nervous. "How long are all of you going to be in there?"

"Until happy hour is over? I don't know."

"Gotcha. Okay, I gotta get going. Gotta do some— things," Al mumbled as he walked away, motioning for the others to follow.

Edwin watched Al turn to look over his shoulder every few steps and heard the grumblings of the others. Edwin didn't know what was going on but he was beginning to get an idea where the cigar smoke was coming from.

A few minutes later Edwin returned with the essentials. He noticed that someone had already closed the blinds and Joan locked the door behind him. Over the next few hours each shared their life's events, the women telling Edwin about what had happened around Fallon and Edwin talking about his own experiences. He was surprised that he enjoyed their company, realizing it had been years since he'd spent time with people his own age.

Outside the craft room there was a noticeable aura of discontent. Darla stalked the halls looking for anyone to hear her divine message, Ellie was waiting to give medicine to missing patients while wondering who all the men were in the lobby, and the men's group finally gave up and shuffled out the door.

*****

Jenna pushed the food cart down the hall while picking at the plate of lunch Ramy had put together just for her. Ellie watched from a distance to make sure Jenna was actually taking the time to eat. Jenna was pretty in a girl-next-door way, but Ellie thought she might be a bit on the skinny side. Perhaps it was envy, Ellie thought. Jenna also seemed to have a following. The men who came to visit went out of their way to engage in conversation with her and doted on their wives to impress her. It was a good problem to have for Ellie, but she also wondered if there was even more about Jenna than simply looks. Ellie walked down the hallway quietly and stopped outside the room that Jenna had just entered, eavesdropping on the conversation she was having.

"Hey, Mr. Cartwright, how is she doing?"

"She's doing okay today. Her thyroid medicine seems to be doing better."

"Good, she must have an appetite then. Mrs. Cartwright, are you ready for some lunch?" Agnes Cartwright stared at Jenna and made some movements with her lips, but no words came out. "I'll take that as a yes."

"She'll eat, she just needs a little help."

"Do you want me to help?"

"Oh no, I can do it. I don't mind at all."

"Okay, well, if you need help then let us know."

"I will. Hey, Jenna, are you working tonight?"

"Every Wednesday. See you there?"

"I'll be there. You got a boyfriend yet?"

"You're the only guy for me, Mr. Cartwright," Jenna said with a wink.

Ellie saw the cart coming out the door and pretended to be writing in a chart as Jenna came into the hallway.

"How's it going?" Ellie asked.

"Good. Real good."

"Does anyone need any help?"

"Not so far. Most of my patients have great families and they show up to help right on time."

"I've never seen anything like it, you're lucky. But listen, have you been getting enough rest? You look a little tired."

"I work some at night, too. I'm saving for nursing school."

"Alright, well, don't spread yourself out too thin."

"I won't, it's just part-time at night."

"Make sure you eat. You know you can eat here?"

"Are you kidding? Ramy is shoving food down my throat every five minutes. Maybe I shouldn't say that."

"It's okay. We seem to be feeding half the town here," Ellie said with a frown. "Look, you take what you need, okay? I promise you I don't mind."

"Thanks, Ellie. Gotta go, this food is getting cold."

"Go," Ellie said and then went into Agnes Cartwright's room.

Al was dutifully spoon-feeding soup to Agnes with a handkerchief tucked into her shirt as a bib.

"Isn't that sweet?"

"Whatever I can do for my lovey."

"Are you going to take her out somewhere tonight?"

"No, I didn't plan on it."

"Oh. Uh, I just happened to overhear that you were going out tonight. I thought maybe you were taking your wife."

"No," he said and then began squirming and stuttering. "We, uh, some of my friends and me, we go down to the church on Wednesdays. You're a spiritual woman, aren't you Ellie?"

"Not really."

"Well, that's okay. Me and my friends like to go to church on Wednesday nights. Every Wednesday night. Without fail."

"That sounds like good, wholesome fun. Probably keeps a young man like you out of trouble."

"Oh, yeah, it does. We like to keep things clean and —" he began to say, but his hand was shaking now and he was spilling the soup on Agnes' chin. "Shit, I messed that up. Like you said, good wholesome fun."

"Gotcha," Ellie said. "I'll leave you two alone so you can concentrate."

"Sounds like a good idea."

Ellie nodded and left the room. There was something odd about the whole encounter, but she chalked it up to the curse that seemed to be haunting this place, where nothing was what it seemed to be. Ellie looked down and saw Jack standing by her side, cautiously waiting for something.

"Hi, Jack."

"Hi, Grandma. What are you doing?"

"I'm making my rounds."

"What are rounds?"

"I check on all the patients. I go around to all the rooms and make sure that everyone is doing okay, so I call it my rounds."

"Okay," he said, standing very still and seeming to wait on something.

"So, what are you up to, Jack? Are you doing okay?"

"Yes, ma'am. I'm making my rounds, too."

"You are?" Ellie said. His bright expression was priceless and his mimicking of her gave her a sense of pride. "Well, don't let me hold you up."

"Okay," he replied and zoomed past her and into the Cartwrights' room.

"There's my boy!" Mr. Cartwright exclaimed. A moment later Jack peeked outside the door to see Ellie still standing there and quickly disappeared again into the room. As Ellie walked by, Jack was standing next to Al with his hands in his pockets, looking guilty.

Ellie smiled, knowing there wasn't too much trouble he could get into there. She thought it was sweet that so many seemed to be bonding with him. She went to the next room to change the sheets.

"You got something, Jackie boy?" Mr. Cartwright asked quietly.

"Yeah," Jack replied and pulled a piece of paper out of his pocket. "It's from Mr. Chandler."

"Oh, okay. Let's see it."

Jack handed the piece of paper to Al, who unfolded it and read it to himself. Jack looked over his shoulder but was unable to read the message. The words read:

SHUT THE HELL UP ABOUT WEDNESDAY NIGHTS, AND DO SOMETHING ABOUT EDWIN AND THOSE WOMEN. TUESDAY IS OUR DAY IN THE CRAFT ROOM! CARY

Al folded the piece of paper and put it in his pocket.

"What's it say, Mr. Cartwright?" Jack asked.

"It's some good advice. And it says to give that boy a dollar for being good."

He pulled a dollar bill from his wallet and gave it to Jack. Jack pulled out a wad of bills from the cargo pocket of his shorts and added Al's to the stack, tucked it back into his pocket and then gave Agnes Cartwright a big hug.

"Thanks, Mr. Cartwright."

"You're welcome, Jack, you're a good boy."

"I gotta go now, I gotta do my rounds."

"Okay, we'll see you," Al said with a wave as Jack left through the door. "Ain't he a sweet little boy?"

Agnes Cartwright smiled and closed her eyes to sleep.

Jack left the room and started riding down the hall again. Ellie heard him chanting some words, repeating them over and over as if he were singing a song.

"Let it ride in three! Eight, skate, and donate," he said.

Ellie frowned. There was something about him lately that concerned her. And where did he get that backpack, she wondered. She'd ask him tonight when she finished work if she remembered.

Chapter 17

Edwin knocked on the open door and Eloise looked up from her recliner with a raised eyebrow.

"What the hell do you want?"

"Company. Are you bored?"

"Of course I'm bored, the only thing I have to look forward to every day is listening to Belle talk about you and Darla trying to give me a sermon. Are you going out on the boat?"

"Yeah, want to go?"

"That's a stupid question, give me a minute to gather my things."

"I'll be back in a few minutes. Want a sandwich or something to take with you?"

"How long are we going out?"

"Until somebody tells us to come home," Edwin replied and Eloise laughed.

"Better make it two sandwiches then."

Edwin turned around and saw Jack coming to the doorway with a hand full of envelopes.

"Hi, Grandpa Edwin, I'm making my rounds."

"Good for you, is Grandma paying you?"

"She doesn't have to—" he started to say but Eloise gestured with her fingers for him to keep quiet.

"Okay, then, I'll leave you to it."

Edwin headed for the dining room and Jack looked up at the number on the door and matched it with the number on the envelope.

"This is from Miss Joan, I think," Jack said as he handed the envelope to Eloise.

"Miss Campanella?"

"Yes ma'am. It's a birthday card and she wants you to come over. She said I could come over, too. She's going to let me help blow out the candles."

Eloise raised her eyebrows for a moment and then opened the envelope. Inside was an invitation to Joan's room for her birthday the following week. Eloise took a piece of paper from her notepad and wrote a reply, then took a quarter from her wallet and gave it to Jack.

"Take this back to her and that quarter is for you."

"Thanks, Miss Eloise."

"And thank you. Run along now."

"Okay."

Fifteen minutes later Edwin and Eloise were pulling away from the dock. The warm breeze and the sound of freedom coming from the motor had a soothing effect. It peeled back the feeling of age and inevitability from both of them. Edwin reached into the small cooler and pulled out two beers, one for her and one for him.

"So, what did Jack bring you?"

"An invitation. Joan's got a birthday coming up and she

invited me."

"Yeah, I'll be there, too."

"You?"

"Sure, why not. I try to make her feel special. She's lonely, you know."

"I know. She's been that way ever since Margaret died and Darla opened her big fat mouth."

"I hadn't heard about that. What happened?"

"She told a story about something going on with Margaret and Joan back in school, some kind of stupid love thing that kids do."

"Darla told them that? It's none of her business."

"Since when did that stop her from doing anything? You know Darla, loves to put people in a corner and make them confess. She thinks she's saving everyone. She had some theories about you being tied up in that mess, too."

"I'm not surprised."

"Well, do you know something or not? Come on, out with it."

Edwin said nothing for a moment, slowing the boat down as they pulled into a cove. There were overhanging branches providing shade and as they came to a stop Edwin tied the boat to one and turned off the engine.

"Just between you and me?"

"I won't say a word."

"Joan and Margaret were seeing each other and Margaret's mother caught 'em. Margaret's sister, Norma, knew about it, too, but she didn't get all bent out of shape. At least not the way her mother did. Margaret took a beating from her mother a couple of nights in a row. She was afraid to go home after school one day and I told her I'd take her home. I took her in the house, although I didn't know what I'd do if her mother started beating her again. I went in anyway and it was like a light went on above her mother's head. She thought that Margaret had a boyfriend and invited me to stay for dinner. Margaret was all for it and I'd been kicked out of my house the night before."

"What were you kicked out of the house for?"

"I had a nudie picture in my room, you know how my mother was. Anyway, Mrs. Thumpacker knew I'd been kicked out and said I could stay there for the time being. She even made a pallet in Margaret's room for me to sleep on. I don't know what she expected but she was always wanting to know if we were getting along okay. She'd give me money to take Margaret out on dates. I think I was supposed to show Margaret the ropes between men and women."

"Did you have relations with her?"

"Not then, it wasn't like you think. I didn't care about what was going on between Margaret and Joan. I'd take Margaret out and we'd pick up Joan and then I'd leave them in the car while I went into the pool hall. That went on until one night Mrs. Thumpacker sent Norma to find us. Somebody in the family had died and she wanted Margaret to come home. Anyway, Norma found my car and the two girls in the back seat kissing, and then found me inside playing pool. She was upset but we talked for a long time and I got her to calm down. She was more worried about what would happen with her sister if word got out than what they were actually doing. I agreed with her but what can you do? I mean, who the hell was I to tell 'em they were wrong?"

"Did Norma tell her mother?"

"No, but she threatened to if she ever caught Margaret with Joan again. And she wanted me to move out, so I did."

"Why did she want you to move out?"

"Because she knew I had a crush on her. She'd catch me looking at her all the time and I think that was too much pressure on her. I honestly think that she thought I was having sex with Margaret at night in her room and was angry or jealous or something, especially when she'd catch me looking at her. I can understand it. Maybe she thought I was a two-timing pig, I don't know," Edwin said. "So, I can also understand why Joan's so touchy about this. It's been a long time, but Darla still doesn't want to let her live it down."

"When did you sleep with her?"

"The same time I slept with Margaret."

"You were the most horrible boy, did you know that?"

"Yeah," Edwin replied. "Or at least I was back then. I think everyone thinks I still am. I'm not, really, and I don't think I was all that bad back then, either. It just seemed to be my nature."

"You were a stinker. A gentleman, though. You held the door for me once without trying stick a wet finger in my ear."

"I must have been off my game that day. Maybe I had my charming moments."

"I heard a rumor about Norma, too."

"Don't you people ever just shut up for a minute?"

"Don't you ever wonder about the past?"

"Not mine, no. I guess I don't need to, everybody else is doing it for me."

"I want to know about Belle, too. What did you do to have her all up in arms?"

"Why do you care? Why does anyone care, it was so long ago?"

"Because I like to know the truth," Eloise replied. "You know, the one thing I always knew I'd get from you was the truth. You were too brash to lie, it didn't fit your image."

Edwin put his head back and closed his eyes. This was the subject he'd been avoiding with Joan, trying not to remember the time he'd had with Norma. But with Eloise it seemed like a catharsis of anguish that had been pent up for years. Somehow, he didn't mind telling her and felt safe doing so.

"Norma and I had a fling for a weekend, that was it. We'd talked on the telephone for two hours one night while I was in the Marine Corps. I came home to spend some time with her and after four days we were about to kill each other."

"When was this?" Eloise asked.

"A little over a year after high school. I think she had run into some relationship problems and God knows what else and was lonely. She called me out of the blue, I don't even know how she got the number for my barracks. We talked about everything and I don't know how but the subject of marriage came up in that phone call. Can you believe it? I bought a ring and everything, proposed to her within five minutes of walking in the door of the room she was renting. But like I said, it went terrible. She dropped me off at the bus station and that's the last I saw of her."

"Must have been a lonely ride back, sounds like you were a little more invested in it than she was."

"I guess so. Just before I was about to get on the bus, some guy came up and shook my hand. He'd had a few drinks already and saw me in my uniform while he was driving past the bus station. He invited me to the retreat, you know, this place before it was Kranz Gardens. I came in with him and then he started partying with some other people and then he snuck off with some woman. Next thing I know, Belle is hanging all over me drunk as a skunk."

"Belle? She hated your guts."

"Alcohol, what can I tell you?"

"Did you sleep with her?"

"Yeah, took her upstairs and left her there. She was so drunk she didn't wake up afterwards. She must have some memory of it though. Darla was so angry."

"Were you there when the police arrived?"

"What police?"

"Belle got into a bunch of trouble one night, passed out in the room of some man. He said he didn't even know she was in his room and his wife came in while he was in the shower. She took a golf club and started beating him and that's when somebody called the police. They got there and the whole place got shut down. Naked women in the pool, a little casino gambling in the boat house, and a stripper in one of the rooms. They had to take Belle in an ambulance because she was too drunk to stand up.

Darla wound up down at the police station, too, but she said she was just giving statements to the police. I guess I believe her, she's never done anything to break the law. She might do things to make us want to kill her, but I don't think she'd break the law."

Edwin was smiling while Eloise recalled the events.

"I never knew any of this. You know, I've only been back to Fallon a few times since we were kids but I never came to see anyone. I just drove through some of the old neighborhoods and by the school and then went on my way. I never kept up with anyone. It's funny, Darla's the one that gave us the key to the room. I made her do it and she was furious. I knew things were getting a bit raunchy out by the pool but it must have gotten worse. But I'll never forget Darla's face when I left that night after dropping off the key with her. You know, she looked hurt."

"Well, you were lucky you stayed away as long as you did. When Darla gets hurt, she gets even."

"Who cares, it's all old news now. So, how long before they opened the place back up?"

"They never did. The owner kept the place from collapsing but they never did anything with it again and thank God. That retreat turned the whole town upside down."

"I thought it was exclusive, kind of a hush-hush type environment. For the life of me I don't know what Darla was doing working there."

"She told me that Jesus went to where the sinners were and that's where she wanted to go. Thought she could save the whole lot of 'em. I sometimes wonder if her daddy put her up to it. Whatever it was that happened that night made her even more vicious than ever. It's like she had this personal animosity toward the building. It didn't seem like a God or Jesus thing, it seemed like a Darla thing. Anyway, it affected a lot of people once all the hullabaloo was made public. The whole town just got more curious about sex, especially the ones our age at that time. More people from around here were getting involved than you would have thought, and there were a lot of girls from this area that had to move away. I still see it to this day, it's like some of these women around here don't want to let it go. I got married a few years out of high school and stayed away from all that, but my husband didn't."

"Who'd you marry, anyway?"

"Jerry Helton."

"Oh, you're kidding? I couldn't stand him."

"He didn't like you either. We divorced after about ten years and he died before he was fifty. Best funeral I ever went to."

"That's funny. It looks like I'm going to have to go to the library and do some research, see what all happened here."

"Before you do that, give me a sandwich and tell me about the rest of your life and I'll tell you about mine."

Edwin nodded, grabbed a sandwich for both of them and they spent another two hours recalling their pasts.

*****

Karen Trimble was getting desperate; the phone wasn't ringing like it once had with job offers. The word had gotten around that she was difficult to work with and even the best references couldn't overcome the stigma. To make matters worse, she didn't qualify for any help for her mother.

"Here's one, Mom," Karen mumbled as she gleaned the classifieds. "It's a new nursing home here in Fallon. 'Pristine, villa-like views of Lake Fallon. Get ready to grow with us.' Sounds interesting, what do you think?"

Norma said nothing, staring at Karen without moving. It had been two months since she'd had all of her medications. Things had been tough before, but not this bad. Norma's medications had been taking a toll on Karen's budget and her unemployment benefits had run out the previous month. Karen was hesitant to go to the emergency room, fearing both the shame of not getting hired and the possibility that someone might accuse her of elder abuse.

"Who knows, maybe I could get you in at a discount. I certainly can't leave you here alone while I'm working. 'Apply in person between 1 and 5 PM on Friday or Saturday'. Shit, I could go now."

Karen looked over at her mother and knew she couldn't leave her alone this way. She walked over and loosened the buttons on her mother's blouse, hoping that a breeze would help cool her off. She took the hand-towel and wiped the sweat off her forehead and face, then dipped a washcloth into a cool bowl of water to moisten her face and neck.

"Bear with me, Mom, the electricity is supposed to be turned back on by this afternoon—" she began but was cut short by the immediate whirring of the fan, microwave timer, and television turning on. "Finally!"

Karen turned the box fan toward her mother and removed Norma's blouse and bra, blotting the sweat from her gray, matting hair. As she moved towards her shoulders, a red tinged streak of sweat coursed down from under her left breast. Karen could see that the bra had rubbed her raw to the point that she was bleeding. Karen broke down in tears.

"I'm sorry, Mom, we can't keep living like this, but I don't know what to do about it. I hope you believe me."

Karen put her hands together, bowed her head, and began to pray. When she looked up, she could see Norma's eyes fixed on her. Her face hadn't changed, it rarely did when her condition was this bad. But Karen thought she could see pity in her mother's eyes, and compassion. Karen read it as forgiveness.

"I'll get it, Mom, just watch. I'll get that job and somehow I'll make sure that you're never uncomfortable again. Remember, you always told me that no matter what, I would always have someone who loved me. Well, that goes for you, too. I'll always take care of you."

Karen looked out the window and was immediately inspired. She walked over to the counter and thumbed through the phone book for the number of the church across the street. Without hesitation, she dialed the number while impatiently tapping her foot.

"Hello?" a voice answered.

"It's a miracle!" Karen shouted.

"What's a miracle?"

"It's a miracle. I needed someone and you happened to be there. Praise God!"

"Yes, praise God, indeed. I don't quite follow you though, is there something I can do for you?"

"Yes, yes! It's all in a day's work for our Savior, isn't it? I prayed a few moments ago for help and His blessing for a new job and I think He wants me to have it. But I can't leave my mother alone to go apply for it. I knew that if I called and someone there answered, then it was meant to be."

"I'm still not sure—"

"Oh, I'm sure. I'm positive! You were sent to pick up that phone when I called just as sure as you're meant to watch my mother for an hour."

"No, look, I always answer the phone. I'm the secretary, I—"

"You're a blessing is what you are, the chosen one for this miracle."

"You can't be serious."

"Yes, very serious. I live right across the street, in the green house. My mother's an invalid and I can't take care of her without a job. And when it all comes down to it, we won't survive without your help."

"Across the street, you say?"

"Yes, the green house. You've probably seen me taking my mother—"

"I have, yes, but I don't know that I'm qualified to watch her. I mean, what is her condition if you don't mind me asking?"

"It's like being in a catatonic state, always. Look, I'm really running out of time and I know that I'm imposing—"

"Ma'am, I simply can't just leave the office here."

"No problem, I'll be right over," Karen said and hung up the phone before the woman could respond. She spun around and looked at her mother with a sly grin. "We're gonna make this happen, Mother," she proclaimed as she grabbed the first aid kit and began dressing her wound. "I'm gonna dazzle 'em this time. I'm gonna watch my P's and Q's, and I'm gonna be the best worker they've ever seen." She stopped for a moment and looked into Norma's eyes. "You're gonna be so proud of me," she said as she hugged her mother's neck tightly.

Within minutes Norma was dressed and Karen pushed her in her wheelchair quickly across the street. The side door was held open by an anxious-looking woman as the two made their way up the wheelchair ramp.

"Mysterious ways," Karen said with a smile as she breezed past the woman and into the vestibule of the church.

"Very mysterious."

"Listen," Karen pleaded, "I know what I'm asking is extraordinary, but what I have to do is that important. Please believe me. I just need this one break, I can feel it. Please don't think badly of me."

The sincerity in Karen's eyes and the humble state of Norma made it hard for the secretary to protest.

"I get the sense that you're desperate and I'll help, but please try to hurry. I have appointments to get to in two hours."

"Not a problem." She took the woman's hands in her own and held them under her chin. "I promise to be back in no time, and I'll even come to church this Sunday."

"Sunday?"

"Yes, I always see you folks coming in and out on Sunday. Quite a crowd, and I want to be a part of it now."

"Let's take one thing at a time. You run along, the clock is ticking."

"It is. And a miracle awaits!"

The woman watched the door close, wondering if she would ever see Karen again. She looked over at Norma, who was staring at her.

"She's quite the gal," she said. She waited for a response but there was none. "Can I get you some coffee? Anything?"

Norma's silence was a bit unsettling, but worse was the possibility that something might happen to her that she couldn't do anything about. The best thing she could think of was to keep her close by.

"Perhaps you can keep me company," she said as she began pushing the wheelchair into her small office.

There was a quiet peace about Norma's face. Her scalp and hair were still damp with sweat from the hot and humid Texas air. Her sweaty blouse was untucked and it was obvious she wasn't wearing a bra. Whatever was going on across the street wasn't boding well for Norma, but the secretary still got a sense of contentment from Norma's face.

"I think we need to pray for your daughter. If what she says is true, then both of you need all of the blessing you can get. We also need to let her know that we're LDS, we worship on Saturday."

Norma's eyes grew softer, as if to smile or even laugh and the secretary knew that she'd gotten through. The secretary smiled back, pulled up a chair, and grabbed a book off the shelf. She looked into Norma's eyes once again before opening the book to a marked page.

"Do you like Shakespeare?"

*****

Larry walked into the laundry room ready to remove the sheets from the dryers and start folding them. He grabbed the

209

handle of the first on and noticed it was unusually cold. He opened it and found that the sheets were still wet.

"Dammit. I started these an hour ago," he mumbled and then checked the other dryers. "All wet. Son of a bitch."

Larry closed the door and pushed the button to start the dryers and nothing happened. No display, not even a peep. The circuit breaker panels were in the laundry room and he found one that had tripped. He pushed the switch over and it tripped again, but on the second try it held and the dryer displays lit up. Her turned the dryers on and began to load up the washers with more laundry.

As Larry was dealing with the dryers, Darla decided to kill some time until Eloise was out of the shower. She took a purposeful stroll outside all the way down to the opposite end of the building. An old memory was haunting her brought about by the recent fire alarm. She had had an uneasy feeling during the renovation of the retreat. Tearing out old things and putting in new, God only knew what might be found if they dug deep enough. Perhaps, she hoped, they did it so quickly they might have either overlooked or disregarded any peculiarities.

Darla reached the other end and peered through the window of the side door. Her level of excitement grew as she saw that the door to Joan's room was open and Joan was at the far end of the hall close to Belle's room. Darla looked into the laundry room first, but saw that Larry was in there. Instead, she darted through the door of Joan's room. Joan kept very few things in there, but there was a bookcase with rows of diaries neatly sorted by year. They were Joan's most prized possessions, containing her memories and secrets, as well as letters sent to her from others. For Darla they were like a gift from God, tools to be used to cast the demons from Joan's past and bring her to the Light.

Darla pulled three of Joan's diaries off the shelf, those from her high school years, and tucked them in her purse. She slid the bookend over to close the gap as if nothing were missing and rushed to the door, peering out to see if anyone was coming. The hall was clear but as she stepped out, another resident whom she'd never seen before came out of her room with her walker. She looked at Darla for a brief moment and then went her own way.

"That's good," Darla said under her breath, "Mind your own business."

"And you mind yours!" the woman said over her shoulder.

Darla did an about-face and left through the side door from where she'd come.

Chapter 18

It's quiet, Ellie thought. Maybe too quiet. Or maybe she was settling into a rhythm and things were going a little more smoothly. Breakfast was over, rounds had been made, and the smell of fresh paint told her that Larry was somewhere touching up a wall or some trim, or anything else that made him feel useful. He'd given up his remodeling business to help her realize her dream, and she knew it had driven him crazy not to be part of the renovations. She could hear the washers and dryers going on down the hallway, a task he took care of that took a huge burden off of her shoulders. She felt sad; she couldn't think of the last time they'd talked or even eaten at the same table together. She promised herself to find more time for both him and Jack.

"This is a good time to take on the accounting," she mumbled to herself.

Ellie went to her office and sat down behind the computer

feeling motivated and excited, maybe even a little important, to be taking the first steps of handling the company like a manager should. She clicked on the icon for the accounting software and as the program opened before her, the feeling of accomplishment vanished. She stared at the blank spaces in the forms, spaces that should be filled with numbers. Where those numbers were supposed to come from, she had no idea. She had receipts, invoices, checks, and every other form of paper piled high on the desk, and the best she could do is move them aside for a tissue to wipe her tearing eyes. But she was determined to do it and would have, too, if the fire alarm hadn't started ringing again.

"Belle!" Ellie yelled as she ran out into the hallway.

Ellie hadn't made it twenty feet before the phone began to ring. She knew if she picked it up she would be answering to the fire department again. If she didn't, they would be coming as fast as they could from all corners of the county; there was nothing worse than a fire in a building where most people moved only at the speed of a fart. She was angry that she still hadn't figured out who the mystery person was who enticed Belle to set off the first alarm.

"Hello?... Yes, I haven't begun to look, but I bet... Yes, I smell something, perhaps you should come," she replied on the phone and hung up quickly. Larry came around the corner casually but wrinkled his nose as he got closer to Ellie.

"Do you smell that?" Larry asked.

"Yeah, but I don't see any smoke," Ellie replied.

"Let's get everyone outside and then I'll do some checking."

Many of the residents were already in the hallway making their way to the exit doors and Jenna was pushing Belle in a wheelchair.

"It wasn't her," Jenna said over her shoulder to Ellie. "I was with her when the alarm went off."

"Yeah, something else is going on," Ellie replied. She glanced at the front desk and saw Edwin talking to someone with no regard to the flurry of activity going on around them.

Five minutes later the first fire truck arrived as Ellie wheeled the last resident out. Larry was focusing on the laundry room and it quickly became a gathering point for the firefighters. Soon, Ellie was given the approval to bring everyone back in, which was reassuring and a welcome relief from the afternoon Texas sun. She passed by the front desk once again, but nobody was there. There was going to be hell to pay on Edwin's part, she would be sure of that.

"What's going on?" she asked, peeking over Larry's shoulder.

"Some old wiring," Larry replied. "We rewired this whole building to make damn sure something like this didn't happen. Look at that, a bare wire wrapped around a nail in the wall. The contractors must have gotten this one mixed in with the new wires."

"That ain't all," one of the firemen said. "Look at that bottle with a rag stuffed in the top of it. Somebody was trying to set this place on fire a long time ago. I'll bet there was some kerosene or something in that bottle, but it's evaporated by now."

"You mean somebody here tried to burn this place down?" Ellie asked, horrified.

"A long time ago, maybe, but this is all old stuff. Somebody probably did this after the place closed, for insurance or something. Pretty shitty attempt if you ask me. Kid stuff. I remember an old film in science class that showed some kids with a wire wrapped around a nail that got hot, I bet that's where they got the idea. We're lucky this didn't happen way back when, before they had circuit breakers and stuff like that. I think you'll be fine," the fireman said.

"This was the only wall in the whole building that wasn't stripped down to the studs and drywalled," Larry said. "Looks like I'll be working on that next week."

"So, we're out of danger?" Ellie asked.

"Yeah, get your electrical contractor to come back in and take

214

that wire off the circuit."

"I'll call 'em now," Larry said.

"I gotta find Dad," Ellie said.

Ellie walked down the hallway and saw Edwin leaning against a pillar outside the front door.

"You know, you could have helped while all that was going on. I kinda thought you'd jump in when you knew I needed the help."

"I was helping."

"You didn't do a damn thing except blabber with that woman, whoever she was."

"Your new nurse."

"What?"

"I just hired her, she's starting tomorrow."

Ellie was stunned. She thought she'd made it very clear that all decisions were to go through her from now on.

"It's a two for one; her mother needs care and Karen is a nurse."

"I can't believe you've done it again, Dad. I mean, I don't know how else to put it other than I want to make the decisions around here!" she yelled.

"You told me you needed help and I told you I'd already put an ad in the paper."

"I didn't even get to interview her."

"You were busy. Besides, I don't need instructions to take my own initiative. You keep procrastinating and things keep getting worse. You need help, plain and simple, and I want more freedom. You're not keeping the books up like you should, you're running yourself into the ground, and there's no need for it. Plus, I know this girl's mother, we went to school together. They're going to have an apartment on the third floor."

"No!"

"Oh yes."

"Fine, you be her manager. It's between you and her, you can both take Glamour Hall."

"Okay, and you get the books in order. You'll have time now. If they're not right in three days, I'll get an accountant."

"We don't need a damn accountant," Ellie yelled. "Goddammit, I wish I'd just kept my old job!"

Ellie stormed off in tears. She was loud enough that Ramy heard her from the kitchen. He watched as Ellie stomped past and slammed the door to her office shut. Ramy walked out and joined Edwin.

"Miss Ellie's goin' crazy, Ramy's seen it before. She's in over her head."

"For the moment," Edwin replied. He felt a sense of satisfaction and some relief. He didn't like stirring up Ellie's emotions, but he knew that something needed to be done for her to finally face reality. "She'll see things begin to get better once she sees we can all be one happy family."

"You gonna fill dis place up quick. Is it makin' any money?"

With anyone else Edwin would have told them to mind their own business, but he had a sense of kinship with Ramy. Plus, Ramy had the right to have an interest in the company's success as well.

"Oh yeah, we're doing better than I expected at this point."

"You was talkin' to a woman at the desk."

"I was. She's a new nurse, she'll start tomorrow."

"What's her name?"

"Karen Trimble."

"Sure is a pretty name for a pretty lady. Is she married?"

Edwin smiled, surprised by Ramy's interest.

"No, she isn't. And if she's anything like her mother she can be a pain in the ass. But, if she has some of her father in her she's a bit more sensible."

"You know her parents?"

"I knew her mother and I've got some suspicions about her father."

"Ramy got some news, too. Ramy's daddy gonna be here tomorrow if dat's still okay."

"That's great news, the more the merrier. I'll be glad to see him," Edwin said, and then hesitated for a moment before he spoke again. "You never say 'I' when you talk, you always refer to yourself as Ramy. What's that all about?"

"It's an old habit. Ramy used to say 'I think dis' or 'I think dat' and nobody listen. One day Ramy was listenin' to the radio to hear dat man everybody liked and he used to say "Jimmy Dooley here tellin' you to go shop at the discount store' or 'you tell 'em Jimmy sent you'. Well, Ramy tried it out and it worked. People listen just to hear Ramy say his name over and over again when they ain't never listened before. It just stuck wit' me. Does it bother Mr. Kranz?"

"Not a bit. I was just curious. Interesting story though, I never thought of it that way. And Beau's coming in tomorrow?"

"Dat's what he say."

"I can't wait. Thanks, Ramy."

*****

Joan sat down at a table by herself in the dining room with her tray. She was eating early today so she could see a special television show that evening. There was another group of women at a table close to hers and she listened in to their conversation.

"That fire was two doors down from your room? Bless your heart, you must have been scared to death."

"I didn't know anything about it until Ellie came to the door. We went out the side door and it was hot as blazes outside. I probably burned up more out there than I would have in here."

"Did you find out what caused it?"

"Ellie said it was a wiring problem, but I'm not so sure. I saw that preacher woman down on that end, I know she was coming and going out that side door, I could hear it slam every time."

Joan's ears perked up, certain she was talking about Darla. She stopped chewing to make sure she heard it all.

"Nobody else uses it. It wasn't ten minutes later that the alarm went off. I don't know, probably a coincidence, but something just doesn't seem right about it."

"Did she say anything?"

"Come to think of it, the little hussy told me to mind my own business. She didn't think I heard her but boy, let me tell you, I gave her what for. I told her not to ever talk to me that way or she'd be damned sorry for doing it."

"And I know you, you'd be the one to do it, too!" one of the other women said.

"I had a good mind to slap the fire out of her. The good Lord told me not to or she'd still be on the floor right now."

Joan turned her head away to giggle so the others wouldn't see it. She wished she had been there, watching Darla get her comeuppance. To see her confronted and scolded was a dream for half the town, but hearing about it would suffice for now. Joan continued to listen but didn't learn anything new. What she did hear, though, was good enough to be put into her diary that night.

*****

Edwin looked at his hands, the skin thinning and drying with age. No matter how much he wanted to avoid it, no matter how much he exercised, his aging seemed to be picking up the pace. It might have been happening a little slower than the others, but it was happening nonetheless. It wasn't that he ever tried to deny it, but now it was troublesome because the moment Karen Trimble had handed him her resume everything had changed. He was barely able to control himself after the interview and had been sitting right there on the dock since she left, thinking about what would happen tomorrow. As innocent as it was, he felt guilty, even ashamed, for having sat with Hester on that bench yesterday.

He felt like he'd cheated on the only woman he'd ever loved.

"You're not going skiing today? Snorkeling? Alligator wrestling?" Darla asked, startling Edwin back to the present. "I've never seen you sit still for more than five minutes and you haven't moved for the past two hours."

"What do you want?"

"Mind if I sit down, my knee is bothering me," she said as she sat on the bench.

"You should exercise, you know, it'd be good for you."

"I'm not into that and it's too late for good habits," she replied. Edwin shrugged, never taking his eyes off the horizon. Darla wondered what was on his mind. "Your daughter's doing a heck of a job in there. She'll be full by the end of the year, you should be proud."

"Yes, I'm proud of her. Very proud."

"Edwin?"

"Yes?"

"Hey, look at me."

"What?"

"What's up with you? Where's your bite? Where's that Edwin spirit?"

Edwin had a blank stare for a moment. It would have been nice to have someone to talk to, he thought, but that wasn't like him, and if he were going to confide in anyone it sure as hell wasn't going to be Darla.

"Sorry, I'm just thinking. A lot of things happening around here, I guess. Life is catching up to me."

"Your past coming back to haunt you? All your dirty laundry is being aired out, right in front of your daughter. I can only imagine."

"No, that isn't it. That stuff I can live down. It's just trivial shit, some of it's even funny."

"Then what's eating you?"

"Time lost, I suppose."

"Oh, don't start that. We've all had enough of it and you seem to still be making pretty darn good use of yours where the rest of us can't."

"You mean won't."

"Doesn't matter, I don't want to do half the things you do."

"And the other half you're afraid to. Look, I'm not going to argue with you, Darla, I just feel like there are certain opportunities I've missed. That's all."

"Haven't we all?"

"I don't know, I'm not sure how anyone else views their life, I'm only concerned with mine. Don't you have some souls to save or something?"

"Don't make fun of my work. At least I'm trying to help people into the afterlife."

Edwin looked away from her and began staring at the water again. He rubbed his hands slowly, his manner seemingly focused one moment and bewildered the next. They sat quietly for a few minutes and then he began to speak.

"We're too old to hope for second chances, aren't we? I know that and it makes sense, and even if we did get a second chance, the things we could do are limited. But damned if I don't feel compelled to reach for that brass ring anyway, if I have the nerve to actually do it."

"You've got more nerve than anyone I've ever known, Edwin. Sometimes for the worse. What in the world is eating at you?"

"An old ghost. One that knows me better than anyone else," Edwin said as he stood and held out his hand to Darla. "It's a shame you never knew who I really was. Come on, I can't leave you out here alone."

"Where are we going?" she asked. There was a look of disbelief on her face and blushing on her cheeks.

"Back inside, I've got a few things to do before tomorrow."

"Oh, I see. Well, I don't want to be the one to hold you back."

"Why, where did you think we were going?"

"I don't know. For a moment I thought when you were talking about second chances and not leaving me out here by myself, I—"

Edwin nodded at first to show her he understood, and then shook his head.

"Sorry about that, I'm just not thinking clearly right now. Come on, I'll buy you some lunch. I know a Cajun that makes some great food."

"Is this a date, Edwin?"

"If you'd like to think of it that way, you can. I'm just hard up for company right now."

"Lucky me," Darla said. "I guess I should take what I can get."

Darla took his arm and for the first time in quite a while she was having strong, emotional feelings toward a man. The giddiness she felt made her realize why so many others had fallen for him in the past and how she might have said yes to him if he'd just asked. On the other hand, it also stirred feelings of guilt. Those feelings would have to be dealt with later, perhaps she could find someone to convert to make up for it. But for now, she was enjoying the youthful rush that was putting a spring in her tired step.

Edwin's thoughts were far from Darla. They were on a girl from a long time ago, someone who took his heart and never gave it back. She was about to be like so many of the others that were here at this very moment, under the same roof with him. But she, of all people, would have been the one that he never thought he would see again. Like Darla, he had second chances dancing around in his mind. Silly and lacking any pragmatic value, but they were second chances that helped one stay young at heart and happy to still be alive.

Chapter 19

Karen crested the hill on her way back home, seeing that the town of Fallon wasn't quite so small anymore. The white church spire that once stood prominently on the outskirts of town was still visible but dwarfed by other buildings. Nonetheless, seeing the church guilted her into another bout of indigestion. She pulled into the drive-thru of the drug store and wrote a check for her mother's prescriptions from an account that was within pennies of being overdrawn.

"I know," she said while looking up into the sky, "I owe You. I'll start tithing once we get some money coming in. I'm hoping You'll see to it that I make enough to make ends meet and still have enough to give to the church. I don't want to seem greedy. I'm not, You know I'm not. And I'm not the best person, but I haven't had the best of luck. I'm just asking for a little credit for taking care of my mother. Splitting the lottery this weekend wouldn't be bad either. Okay, sorry I'm bringing all this other stuff up. I get to eat, my power is on, and I've got a job and a free place to stay. I'm grateful, and I hope You forgive me for my sins, even the ones I may have committed thinking about the lottery. And lying about the tithing. Well, thank You. Amen. Oh, and forgive me for what I'm about to do."

Minutes later Karen had a large bag full of Norma's medications that would last her for another month and was worrying about how soon the check would appear at the bank. She drove the rest of the way thinking about the new job, how the place looked, and how much money she was going to save. She'd only seen the lobby but that alone was a giant leap from the rental they lived in now. She pulled into the drive, ran into the apartment to see if it had cooled off, then ran across the street to the church.

"I'm back," Karen said as she rushed through the office door. "Everything okay?"

"We're fine," the secretary said. "Your mother seems to enjoy being read to. Do you ever read to her?"

"I do; she's especially fond of Dickens. Before she got sick, she reread his books often. So, now I read her a Chapter or two every few days."

"Do you ever pray with her?"

"I pray for her, that's about the best I can do."

"I'm sorry, dear, I didn't mean to upset you. I just feel like she may want to be a part of the prayer process."

"I'm sure she probably would. I'm sure she would probably like some big miracle to come streaking down out of the sky to make her better, or somebody to come along to take care of her while I'm trying to work and support us. Wouldn't that be nice? But frankly I think she barely comprehends things going on around her and the best I can do is to make her comfortable and keep her in fresh diapers. Does anybody ever think about that? That's what I do on top of everything else. So, forgive me if I don't find the time to have a communal prayer with her."

The secretary folded her hands and put them in her lap, looking at Karen with compassion.

"I think you're doing a wonderful job and God has blessed your mother with a wonderful daughter. I hope you get this job, and if it's God's will—"

"I did get the job. I've given my thanks and I know that it's up to me to follow through and show my appreciation for the blessing."

The secretary sat quietly, deciding that either her suggestions were falling on the wrong ears or that it was just bad timing. Karen realized she was overreacting, but she also realized that letting her pent up anger and frustration free felt good.

"Look, I appreciate what you've done for me and what you're trying to say. It's been a rough day and I'm ready to be finished with it. Please understand, I cannot find God's grace in everything that happens because I don't think He brings things into our lives to purposely enrich it any more than He sends bad things to ruin it."

The secretary nodded and put one hand on Norma's shoulder and held the other out for Karen's.

"Whatever life brings you, honey, I hope it's everything you've wanted and everything you need."

"Me, too. I have to run."

"If you need help again, just call me," the secretary said as Karen wheeled her mother out of the office.

"Thanks, I will. And God bless you."

Within minutes the two were back in the apartment and Karen began gushing about what had happened.

"I did it, Mom. You'll be there with me and I can check on you whenever I need to. We get a room to ourselves and it's a beautiful place on the lake. I know you don't like the lake, but it's very quiet and pretty, and I think you'll be happy."

Karen kept thinking about what the woman at the church had said about praying with her mother. How many times had she done just that when her mother became ill? How many times had she begged for a cure? How many times had she cursed that she'd never had a father who could have and should have been there to take care of his wife? And how many times had she cursed that her father had never been there for her? She'd never found reason for blaming her mother for bringing her into the world, and all the trouble to go with it. But that ghost, that silent partner that she'd never seen, he was the one who had never been there for her. For them. He got all the blame.

"Little good it does to think about that now," Karen mumbled. "Besides, fuck him. We'll get by, won't we, Mom?" Norma could only stare back. Karen held up the bag from the pharmacy with a smile. "Look! I was able to get your meds."

Karen began packing the few belongings they had. It was three in the morning before she became tired mentally. Her fifty-seven-year-old body had wanted to give up hours before, but she wanted to wake up ready to move. The more she thought about how she got the job and how everything fell into place, the more she felt that karma's good side was finally coming around to her.

"Maybe there is a force in the universe that comes about in the right time and the right place. Who knows," Karen said on reflection, "Maybe there is a God."

*****

Edwin sat at the front desk watching and waiting for any sign of Karen's car coming down the road. He tried to convince himself that he wasn't anxious, but after almost sixty years he was about to come face to face with the woman he'd been willing to throw his whole life away for. He was still sweaty from his run, certain that his clothes were beginning to smell, but it was exactly the way he wanted Norma to see him when she arrived: active and virile, but more importantly, happy, successful, and independent.

His biggest regret was not having given Karen an exact starting time. He had no idea when she would arrive.

"Hot chocolate?" Ramy asked as he came to the edge of the desk.

"Yes, thanks," Edwin replied, taking the cup and being careful not to let the marshmallows tip over the side. "Big day for you today."

"Ramy's excited. Ramy ain't seen his daddy in a few years, be good to take care of 'em so he don't worry no more and Ramy don't worry no more."

"Yeah, it'll be good to have him here. All these other people are driving me nuts. Good hot chocolate, Ramy, thanks."

"Why don't you drink coffee and make it easy on Ramy?"

"I don't touch that shit."

"Why not?" Pastor Carl asked. He was leaning against the wall behind both of them, finished with his shower after running with Edwin.

"My mother used to wake me up at six o'clock every weekend morning to make her coffee and serve it to her while she lay in bed. I swore I'd never drink the stuff."

"Did you ever try it?" Ramy asked.

"Yeah, I did. I was stuck at a bus terminal without a dime to my name. They had free coffee and the bus was late so I drank one cup after another. Gave me the shits for about three hours, I thought the other passengers were going to kill me in El Paso for taking up the only bathroom on the bus."

"It can have that effect," Carl replied. "Did you ever make it for her later in life when she came to visit you?"

"No, I didn't even keep it in the house. My wife did but I told her to hide it so Mom wouldn't know. She said I was being silly and I told her 'Fine, you get up and make the shit for her every morning'. Mother was beside herself that I would make her go to a drive-thru to get her coffee and wouldn't buy a cheap coffeemaker. I call it getting even."

"So, you waited on your mother as a kid. You couldn't have been as ornery as people give you credit for," Carl said.

"I wasn't such a bad kid. I got into trouble some, but I don't think I was too rotten."

"Ramy goin' back to the kitchen. Everybody had breakfast?"

"I'm good, how about you, Carl?"

"I'm fine," Carl said, but Edwin could tell he was being polite.

"Go have a danish or something. It's not going to break us."

"If you insist. I'll be right back."

Edwin continued to watch the road for signs of a car when the phone rang.

"Kranz Gardens... Yes, hello Karen... Bullshit, I'll be right over," he said and hung up. Edwin picked up the file laying on the desk and found Karen's home address on her resume.

*****

Joan was ready for war. She had an enemy, a motive, and certainly the energy at this point, she just didn't have a strategy. She'd always been impulsive, but this called for plans. Hasty plans but calculated, and soon; nobody around Kranz Gardens really knew how much time they had left.

"That self-righteous biddy stole my diaries," she mumbled to herself, seething with every syllable. "She acts like she's the Almighty and then steals from someone. And she'll say it's for a good reason, too, you watch her. She'll find a way to use it against me like she's always done and then sit there and gloat. The whore of Babylon!" she yelled and then realized that she'd gotten carried away.

It was a lonely existence for her. She ate alone, watched television alone, and tried to mind her own business. She meant no harm to anybody but dammit if everything she'd ever done seemed to go against her. Since high school her friends had begun drifting away, one by one. People would still talk to her but there was a distance kept and she wondered if it was because of her relationship so long ago with Margie. Nobody was to have ever known but she assumed the secret had been exposed. Or, perhaps she had changed. But even if that were the case, she felt that since her time with Margie she'd changed for the better. Whatever it was, she didn't deserve to be an outcast and she certainly didn't deserve to have Darla stealing from her and spying into her diaries.

Joan walked to her door and looked out, wondering what her next move should be. It was quiet, even on the other end of the building in Glamour Hall. She pulled a chair up to the door so she could watch her neighbors like she used to do on the front porch of her house when she'd lived in Brooklyn. The only person moving around was Jenna, going from room to room handing out medication. And then it happened. Inspiration, opportunity, and divination all rolled into one as Darla walked out of the dining room, down to Eloise's room for a few moments, and then over to Belle's room.

Joan stood and began walking down the hallway as if a spirit were guiding her. She didn't want to confront Darla, not at all. Joan didn't think confrontation was in her, only crying, hurting, and cowering. This spirit felt sneaky and underhanded, just what she needed to accomplish her goal. She didn't even care if others found out what she did, her satisfaction would be to get even. She made her way down the hall where the door to Eloise's room was open. Jenna's medication cart was still in the hallway blocking the view into Belle's room and she could hear her talking to Belle and Darla.

"Eloise?" she called out softly, but heard no answer. She walked in the room and heard the shower going. On her way out, she saw Eloise's purse laying on the counter with the wallet on top and cash exposed. She suddenly became flushed with excitement. It wasn't the money, she had plenty of that, but it was an opportunity here that she wasn't sure what to do with. She grabbed the wallet and peaked out into the hallway. They were still talking across the hall so she knew the coast was clear. Joan looked both ways and went halfway down the hallway and then turned around and went back, turning Eloise's purse upside down so that she would see someone had been there. She checked the hallway again and quickly made her way back to the dining hall. Within minutes she had a plan. She took the cash out and then laid the wallet on the front desk and made her way to her room without being noticed.

What she had just done was diabolical and anonymous. It was almost spiritual in a sense how everything came about perfectly. Joan laughed to herself, thinking that even Darla might have found it to be the work of God. Now she needed to write a note.

*****

Edwin pulled into the driveway of the duplex. According to the address on Karen's resume, the side with overgrown grass weeds belonged to her. Edwin sat in his car for a moment wondering how in the hell Norma had come to this. As he opened his car door, he saw Karen coming out of the front door to meet him.

"Mr. Kranz, this is kind of unusual and I have to respect my Mom's wishes."

"Go to work, I'll handle this."

"Excuse me?" she replied. "Who the f—"

"This may or may not come as a surprise to you, but I know your mother very well and I think I can clear this up."

Karen's feeling of outrage vanished, replaced by fascination of Edwin's interest in her mother.

"Believe it or not, this has been a long time coming."

"I don't understand, Mr. Kranz. What is it that you think you can do?"

"I'm just telling you that I can work all of this out. Do you trust me?"

"Not really. Not yet."

"Well, you need to."

"Mr. Kranz, you may get your way with everything else, but I'm not going to be railroaded into doing anything that makes my mother uncomfortable."

Edwin looked at her, trying to suppress a smile. She was stubborn and stood her ground, traits he understood and liked. He knew exactly why she was protesting and if the tables were turned he'd feel the same. He had to find a way to win her over.

"Listen, I can't just leave you with her, she has needs, things you wouldn't know how to deal with."

"Tell you what, give me fifteen minutes alone with her."

"Fifteen?"

"Karen, there's a lot more going on here than you know. And both of you will benefit greatly if I can get through to her, right?"

"Ten minutes," she said defiantly as she opened the door behind her. Edwin stopped short of the doorway as Karen walked over to lean on her car.

"Norma?" he called through the door while walking in. "It's Edwin."

Edwin disappeared through the door and closed it behind him. Ten minutes later Karen had gathered Norma's essentials for the night, put on her scrubs, and was following Edwin back to Kranz Gardens.

It was an oddity, Karen thought, to see her mother sitting in a car with a man. As she followed behind them, it appeared that neither of them spoke. Perhaps Edwin was right, perhaps there was much more going on and at a deeper level where words were unnecessary. Karen couldn't decide if it was romantic or sad, or perhaps a combination of both. What she was convinced of was Edwin's interest in Norma, and that was more than she could have ever asked for.

Old Flames and Brimstone

Chapter 20

Larry looked at the charred wall in the laundry room, assessing the damage and realizing it could have been much worse. There were a few studs that would need to be braced for support and a drywall patch to replace the burned paneling. The laundry room was the only space that hadn't been completely gutted during the renovation and Larry began removing all the paneling from around the old circuit breaker box. Most of it was still intact, the part that burned appeared to have been loosened at some point.

"What are you doing, Grandpa?" Jack asked.

"Just fixing the wall, buddy, what are you doing?"

"I'm making my rounds. Ramy said for me to tell you that he saved some lunch for you."

"That sounds good. You stay out of trouble now, don't aggravate anybody."

"What does that mean?"

"Don't bother anybody. And don't steal their money," Larry added with a wink.

"Grandpa!" Jack exclaimed and then laughed.

"Okay, go on now."

Larry looked inside the box and found no wires going in and out, just an old, large envelope. The flap on the end was held down by a piece of string wrapped around a tab. There was something inside, something solid and heavy. He loosened the string and opened the flap, letting the contents fall into his hand: Two film reel cases for an 8mm projector.

"What the hell is this?" he mumbled to himself.

Both cases had the letters H.H. written on the outside and each contained a reel of film.

"I'll be damned. Somebody was hiding something in here."

Larry felt a tingle of excitement, remembering the stories he'd heard about the place and thinking about what might be on the tapes.

"Somebody planned on burning this place down," he mumbled. He was stunned, staring at the wall, and hadn't heard Ellie coming up right behind him.

"What?" she asked.

"Not sure yet, but I think I may have found a clue to the mystery around this place."

"I don't care about that right now. We have a huge problem.

*****

Beau Vicnair was cranky and making it impossible for LeBlon and Donnell to enjoy the ride. They had left New Orleans at four in the morning and he'd been complaining ever since. Nevertheless, they remained quiet and respectful. Beau knew they were ready to toss him over the next overpass and he tried to hold his tongue as best he could. They crested the hill that ran through the trees and got their first glimpse of Kranz Gardens.

"Looks like a nice place there, Uncle Beau," LeBlon said.

"It does at that. If you gonna die somewhere it might as well be someplace dat ain't hot with flies diggin' into you right off the bat."

"Let's don't talk 'bout dat now. Look at dat lake, I bet dat's where Ramy been fishin'. He said he pulled out some thirty or forty pound catfish out of dere, said he could find areas to flood to get crawfish."

"Yeah, dat's what he said," Beau said absently. There was a day not too long ago that this would have been a conversation he could have carried on for hours, but lately he seemed removed from everything.

"Well, we're here. Let me go see if they got a wheelchair—"

"I don't need no wheelchair, I got my walker. Just pull under dat roof thin' stickin' out by the front door and help me out."

"Alright, Uncle Beau."

The car came to a stop under the carport, and they were mesmerized by the beauty of the building.

"You gonna love dis place, I bet dey even got a masseuse in here," Donnell said as he looked around.

"What da hell am I gonna do with a masseuse?"

"I don't know, maybe massage some of that meanness out of you, I guess."

"I'll start gettin' your stuff from the trunk," LeBlon said. He worked the key back and forth until he heard a click, and then pounded his fist on the trunk to get it to open.

Beau was halfway out of the car when he saw Ramy quickly coming from the front door. Beau began to cry as soon as he saw him.

"I'm a-dyin', boy."

"Well, you ain't gonna die hungry and unloved. You gonna have lots of people around you. Dey's a lot of pretty girls your age, you can talk to all of 'em. And Ramy's got a good lunch ready for you."

"You been a good boy, Ramy, Daddy's proud of you."

"Stop talkin' like you gonna die today. Ramy loves you and dat man Edwin loves you, too."

As they spoke, Edwin and Norma pulled up behind Beau's car, with Karen right behind. Edwin got out and rushed over to give Beau a handshake.

"It's good to see you, Beau. Ramy's going to get you all fixed up and I'll catch up with you later. I've brought someone else and they need to get in, too. Do you mind?" Edwin asked.

"You a damn good man, Edwin," Beau said as he began to tear up again. Edwin smiled and patted him on the shoulder.

"You'll be calling me a son of a bitch in no time. It's good to have you here."

Beau watched Edwin and Karen as they began to get Norma out of the car, not taking his eyes off the three of them.

"Edwin, dat girl look just like you," Beau said, catching Karen by surprise. Edwin gave him a sideways glance and Norma said nothing. "You know I'm right. Swamp blood in me always tells da truth."

Edwin never got a chance to reply. Somewhere in the confusion Ellie had made her way outside with Larry and she was toe-to-toe with Edwin.

"Where have you been?" Ellie asked.

"Helping out, what's the matter?" Edwin replied.

"Who are all of these people?"

"Beau Vicnair, Ramy's father. I don't know the two gentlemen with him. And this is Norma Trimble and her daughter Karen. Karen is your new nurse."

Ellie rolled her eyes, clenching and unclenching her fists. She wanted to tear into him, but the timing was bad.

"Hello, everyone," Ellie said while glaring at Edwin. She stuck her hand out to Karen who took it. Ellie half shook her hand and half pulled her along as she turned to go inside. "I need you, come with me."

Karen turned and looked at her mom who nodded and motioned for her to go ahead.

"Miss Karen!" Ramy shouted, causing both Ellie and Karen to stop. "Ramy gonna make sure your momma gets fed good, and you let Ramy know when you're hungry, too." Karen stared at him for an extra second before speaking.

"Yes, thank you Ramy, I—" she began but Ellie pulled her into the building.

"You're sweet on dat girl, ain't you?" Beau said.

"Ramy's got some thoughts. Come on, you got a room just waitin' for you. Donnell and LeBlon can stay the night, too."

"Nah, we gotta run, Ramy," Donnell said. "Can we get somethin' to eat before we go?"

"You talkin' to Ramy and wonderin' if you gonna get somethin' to eat? Course you will, come on in. If LeBlon waits for a while, Ramy got someone to introduce him to. A mean girl, likes fishin'."

"I got all day," LeBlon said as he pulled a comb from his pocket. Donnell looked at his watch and then shook his head as he smiled.

The Vicnair clan made their way to the dining room, leaving Edwin to push Norma inside. As he turned her toward the front door, he stopped as Jack had planted himself directly in front of Norma. He stared at her, mesmerized, and before Edwin could scold him for staring, Norma held out her arms and Jack ran to her and gave her a long hug.

"What's your name?" Jack asked.

"Norma, and what's yours?"

"Jack. Can I call you Miss Norma?"

"Yes, you can."

"Can I come see you after my rounds?"

"I hope you do."

Jack gave her a kiss on the cheek and released his grip around her neck. He stared at her for another few seconds and then ran back inside.

"My great-grandson."

"A sweet little boy," was all Norma said as Edwin pushed her inside. He grabbed a plate of lunch for her and took her to his room. Edwin pushed her wheelchair up to the table and sat across from her.

"What happened?"

"With what?"

"The scars, the burns. What happened?"

"You don't waste any time, do you?"

"We're not getting any younger," he replied.

Norma put her head back, stared at the ceiling and realized that at the moment she was defenseless and that nothing was going to satisfy Edwin short of everything. She decided she would let him have it with both barrels.

"I met a man named Jonathan. A good man, one that was everything I wanted. He was ready to take me and Karen in. He was going to adopt her, give her his name. She was so young she would have never known the difference. But before him I'd dated another man, Billy, who didn't want to let go. Sort of like someone else I know."

"Hey, I told you in the car I wouldn't start if you didn't."

"We're only having this conversation because you want it, Edwin." He bristled at her rebuke but remained silent. "Billy caught us one night. I'd left Karen with my sister and Jonathan and I were sitting by his fireplace having wine. Up until then I hadn't had relations with anyone since you'd gone and Billy had been angry about that. Anyway, Jonathan was reaching into his pocket for something at a very romantic moment and then the door busted in. Billy beat Jonathan with a tire iron until he didn't move anymore and then took a knife to my face. He stabbed me twice in the stomach and in one of my breasts. I lost consciousness somewhere in all that, but one of the neighbors heard the commotion and came in while he was lighting my hair on fire with a cigarette lighter. That's how the burns and scars got there. You remember how thick my hair was?"

"I do."

"Anyway, Billy ran out the back door and they rushed me to the hospital."

"What about Jonathan?"

"He was dead before anyone got there. They told me..." Norma said as she began to cry, "They told me that he had two rings in his hand, one for me and one for Karen."

Edwin got up and pulled a chair next to her and put a hand on her shoulder. She grasped his arm and cried grievously as if she hadn't allowed herself to mourn the event since it had happened. Edwin sat patiently, lightly squeezing her neck every so often in comfort. They were experiencing similar pain, just for different people. The woman he'd longed for was sitting before him in his grasp as she longed for another person and another time. She would never be able to understand the memories that were flooding back to him and he wasn't going to try to make her. But there was something that he had to know, and as she began to regain her composure he pulled his hand away.

"So, I have a question for you. I did the math and I can almost bet that Karen is mine."

Norma sat quietly staring at him. She had hoped the question wouldn't arise, but she also knew that Edwin rarely missed a thing. The problem was that she'd never considered an answer until now.

"Yes," Norma replied. Edwin nodded and gathered his thoughts.

"I can think of all kinds of reasons that you would have never told me. Was I that bad back then that you couldn't bring yourself to let me be a part?"

"You were married by the time I was ready to tell you, Edwin. I didn't want to mess up your life, not the way mine was."

"I would've taken care of her. I would've—"

"You would have tried every way in the world to get back with me and that's the main reason why I never told you."

"You seem pretty goddamn sure of yourself, what makes you say that?"

"Because I know I hurt you. I could see it in everything about you the day I left you at the bus station. And the day I called a few years later, I could tell you still weren't over it. And you weren't what I wanted, Edwin, but I wouldn't have known that if we hadn't spent those days together. I still cared about you, you were a friend. There was something special about you—"

"But not special enough."

"No, that isn't it. You were different from what I wanted. I was looking for someone specific, and I think you were lonely. I don't know why, God knows you had plenty of women to choose from, but you had to have been lonely."

"I was lonely? Who called me out of the blue and talked to me for two hours on the phone? And you're the one that brought up marriage, so that's where you're wrong. And stupid me, I thought there was something special about you. You were the only person I ever wanted. It just seemed like you changed so much in just that short time after I went into the service. I couldn't do anything right, you complained and lost your temper every time I opened my mouth. I didn't have a dime to my name and I think that irritated you even more. The worst part, for me anyway, was that we didn't seem to have that much in common anymore. That time was everything to me and it seemed to sour right off the bat."

"It was three days, Edwin. Three days, there wasn't time to even put anything together, much less have anything fall apart. It was a time to find out about each other, that's all. It just didn't work out."

"I was just another pair of shoes."

"What?"

"You told me that spending time with someone was like trying on a pair of shoes to see if they fit."

"Isn't that what dating is? Spending a weekend together to get to know each other?"

"To you, maybe. It was more than that for me," Edwin said. They sat quietly for a moment and then Edwin spoke again. "Let me ask you one more thing: Why did you call that day? You knew I was married, the person who gave you my number told you that, but you called anyway."

"I was desperate. I was hoping you were divorced or something. Don't take that wrong but nobody wanted a young woman who was tainted with a toddler already. I thought that I could give it another try, maybe you'd changed. When you told me you were still married and I sensed how angry you were, I knew I'd made a mistake."

"I would've dropped everything and taken you if you'd just been honest with me."

"It wouldn't have been right, Edwin."

"Maybe not, but perhaps the same outcome. My marriage didn't last much longer after that and you probably hadn't changed either."

"I'm not sure what you think was wrong with me," Norma said.

"Well, you certainly weren't the same person I knew in school when we had that weekend together."

"I grew up. But I was still a nice person."

"You may have been a lot of things, but you weren't a very nice person. You took every occasion to be critical of me—"

"Well, you were being such an ass about everything," Norma said.

"Thank you. Does that make you feel better? Been waiting to say that for a long time? That's exactly what I was talking about. You and your silly pride and your cavalier attitude, telling everyone you were a bitch and proud of it."

"So, what's wrong with that?"

"Didn't get you very far, did it?" Edwin replied, and Norma glared at him. "Be that as it may, I made a promise to you and myself before you dropped me off at the bus station and I'm glad to be able to keep it."

"I don't remember any promise, I just remember you slamming my trunk when you grabbed your bag."

"It only matters to me, I'm sure, but I promised that if you ever came back into my life, I'd do everything I could to take care of you. No strings attached except for one."

"What is that?"

"You tell Karen the truth."

Norma sat still for a long time, looking out the balcony window and into the distance.

"That might be difficult, perhaps we should give it a little time. Let her get to know you,"

"Alright, a couple of weeks."

"Edwin, for Pete's sake, why have you always been in such a rush for things?"

"I'm guessing that you didn't have a lot of good things to say about me, did you? And why the rush? Because I want her to understand why I'm ready to open a whole new world up to her, one that she probably never imagined. Two weeks, Norma, or I'll tell her myself. I lived my whole life doing things I thought you'd find appealing, trying to impress you I suppose, and I'm tired of it. I'll do what I want now. You'll have to excuse me while I make some phone calls, I've got to get some movers to get your stuff in here by tomorrow."

Norma sat in her wheelchair staring out the window, trying to give the impression that she was ignoring him. But she listened as he made his phone calls, bullying the moving company into turning on a dime to do what he wanted. She listened to him call his accountant and discuss how to position his assets so that he would have extra cash on hand. None of this was the Edwin she had known before. Long gone were the days of his carefree spirit and willingness to worship at her feet. He now took charge of things, understood things, made things happen. Had he been like this years ago she would've never let him go. But if what he'd said just a moment ago had any truth to it, she'd made him this way. He'd obviously worked long and hard to become the man she saw before her. And years ago she'd let it all slip away.

*****

"I'm Ellie, or did I already tell you that?" Ellie said while taking Karen to the medication room.

"You did," Karen replied. "Something seems amiss, did I do something wrong already?"

"No, but my father hired you without consulting with me and thank God he did, just don't tell him I said that."

"He's quite the man."

"You don't know him, he's doing his best to drive me insane. Okay, forget all of that, I've got a mess going on, but I need to know what you can do."

"RN with thirty-five years experience. I've also got a degree in accounting and an associate's in business. I've worked the last ten years in nursing homes that were shit-holes, if you don't mind me saying. This place is nice."

"Thank you. I'm trying but some people aren't making it easy on me. Anyway, it's you, me, and an assistant named Jenna."

"Jenna Pack?"

"Yes, you know her?" Ellie asked.

"Oh yeah. She's good. A little wild, but she's good."

"She's been great for me. Haven't seen the wild side of her."

"You probably won't. She's never late, takes great care of the patients. Look, I'm not trying to give you the wrong idea about her. I love her to pieces. That sounds like her singing now."

"Yes, it does. People on the floor swear she's good and that she performs somewhere but I can't imagine who'd hire her for her singing."

"It's not such a mystery. She bartends a few nights a week at a strip club and in between acts they sometimes let her sing. Everyone that works there is a bit under-dressed, I think that's why they let her sing. She's not one of the strippers, though. At least I don't think she is."

Ellie's eyes widened, completely caught off guard with the information.

"Okay, then. Sweet little Jenna, who would've guessed?" Ellie stammered. "Never mind that, I have a fire to put out here. Someone stole a purse from a patient and she wants the police involved and the whole nine yards."

"Do it."

"What?"

"Call the police. It'll show that you're being proactive. Trust me, I've seen both sides of this and that's the better way to handle it. They probably won't be able to do anything to recover it but it'll make the people here feel better."

"I'll consider—" Ellie began to say when Jenna walked up behind them.

"Ellie, I found this," she said, holding up Eloise's wallet. "It looks like everything is here but there's no cash. I'm not sure if she had any."

Ellie looked back at her curiously, trying to envision this sweet creature in front of her singing in fishnet stockings.

"She told me she did," Ellie said, trying to clear her head. She took the wallet from Jenna and thumbed through it. "I think she said fifteen dollars."

"Hi, Karen. Are you going to be working here now?"

"Just started, sweetie."

"Cool. Ellie, do want me to take this to Eloise?"

"No, I'll take it. Where did you find it, anyway?"

"On the front desk. It was laying out in the open."

"Lucky somebody else didn't take it. Thanks, Jenna." Ellie turned back to Karen. "Problem solved for the most part."

"I'd still call them. Scare the shit out of whoever did it if they live here."

"Like I said, I'll consider it. Let me show you around. This, of course, is the med room and I'll get you a key. Let's go to the dining room."

"And what's the cook's name, Remy?"

"Ramy. Yes, Third-Person Ramy."

"Ha! That's funny, I noticed that."

"Drives me up the wall."

"I think it's attractive, myself. He seems like a simple guy. Handsome. Can he cook?"

"Heaven's yes, but don't tell him I said anything."

"You don't give men a lot of credit, do you?"

"Ramy was the first employee forced on me by my father when we opened. He had him all lined up before I could even think about it. Then you. I'm scared to think what's coming next."

"Well, so far so good for him. Was Jenna your pick?"

"Yes."

"Well, if Ramy's a good cook I think we're off to a great start. I'm probably the best you're going to find as far as nursing home care and you really can't go wrong with Jenna."

"I wish I were as confident as you at the moment. Here's the dining room," Ellie said as she opened the door. "Over there is the line to go through the buffet, or Ramy will bring a plate to you if you wave to him. That's him and his family there."

Ellie looked at Ramy and saw that he had a fixed gaze on Karen, and Karen seemed to be soaking up the attention.

"Miss Karen, Ramy sent a plate of food up to your momma. Mr. Kranz gonna make sure she eats right."

Karen nodded to him and smiled but Ellie became concerned.

"Can your mother eat by herself okay?" Ellie asked, steering Karen back out toward the lobby.

"As long as she isn't having one of her spells."

"What happened to her?"

"A man tried to kill her a long time ago."

"He wasn't messing around, was he?"

"Not at all. Look, I know he's a touchy subject for you, but your dad is the only man that has shown my mother any kindness my whole life. That's important to me."

"Was it your father that did that?"

"No, I've never met my father. The bastard's never been in the picture."

"Sorry to hear that. I saw my dad. Rarely, but still saw him. Thankfully he paid child support and gave me everything I wanted. Everything but affection, I'm afraid."

"He can have an abrasive side to him, can't he?"

"He can. Okay, let's get you introduced to everyone. This is Glamour Hall."

"They brought the name with them, how funny is that?" Karen mused.

"I'm guessing the old place had one as well? It's anything but glamorous but if it makes them happy then fine with me. I'm going to turn this floor over to you for the afternoon, the charts can be found on the monitors in the rooms. I've got to figure out what to do with the second and third floors. No offense but I didn't expect anyone new moving in here other than Ramy's father."

"I understand. I hope we can figure this out, I certainly didn't mean to cause a firestorm."

"You didn't, my father did. Don't worry, you'll see what a pain in the ass he is soon enough," Ellie said. Karen laughed but said nothing.

*****

That night, Edwin sat out on the balcony feeling the warm

evening breeze blow across his face. He watched the lights from across the bay as they glimmered off the waves that lapped the shore of the lake. Most everyone was asleep now except for Nettie, who was quietly playing her harmonica the way she did every night. Her room was on the far end of the building where distance and the crickets helped smooth out her awful playing skills. As bad as it was, Nettie's harmonica could usually bring a sense of contentment and comfort.

He was tired, having spent most of the day avoiding his apartment and Norma. The movers had done their best and gotten her and Karen moved into the apartment down the hall but they hadn't finished until late that afternoon. It had been hard avoiding the only person he ever wanted to be around for decades.

As much as he'd tried, Edwin hadn't come to grips with what he saw as a lost opportunity with Norma. That and the fact he was getting old. For him, life had been a continuous string of new beginnings, going from one place to another in the military and moving from oil field to oil field. Even after he had retired, new places seemed to get old quickly and he never quite found a place to call home. But that wasn't the worst of it. Throughout those years, he'd dreamt about finding her again and that she'd be the one to help him settle down. There had always been that small glimmer of hope until today. When he saw her that morning for the first time in years, sitting in her wheelchair in the duplex she shared with Karen, his dreams had vanished. It wasn't where she lived or how she looked, it was how she looked at him as he came through the door. It was a look of dread and frustration. He knew she didn't want him there no matter what the circumstances, no matter what the outcome. That's when it struck him that their time wasn't diminishing and the opportunities weren't getting fewer by the day; they had never been there to start with.

Edwin formed a pool of saliva in his mouth, leaned over the rail, and spat as hard as he could. It was a symbol of wasted time and anger, and now the soft music of Nettie's harmonica with its off-key tone and warbled delivery seemed to define how he felt about his life.

Chapter 21

It had been four days since Norma moved in and Edwin hadn't seen her once. There were plenty of explanations for why she might prefer being in her room, but all of them made less sense to him than his feeling that she was simply avoiding him. She had her meals brought to her and never seemed to venture beyond her apartment door. Edwin sat fidgeting at the front desk thinking up a reason to go see her. Larry walked up to Edwin and tapped him on the shoulder.

"Hey, you got a minute?" Larry asked.

"Yeah, what's up?" Edwin replied.

"Let's go down to the laundry room, I'll show you."

Larry had his laptop resting on top of the long table used for folding the sheets and had an old blanket pinned up to one of the walls.

"What the hell is that?"

"Remember when the fire chief said someone was trying to burn this place down? Take a look at this."

Larry pulled the blanket back, exposing the hole in the wall, and opened the file in his cell phone that had the pictures he'd taken before.

"Yeah, I saw all of this."

"That isn't all. See here in this picture, all this newspaper and stuff I pulled out? That was the kindling to make sure that these would burn, too," Larry said while pulling the two 8mm reels from a drawer. "They were tucked up above the newspaper. Look at the initials here: H.H."

"How do you know they're initials?"

"I don't know what else they'd be. Anyway, judging by what I read in the newspapers I pulled out of there, this place was for swingers."

"I'm not surprised. You still have the papers?"

"Yeah, they're in the drawer. But you should see what was on the films."

"I don't know if I want to."

"It's actually kind of funny. Here, I'll show 'em to you. They aren't that long," Larry said as he looked for the file on his computer.

"You've got them on here?"

"Yeah. I had a company in town digitize the film and load it on a CD. They're slow here, took 'em a week. They did a good job, though."

"And they were able to put them on here? Remarkable."

"You really need to catch up with technology, Edwin."

"No, thanks, I've got solitaire and a word processor. That's all I need to understand."

The video began and, in spite of the poor lighting when the video had been shot, it had obviously been done with a decent camera by someone who knew what they were doing. The pictures were sharp, showing details of everything that came within sight of the lens and Edwin was captured by it instantly.

"Look familiar?"

"I can't believe what I'm seeing," Edwin replied and then pointed to a person in the background behind a counter by the pool. "See that girl right there? That's Darla McGee."

"I wondered about that, but I wasn't sure if it was the same person. Man, she was a looker back then."

"That's her. Look at her, she was pissed off back then, too."

"Well, then you're really going to like the rest of it. Let me turn the sound on."

Larry turned on the sound and the voice narrating was the same person shooting the video, giving moment by moment accounts of what he was seeing and doing.

"Look at her, standing there with her chin high and shoulders square. We could turn that stern look into a sultry one with just the twist of the mouth and she'd make every man's head turn. Let's go see what her name is."

The camera made its way up to the counter, the girl glaring at him the whole time.

"What's your name, princess?"

"Darla, and don't call me princess."

"Darla, that's a pretty name. A good southern name. Are you a Southern girl at heart, Darla?"

"I'm a good Southern Baptist girl at heart. Why are you filming me? I'm not one of those naked heathens you were filming in the pool earlier."

"I'm just trying to get to know you. What do you do here?"

"I keep things like room keys and change and cigarettes while the guests swim and do all these other filthy things. I really wish you would stop filming me. If you want

to do something for me, go get me a lemonade or some tea,
I'm dying of thirst."
    "I'll be right back."

The screen went blank and Edwin looked perplexed.
"That's it? That's certainly nothing be excited about."
"That's the first one. I'll load the second and that's where it gets interesting."
"This is remarkable. It's like looking back in time."
"Brings back some memories?"
"Lots."
"Here, tell me what you think of this one. I think there may have been a lot of lemon in that lemonade he brought her."
Edwin frowned and then focused on the screen again. The video seemed to resume from an interrupted point of some data that was lost.

    "So, you're right out of high school. A mature woman
now?"
    "I'm a big girl, I can do what I want."
    "So, what do you want to be, Darla?"
    "I want to be a singer. I want to sing in a rock and roll
band and travel on the road. I want to have fun!"

Darla was slurring her words in the video and the blouse she'd been wearing buttoned to the top of her neck was now loosened by a few buttons.

    "You like to sing?"
    "Yeah, I sing at my Daddy's church. But that music
isn't fun. I like rock and roll. Daddy doesn't like it. He'd
slap me if he found out I liked rock and roll."
    "That's a shame. You're such a pretty girl. Do you
know how pretty you are?"

Old Flames and Brimstone

"No, tell me! Tell me how pretty I am. Do you think I have a nice figure?" she asked.

"You're gorgeous, Darla. You know, I meet women all the time that are pretty but only a few of them have that special look. And you've got that special personality that men look for. You could make a lot of money in Hollywood, I bet."

"You think so? I'd love to be in the movies. I could sing and dance, maybe meet one of those guys like James Dean or Rock Hudson."

"I don't see why not. Let's see what you can do on camera. Put your hand on your hips, give me a mean look."

"Why a mean look?"

"Just help me out here, and look, unbutton another button and raise your collar up. That's it. Now spread your feet out and put your hands on your hips. Very nice. Hey, don't fall over."

"I need another lemonade," Darla said.

"I think you've had plenty."

"No, I need another one."

"Right after we finish with this I'll get you another one. Promise."

"Okay."

"Now, one more button, and let your hair down and put it over one shoulder."

"No, no more buttons."

"It's okay, your hair will be hiding anything exposed. You won't even realize it."

"You sure?"

"Absolutely. Yeah, perfect. Spread your feet a little more. That's good. Turn sideways and look at me over your shoulder. Amazing! Alright, have a seat and I'll go get another lemonade."

The screen went black again and Edwin put his hand up to his mouth.

"She's drunk." Edwin said.

"Not completely," Larry replied. "Now this next part is a bit risqué."

Larry started the third video and Edwin looked away after only a few seconds.

"I don't want to see that."

"That's about as bad as it gets."

"It couldn't get any worse. Just tell me how it ends, I don't need the details."

"She ends up on one of the chaise lounges naked and passed out. He threw a towel over her when he finished. It hid most of her body."

"Are there any more?"

"No, that was all one reel, the other one had some damage to it and they couldn't even get it to load into a projector without it crumbling."

"Probably just as well. Look, don't let anybody else see these. And let me have those newspapers, I want to look at them a little."

"Okay," Larry said, taking the lid off the boxes that had the newspapers inside. "That really seemed to bother you. How come?"

"Because I know Darla, and I know people can sometimes make bad choices because of other people. Nobody deserves to be exposed like this. Nevertheless, save this video."

"Got it," Larry replied.

*****

Karen went to the dining room under the guise of checking on lunch for the patients. It was something she'd done over the last few days and both she and Ramy knew it wasn't really about lunch at all. She was giving Ramy every signal and opportunity to ask her out and so far he was toying with her. She didn't understand why but it didn't bother her. She felt a sense of ease with him and there was no reason to hurry.

"Dere's Miss Karen, doin' a good job takin' care of dem patients, makin' sure dey food is cooked good."

"I never worry about the food, Ramy. It's always good," Karen said.

"Den what you down here for, come to see Ramy?" he asked.

"Maybe. Maybe I like the way you talk. Maybe I like the way you look. I don't know," she flirted. "I could say that I like the way you cook, but you already know that."

"Maybe it's how Ramy make Miss Karen feel."

"No, it isn't that. I feel lonely, like an old maid. Somebody that nobody wants, nobody looks at," she said with a sigh.

"Well, dat's silly," Ramy said absently.

"What do you mean?" Karen asked.

"All dem people dat you care for, you can't be lonely. You workin' way past your shift helpin' all dem out and never take no time for yourself. How Ramy 'posed to find time to take you out?"

"Maybe it's time you asked. I might try to find some time for that."

"Ramy take you out tomorrow night at eight. We let somebody else do the cookin' while we dance and look at dem stars."

"You've got this all figured out, don't you?"

"Ramy's just beginnin' with dat, dey's more in store."

"Well, I'll have to find someone to look after mom…"

"Mr. Kranz gone look after Miss Norma," Ramy said.

"You've already talked to him about this?" Karen asked.

"Ramy had to borrow Mr. Kranz's car and Mr. Kranz wanted to know why. He's happy to help. Dat's a good man, dat Mr. Kranz."

"I guess I can't refuse, can I?" Karen said.

"Miss Karen can refuse dis time, but not later on. May as well be dis time," Ramy said.

"Alright then, where are we going, if you don't mind me asking?"

"A little cajun restaurant dat's got a big back porch with a dance floor outside. Ramy wear some blue jeans and a t-shirt and Miss Karen wear a cotton sundress," Ramy said.

"A sundress? What if I want to wear something different?"

"Well, Miss Karen have to go with someone else if she wear somethin' different. Ramy want to see her in a sundress with dem pretty arms around his neck and dat hair hangin' on her shoulders," he replied.

"You're a bold man, Ramy."

"Ramy knows what he wants and how he wants it. Dey's no need in pretendin' you don't want to make Ramy happy."

"No," she said, amused. "One thing I don't think I have to do with you is pretend. Alright, I'll wear a sundress."

"Ramy got to get back to cookin'. Here's a piece of strawberry-rhubarb pie for you," he said as he pulled a small plate from under the counter.

"That's my favorite," Karen said in surprise.

"Dat's what Miss Norma told Ramy. Ramy made it dis mornin'."

"You're sneaky."

"And you a pretty woman."

*****

Ellie walked through the side kitchen door that adjoined the dining room. At five-thirty in the morning, she knew that it was a little too early for breakfast, but the smell of biscuits baking had filled the hallways and made her hungry. She walked toward the back but something in the corner caught her eye, something that made her heart race from anxiety. Nettie sat in the corner in her wheelchair with a large mixing bowl full of raw eggs sitting in her lap. She stirred the eggs with a wire whisk as she hummed off-key, but there was something disturbing that called for Ellie to walk a little closer to confirm. She quickly went looking for Ramy in the cooler.

"Ramy!"

"Yes, ma'am?"

"Why are you letting Nettie in here, making her work like this? Do you know that she's drooling in the eggs?"

"Yes ma'am."

"What? Really?"

"Yes ma'am. She like to work here, comes in every mornin'. Make her feel good to help Ramy. Make her feel good to contribute. Ramy can't find anythin' wrong with dat."

"Ramy, don't serve those eggs to anyone. If the Health Department came in here—"

"Ramy don't serve those eggs, Miss Ellie. Dey probably not hurt anybody, but Ramy knows better."

"Do you throw them out?"

"Every day."

"You're shitting me?"

"No, not today, Miss Ellie. Dat's Miss Nettie's dozen. Ramy's supplier always have eggs out of date so dey bring 'em here for free. Dey come in every Wednesday with the other eggs. Dem eggs put a smile on her face and she don't feel like a wart no more."

"A wart?"

"Yes, ma'am. She says she feels like a wart to society when she just sits in her wheelchair and watch everybody else with a job. Now she feels good. Now she smiles and smiles. She's a good woman."

Ellie stared at him dumbfounded, but it wasn't just him, or this incident, or any other particular thing. It was a combination of everything that made her feel as though she were overseeing a circus.

"Miss Ellie?"

"What?"

"Are you okay?"

"No, I want to scream and pull my hair out. But I'll live," she replied. Ramy smiled and nodded.

"Ramy feels like that sometimes. Are you hungry?"

"No, I couldn't possibly eat right now."

"Somebody told Ramy you like pancakes. The batter's ready, won't you sit down for just a minute?"

"No thanks, Ramy. Maybe in a little bit," she said as she walked away. Around the corner, she turned to take a parting look at Nettie, only to see that she was no longer moving the whisk in the bowl. She was asleep with her right hand and cuff of her sleeve laying submersed in the egg mixture.

Ellie thought about having a company meeting, bringing everyone together and laying down the law. They had done things like that at hospitals she'd worked for and sometimes it worked. But none of those places had an Edwin in their midst and that was something she couldn't overcome. Tears began to well up in her eyes and she made her way to the back door before anyone could see her cry. After a few minutes, the worst of the emotions had passed and she turned around to see Jack staring at her through the door with a look of horror on his face. Ellie grabbed the door handle as her heart began to race.

"What's the matter, honey? Why are you up so early?"

Jack looked around to see if anyone else could hear him, but didn't utter a sound.

"Jack, what's the matter? You can tell Grandma anything. What is it?"

Jack swallowed hard and balled up his fist.

"Well, yesterday Mrs. Chandler said I should call the police and I forgot. I don't want to get into any trouble."

"The police? Why, Jack? Why does she want you to call the police?"

"She said her teeth are missing. She said Grandpa Edwin stole them after he, uh, after he—"

Ellie began to feel her panic turning to anger as she realized this probably wasn't a crisis after all.

"After he what?" Ellie prodded.

"After he got her pregnant."

Ellie closed her eyes and rubbed her head. Up to now, letting Jack visit with the residents hadn't seemed a big deal, but now she would have to keep him away from Belle.

"It's okay, Jack. Mrs. Chandler is not pregnant, okay?"

"She said it would be my little brother or sister. I want one, how come she can't have one?"

"Well, it wouldn't be your...never mind, Jack. Honey, go have some cookies or something and Grandma will get all of this straightened out."

"Okay," Jack said, his little shoulders slumping.

Ellie watched as Jack shuffled away and she felt guilty all over again for not showing him enough attention. He and Larry had begun bonding more but over the last few days she was seeing less of him and she was only guessing that Larry was watching over him. Something needed to be done but she wasn't quite sure what or how she was going to accomplish it.

Before Ellie knew it, morning rounds were over and the medicines had been distributed. Lunch would be in an hour, the sun would be setting in another few, and then she would scream at her father at the top of her lungs. Maybe Belle Chandler, too, just for good measure. She knew Edwin had no control over what Belle said or did, but the fact remained that he was the impetus for much of what she did. That alone made her want to smother him in his sleep.

Ellie stopped in the hallway and leaned against the wall to rest for a moment and reflect. She was tired and angry, feeling the weight of everything around her on her shoulders. The only thing keeping her from packing her belongings in the middle of the night and leaving was the realization that she hadn't ever eaten this well or felt this much of a sense of accomplishment, even if things did seem crazy. And to top it all off, she had finally been pushed to the edge far enough to do battle with her father.

Chapter 22

Ellie looked at her watch and looked up and down the hallways. Jenna had already delivered the lunch meals and Karen had distributed meds. It was quiet in the hallway for once and Ellie thought for sure she was missing something. She walked from one end of the hallway to the other, peering into the rooms that had doors open. People were content, minding their own business, or asleep. There was a cigar odor coming from somewhere, but she couldn't quite tell where. Sometimes she smelled things that weren't actually there, but she was sure this wasn't one of those times. She saw Cary approaching her.

"Hey, Ellie, have you seen that grandson of yours?"

"Not lately. He's always running about, I'm sure he'll be by shortly. What do you need?"

"Well, uh, I'm just used to seeing him and visiting Belle. I just wanted to make sure he wasn't sick or something."

"No, he didn't seem to be sick this morning. If I see him, I'll send him down there."

"Yeah, that'd be great. Tell him I was looking for him, too. And it's okay if I gave him that backpack, right? We had it left over from one of the grandkids and I thought he might like it."

"I was wondering where he got that from. He loves it, and thank you. It's fine."

"Alright, gotta get back to the meeting," Cary said and left in a hurry.

Ellie worked her way to the second floor to check on things and it was calm up there as well, but now the conversation she'd just had with Cary began weighing heavily on her mind; where was Jack? She looked through the window from the upstairs patio and the first thing she saw was the dock. Ellie panicked and ran downstairs.

"Larry, have you seen Jack?"

"Not for a couple of hours. He's probably making his own little rounds."

"I don't think so, I would have noticed him by now. Something doesn't feel right, Larry."

"Okay, let's get to looking. I'll check outside—"

"Oh, God, I hope he didn't go out on the dock and fall off."

"I'll check, Ellie, settle down a little. We'll find him. See if Edwin's seen him."

"Okay."

Ellie rushed down the hallway and saw Edwin coming out of Eloise's room.

"Dad, I can't find Jack."

"Did you look in the kitchen?"

"No, I'll check there, but I already looked on this floor and the second floor. Larry's looking outside. I want some fucking rails put on that dock, do you hear me?"

"Okay, Ellie, calm down. Let's find him and go from there. Did you look up on the third floor in your apartment?"

"No."

Edwin took a deep breath and refrained from rolling his eyes. "I'll check up there, you keep looking around down here."

"Okay," Ellie said.

Edwin checked in Ellie's apartment and his own. Ramy's apartment was empty and the other rooms were locked. Edwin knocked on Norma's door and walked in. Norma was sitting in her wheelchair on the balcony talking to Beau with Jack sitting in her lap while working diligently on a coloring book. Beau was smoking and had his oxygen flowing at the same time.

"I thought you didn't like people that smoked," Edwin said.

"I don't, but he's as hard-headed as you. I've tried to throw him out twice," Norma said.

"Just a minute, we've been looking for this one and I need to let Ellie know where he is."

Edwin called Ellie on her cell phone to tell her everything was okay, all the while glaring at Beau.

"You're going to blow all three of you up," Edwin said to Beau as he turned off the oxygen flow.

"What the hell, Edwin, I need dat to breathe."

"One or the other, you're a damn fire hazard to have 'em both going at the same time and I don't want Jack to get hurt."

"Here I am tryin' to do you a favor and you do dis shit," Beau said as he snuffed out his cigarette on the sole of his slippers.

"Stop flapping your gums and let's go see a movie," Edwin said.

"A movie? I ain't goin' to no theater to see no damn movie."

"You don't have to go anywhere, we watch 'em in the craft room downstairs. There's booze and if I can find a joint we might try one of those."

"Ain't we a bit old to be startin' in on drugs?"

"We're all on drugs here. Everybody but me, that is."

"See?" Beau said to Norma, "Dis is what I was talkin' 'bout. He used to be fun and then you came along."

"Hey, do you want to go or not?" Edwin asked.

"What kind of booze?" Beau asked in reply.

"Whatever you want. I have a stocked bar in one of the supply cabinets. Someday somebody's going to figure out that all the crayons and finger painting supplies got moved."

Norma stared at Edwin while he talked to Beau. It was hard to read the expressions on her face because of the scarring and disfigurement, but judging from the look in her eyes Edwin knew she wasn't happy at the moment.

"How about you," Edwin asked Norma. "Want to go to a movie?"

"No, I've got all the entertainment I need right here," she said quietly while pointing at Jack.

"How long has he been here? We thought we'd lost him."

"About an hour and a half. He's been coming by every day and keeps me company."

"Are you okay with that?"

"He's the first child that's approached me in eons, are you kidding?"

"Miss Norma got burned like my mom," Jack said, momentarily taking the time away from his coloring. "My mom would want me to take care of her."

"See, what else do I need?" Norma asked.

Edwin stared at her for a moment and nodded his head. He could tell that she was enjoying Jack's company and he wasn't going to argue.

"Okay. If you ever want to, we watch a movie every week. And Jack's okay here?"

"He's fine. I'll have him come find one of you when he leaves, but right now I want to talk to you."

"I'd rather watch a movie," Edwin countered as he began to the door.

"We have to talk."

"We had years to talk and now you want to cut into my movie

time?" Edwin asked. He hooked a thumb over at Beau and shook his head. "I don't know what he's been telling you but that was a long time ago and he's had it wrong ever since."

"I been right on the goddamn money, dat's what I been," Beau cackled with a toothless grin.

"Edwin, please sit down," Norma said. Her words were soft but impatient which irritated Edwin. She had a way of making him feel like a child when she talked.

"Yeah, sit down and let's have dis out," Beau said.

"Get the hell out of here before I toss you over the rail," Edwin replied to Beau.

"I tried to help," Beau said as he stood up. Edwin reached over and turned his oxygen back on. "You said the booze is in one of the supply cabinets?"

"Yeah," Edwin replied, fishing a key out of his pants pocket and giving it to Beau, "And don't drink the good stuff. I bought you some of that blackwater elderberry shit you like. Drink that."

"Much obliged."

Beau shuffled to the door and Edwin turned his chair around, looked out at the lake for a moment and then sat down backwards on the chair. He rested his arms on the seat back and put his chin across his forearms with a heavy sigh.

"What?" he asked.

"I just want to get this over with," she said.

"Get what over with? You're here, I'm not trying to bother you. I came to see if you wanted to go to a movie, I won't do it again."

"Nonsense. You still haven't let go, have you?"

"Oh, yes I have. A long time ago. I learned my lesson and look, no hard feelings."

"Then why did Beau come to give me some sob story about you?"

"He's a damn menace, that's why. A good-intentioned hemorrhoid that keeps bringing up painful shit. Never mind."

"Grandpa Edwin, you say too many bad words."

"He does, doesn't he?" Norma said as she rubbed Jack's back, then turned her attention back to Edwin. "It is painful, isn't it?"

"It's all in the past; a memory. And look at us all now, everyone getting what they need. Not ideal circumstances but we could all be much worse off, right?"

"Edwin, we barely knew each other. How could you have let it affect you so much?"

"You don't remember when I stayed at your house that I always looked at you? Don't tell me you didn't know it. And that night at the dance, a few months before I went to boot camp, and we were sitting in Jerry's truck. Things got a little advanced, so to speak. I didn't want to disrespect you, so I wanted to leave and you wanted me to stay. That was the night, I think, that I conjured up this person that I thought you were. I wanted you to be this perfect, pure woman and I think it just stuck. And then when you called at my barracks, well, I thought everything was coming to pass. We'd both agree that it didn't, but it made me focus. It made me grow up and I did, and now I'm doing better than anybody imagined. Especially you. You thought I was a loser, you had higher ambitions than betting on someone like me. I can't blame you, you seemed to know what you wanted. So, just to clear things up, it may have been just a few days for you, but it was much more than that to me."

"We were different people. You weren't mature at all and—"

"We just covered that. I said I grew up just a moment ago," Edwin replied sharply. Norma slowly nodded.

"Yes, you did. But Edwin, did you really grow up or did you just grow bitter? You still seem so haphazard about everything. Just because you can afford to do things doesn't mean you've moved on."

"What does it matter, Norma? Why are we having this conversation, so that you'll feel better? Do you think I haven't thought about all of this a thousand times and found some closure? I'm not trying to impress you or anyone else. I'm trying to do nice things for people, what's the harm in that? It's your conscience we're dealing with here, not mine."

"You're hurting still, Edwin. When Beau told me everything, it was like someone put a millstone around my neck again after I tried for so long to finally get it off."

"What millstone? Tell me what it is because frankly you didn't seem to have much of a problem casting me aside. Is it guilt? I doubt it. There's only one other thing I can think of that it can be."

"What's that?" Norma asked.

"Doesn't matter. It'll take us back to a dead horse that's already been beaten."

"There is some guilt. I know that I hurt you terribly."

"Stop saying that! And stop talking to me like I'm a damn child! You think you're that special that I've been suffering all these years? Forget it."

"Whatever, but I did feel guilty. I started it all with that phone call. I was lonely and you were so far away from everything in this damn town and I wanted to be away from it all, too. But God help me, Edwin, if I can ever reconcile how all of this could have affected you so."

"That's probably the part that bothers me most," Edwin said while standing up. "How all of it did nothing more than make you feel guilty."

Edwin put his chair back in its place and stood with his hands in his pockets, staring at the floor. After a few moments, Norma could no longer stand the silence.

"So, where do we go from here, Edwin? I don't want to feel like we need to avoid each other, everything seems so awkward."

"Where do we go? We don't go anywhere. That time is up, those feelings are gone. They fell off like rust on an old swing set that sat out in the backyard for years. It got played on once and then slowly got eaten away by time. Nobody there to take care of it and nobody to use it. It rotted away, fell apart. So, all that's left is one man asking one woman if she wants to go downstairs to see a damn movie."

Norma looked at him with tears in her eyes and shook her head.

"I want a swing, Grandpa Edwin. A swing and a little brother. Miss Norma, can you give me a little brother?"

"Not me, honey," Norma said with pained smile while stroking his hair. She looked back at Edwin. "I'll pass on this one, maybe the next movie."

"I'll check back with you when we plan the next one."

Edwin got to the door and opened it when Norma called out.

"Edwin."

"Yeah."

"Something good did come out of it all. We've got Karen."

"No, you had Karen all to yourself. Now I have to make up for that, too. Does she know yet?" Edwin asked. Norma shook her head.

"No reason to put it off anymore."

Edwin closed the door behind him as Norma sat wondering if perhaps it was she who couldn't let the painful feelings go. She also realized she might be chasing away something she'd been longing for for the last fifty or so years: A man who cared for her again, even if it was Edwin.

*****

Ruth pushed Belle in her wheelchair to the craft room door where Joan and Eloise were waiting. Hester leaned against a wall for balance while holding a flask close to her chest.

"Who the hell's in there?" Eloise asked, and then turned to face the others. "The lights are low and the curtains are drawn but I can hear noises."

"Here, let's see who's in there," Ruth said.

She tried the door, but it was locked. After knocking several times one of the curtains moved slightly and Cary's face appeared with a scowl while he waved his hands.

"Go away!" he yelled.

"Open up, this is our time," Eloise said.

"Says who? Get the hell out of here," Cary countered.

"Keep beating on the door until he opens it," Eloise said. "Darla's gonna be here soon wanting us to sit in her damn prayer meeting. Here, everyone beat on the door."

Ruth pushed Belle closer to the door and each began knocking except for Belle, who kept asking if Edwin was in there. The noise brought Jenna around the corner, followed by Eloise's son, Champ, who was making an impromptu visit.

"What's going on?" Jenna asked while looking for the key to the door.

"They won't let us in and we're running short on time," Eloise replied.

Inside, Cary could see that Jenna was about to unlock the door.

"Turn off the screen, Al," Cary said.

Al fumbled with the remote and kept pushing buttons. The volume began increasing and track announcer's voice became louder.

"That's the volume, you idiot! Turn the damn thing off!"

"I'm trying…. It isn't working," Al said.

"Well, pull the power cord out. Do something!"

Cary heard the key sliding into the lock and grabbed the door handle while leaning his shoulder against it. Jenna gave a few pushes but to no avail.

"Champ," Eloise said, "Use that big ol' shoulder of yours and get that door open."

"Who's in there?" Champ asked.

"It doesn't matter, just open the door."

Champ leaned against the door and gave it a gentle nudge,

worried about hurting whoever was on the other side. Cary was still barking orders at Al when Champ's nudge easily slid him out of the way.

"Who are all of these other people?" Eloise asked as men scrambled to gather their race forms and cash.

"They're betting on the races, Mom," Champ said. "And those guys are playing poker for money."

"I didn't know they offered that here," Hester said as she started fumbling through her purse. "I love betting on the ponies!"

"You guys know this is illegal, right?" Champ said. He pulled the lapel of his sport coat aside to expose a badge and a gun on his belt and the room fell silent.

"Champ, put that damn thing away. They aren't hurting anything," Eloise said.

Champ looked frustrated, Hester was still trying to find cash in her purse, and Cary stormed through the door swearing at all of them. A red-faced Al Cartwright was still fumbling with the remote when Darla appeared behind them.

"Good!" Darla exclaimed, "I don't have to come find you, you're all here. Come on, let's go into the dining room and worship the Lord, it's too smoky in here. And what is this, a saloon?"

"Forget it, Darla, just men being stupid again," Eloise said. "Come on, let's all go say hallelujah and get this over with."

"That's blasphemy."

"So what, I'll tell them I'm losing my mind when I get to the pearly gates."

"That's even more blasphemy," Darla mumbled.

As the women moved across the hall to the dining room, Jenna approached Al who was shaking all over."

"Mr. Cartwright, are you okay?"

"Yeah. I just don't want to be in trouble. I've never been in trouble before and I don't want to wind up somewhere where I can't take care of my lovey."

"I think you'll be okay, don't worry. Do you know how to work that remote?"

"Yeah, I know how to work it. I think the batteries are just low."

"I'll get some new ones put in here for you. And look," she said as she put a hand softly on his shoulder, "You guys need to find somewhere else to do this."

"But this is our place. I'm having more fun than I ever did."

"Well, considering what you're doing, you'll probably lose that argument with Ellie."

"Alright, I'll talk to Cary. We'll find somewhere else."

"Just be careful, don't get yourself into any trouble."

"I won't."

Jenna opened the shades and arranged the tables and chairs the way they should have been. She smiled, knowing that no matter how old you get some things were still attractive regardless of the risk. She also knew that some forms of sin would never go out of style, and if they did nobody would ever come to hear her sing.

*****

Darla's sense of boldness had finally returned after the fire in the laundry room. There were no questions asked, no fingers pointed, and no connections made. Up to now she'd felt a little uneasy, but Ellie seemed too busy to even know which way was up.

"I want to talk to you about repentance," Darla began and there was a groan from the women sitting in front of her. "Now don't start, you know we all have our secrets, and each of our secrets is like a lock on the door to heaven. You alone have the key to redemption and God's love. Now, I think I know the answer to this, but does anyone have anything they want to confess today, right here in the open in front of your sisters and before the Almighty Himself?"

"I'd have to confess I was hoping you'd have a wreck coming over here," Eloise said, bringing muffled laughter from the others. Darla glared at her.

"You're so hateful when you're like this."

"Come on, Darla, you know I'm just kidding. Seriously, do you think any of us are going to confess to anything useful right here?"

"Well, are you going to do it at church? By my estimation, you haven't been to church in years so I don't know if you're going to get the opportunity."

"It doesn't matter, I'm not doing it here. Besides, there's not too much left that I could be ashamed of. I never hurt anybody and I never stole anything or caused a ruckus between others. I'm sure everyone in here would probably say the same thing."

"I wouldn't bet on it," Darla said smugly as she gazed over at Joan. "I'd bet some in here have quite a bit to get off of their chest."

Joan began to turn red. She was being targeted by Darla again and she didn't think she could fight her. Darla was too quick, too shrewd. Joan was convinced that most, if not all, of the people in the room knew her secrets but she couldn't understand why Darla felt as though she had to repent in public. But she felt she had to do something, she hated being bullied.

"Why don't you tell us, Darla? You seem to think you know so much, why don't you tell us who has some deep dark secrets? And maybe you can tell us how you came about those secrets? Was it some sort of divine intervention? Did God give you some kind of all-knowing power?"

The rebuttal took Darla by surprise and Joan suddenly found herself feeling bold. Darla didn't have the quick response Joan expected and she looked guilty.

"Now Joan, you know I'm just a vessel for the scripture—"

"What book of the scripture tells you what some of us might

need to confess?"

"Well, of course no book in the Bible tells me that, it's just that I... we all have our little secrets and I'm sure that some of you have one or two, or more."

"Then I have a suggestion for you: Why don't you get the ball rolling and give us a confession of your own?"

"Good luck trying to get something like that out of her," Hester said as she took a drink from her flask.

Darla turned to look at Hester just in time to see the flask leave Hester's lips, and Darla's eyes began to smolder.

"What is that?" Darla asked angrily while pointing at the flask.

"Holy water."

"I'll not have that in my prayer meeting!" Darla said as she charged over and tried to grab the flask from Hester's hand. Hester pulled the flask away and caught Darla's wrist with her other hand.

"You try to take this and I'll break your hip, you old prude."

There was silence in the room as everyone realized that Darla was being challenged and things were getting ugly.

"If you don't like being a part of this then why do you come?" Darla asked.

"You drug us in here, we were going to watch a movie. That's a lot more fun than somebody trying to make us feel like dirt every day."

"That's not what I'm trying to do. Hey, where did Joan go?"

"She walked out while you were trying to steal Hester's flask."

"I wasn't trying to steal it, I just don't want her drinking while we serve the Lord. No matter. I think we can bring the horse to the water again and finally get her to drink. There's no end to God's perseverance. Meanwhile, we can all continue—"

"Nah, I'm done," said Eloise. "I'm hungry and I gotta check my blood sugar."

"Me, too," said Hester with a giggle.

"Where the hell is Edwin?" Belle mumbled.

"I don't know," Darla said as she watched the other women file out of the room. "But I'm going to make sure you see him soon. Come on, let's get you back to your room."

"Take me to his room, he'll want to see me."

"All in God's time, Belle."

"I'm running out of time," Belle said, and the inflection of her words sounded ominous. Even in her mind's deteriorating state, Darla sensed that Belle still had the capacity to know she was slowly slipping away.

Chapter 23

Joan went back to her room, closed the door, and wrapped her arms around herself in a congratulatory hug. She could hardly contain her pride for taking on Darla and winning. She'd put Darla on her heels and was now ready to keep her there. She poured herself a drink and sat by her window, where the sunshine seemed brighter, the grass seemed greener, and the birds chirped in harmony with her happiness. A few minutes later she saw Darla's car drive away quickly and knew things probably hadn't gone much better after she'd left the dining room. The wheels in her mind began to spin.

"Now, where is that boy?"

Joan walked down to the dining room and peeked around the corner. There were cookies left over from lunch on a cellophane-wrapped plate and about half a pot of coffee on the warmer. She poured a cup and sat down, dipping one cookie after another in her coffee while waiting. Jack was never still for a moment and sooner or later he would come around. Within a few minutes, he walked through the door.

"Hi, Miss Joan," Jack said.

"Hi, Jack. How are you doing today?"

"I'm okay. I'm hungry, too," he said as he walked straight to the cookies.

"Can I give you a little job to do?"

"Sure, and I won't tell anybody!"

"I know you won't, sweetie. Can you take this envelope to Miss Eloise? But don't tell her I gave it to you."

"Right now?"

"Oh, no. You go ahead and enjoy your cookies, you're a growing boy. This can wait until you're done."

"Thanks, Miss Joan," Jack replied, spewing cookie crumbs from his lips as he spoke.

Joan nodded and left the room quickly. She didn't want to be in the same room with Jack if he were to get caught.

Jack laid the envelope down and stared out the window as he nibbled, looking at the lake and the boat and wondering when his Grandpa Edwin would take him out again. He heard a rustling behind him and turned to see Eloise wheeling herself into the dining room.

"Miss Eloise, this is for you," he said, grabbing the envelope and running it over to her.

"Who is this from, Jack?"

"I can't tell you, she told me to promise to keep it a secret."

"Well, I guess there's no harm in that," she said as she began to open the envelope. Eloise pulled the note from within and read it. Then she looked back over at Jack, trying to be as sweet as she could. "Are you sure you can't tell me who gave this to you? I'll give you a dollar."

"No ma'am, I can't. I promised."

"How about two dollars?"

Jack stared at her and shook his head as he continued to shove more of the cookie in his mouth, but his eyes narrowed ever so slightly as she upped the ante.

"Five dollars?"

Jack looked around the room to make sure nobody else could hear him. He stared at her a few seconds more, contemplating, and then got within a few inches of her ear, cupping his hands around his mouth.

"Ten dollars."

"You little shyster!" Eloise said with a laugh. "You're as bad as your grandpa! I'm not giving you ten dollars to tell me that Joan gave you this."

"How did you know?"

"Well, some things I can just guess. You come by my room later and I'll give you a dollar."

"You promise not to tell anybody?" Jack asked. The look of sincerity made Eloise feel guilty for tricking him.

"I promise I won't. When did she give this to you?"

"A little while ago. Please don't tell her."

"I won't," she said, opening her arms and motioning for him to get closer. She gave him a long hug and handed the note back to him, then let him go. "Go on now and eat your cookies."

"You don't want the note, Miss Eloise?"

"No, I don't need it. You can tell her you gave it to me, okay?"

"Okay," he said and then shoved the letter down into his pocket.

Jack sat down, no longer feeling hungry. He'd kept his word, but the secret still got out. He reached into the cargo pocket of his shorts, pulled out the roll of cash and counted it to see how much he'd have after he was paid by Miss Eloise. Ever since Miss Nettie had moved in, he'd fallen asleep while listening to her harmonica through the open window and he wanted one just like it. He didn't know how much they were, but he figured he was close to having enough.

Joan sat in her room, feeling both exuberant and fearful at the same time. There was no telling how long it would be before the contents of the note found its target or what the reaction would be. She opened her address book, found the name of an old friend, and invited her out for a dinner date.

*****

Darla sat in Belle's room, still fuming about being snubbed in the dining room the previous day. Joan had gotten the best of her, which was bad enough on its own, but to have the rest of the group walk out showed a complete lack of respect. Her only solution was to instill the fear back into Joan and make her look vulnerable so the others would get back in line. The problem was how to do it without confessing she'd stolen Joan's diaries. She was frustrated and at the moment Belle wasn't making things any better.

"Where is he? I want to see him. I got something to say to him," Belle said.

"I don't know," Darla replied while thumbing through a magazine. "He's around somewhere."

"Well, go find him, whatever your name is. Drag him in here by his damn ear!"

"I wish I could. I wish your husband would get here, too. I've got other things to do."

"He's probably out whoring around, giving everyone the clap. Probably out with that Joan woman, I heard they've been going skating," Belle said. Darla looked at her curiously, wondering how the new ideas came together in her head day after day.

"That's a new one. Where do you suppose they've been skating?"

"Down at the goddamn ice rink, where do you think?"

"Ice skating, no less? Okay," Darla replied. She heard feet sliding down the hallway, an annoying trait that Cary had, and went to the doorway to look. "There he is."

"Who? Is that Edwin?"

"No, it's Cary, he's come to take over."

"Shit," Belle said. "Shit, shit, shit."

"Belle, stop it already."

"Where is he?"

Cary got to the door looking angry and tired. They were taking shifts watching after Belle and the strain was wearing on both of them. Their daughter came infrequently during the week and the grandkids on the weekends, but it wasn't enough. Ellie had installed a Dutch door with a lock to keep Belle from wandering out of the room, but Belle had begun putting things in her mouth and playing with the outlets in the room.

"Asking about Edwin?" Cary asked.

"She won't stop for a minute. She thinks you've been out ice skating with Joan."

"Damn loon. Where the hell would we go ice skating in Texas in the summer?" he asked.

"Cary, she's your wife, show some respect. She probably doesn't have long and you'll regret all of this."

"No, I won't. Her brain is all rewired and all she talks about is that bastard at the front desk. How do you think that makes me feel?"

"He's at the front desk now?"

"Yeah, why? Do you want some of him, too?"

"You're disgusting. I'll be right back."

Darla opened the door to let Cary in and then stormed down the hall. She found Edwin in his running clothes behind the desk, his feet propped up on the file cabinet. He looked young, much younger than the rest of them, and she could easily place his features back to her memory of him the night he was wearing his uniform. He glanced up at her and she could see that handsome boyish face hiding behind a few wrinkles, disarming her momentarily.

"What?" he asked pointedly. His tone put her right back in the mood she'd started with.

"You're a coward."

"I could care less about what you think of me."

"You scarred that woman for life and you don't care a wit."

"Which one?"

"You know who I'm talking about. Belle."

"How do you figure that I scarred her? She was a grown woman and made her own decisions."

"You manipulator! You left her vulnerable in that bed instead of taking care of her. Do you know how much trouble you caused? This place closed down because of you and she married a pig of a man just to try to save face and you're able to wash your hands of the whole thing like nothing ever happened. You haven't even laid eyes on her since she's been here, have you?"

"I saw her going across the hall one day."

"I'm talking about going to see her, talking to her."

"For what? I did a lot of things with people from my past, but I don't go around looking them up to talk about it. And why do you care? Why didn't you keep her from getting drunk that night?"

"I was working, and besides she was a big girl, she should have—"

"Should have known how to take care of herself except for when it came to me, right? Darla's never responsible for anything but holds everyone else to some heavenly standard. You're a damn hypocrite."

"I am not. When it comes to a woman's heart, they aren't responsible for what happens."

"Let me write that down so I can use it later. I really can't believe you just said that."

"It's true," Darla replied, knowing that her last comment sounded childish but deciding to stick with it. "And, I think you owe it to her to go down there and face the music. She wants to

279

talk to you and I don't think you have the guts to do it."

"Fine," Edwin said. He put his feet down on the floor and stood up, his fluid movements once again catching Darla by surprise. "Let's go see Belle and get this out of both your systems."

"You're kidding?"

"No, I'll be there in about two minutes. I had something made for her in the event this would happen."

"He's coming to see you, Belle!" Darla yelled as she rushed down the hall. "Edwin's coming to see you!"

Darla stood outside of Belle's door waiting desperately for Edwin to come. Karen, hearing the commotion from across the hall, walked over to Belle's room to see what was going on.

"Where is he, I don't see him? Hey, nurse, go find that bastard Edwin Kranz."

"What kind of trouble are you starting today, Belle?"

"Edwin's finally going to come and see her after all these years and she's going to let him have it!"

"Really? And what kind of trouble did Mr. Kranz cause for you?"

"Come here," Belle said, motioning for Karen to come in the room. Karen obliged and stood at the end of her bed. Belle had a childish grin on her face as she lowered her voice. "He used to kiss my privates."

"Uh," Karen hesitated, momentarily unable to think of anything else to say, and then broke out into laughter. "That's quite the, uh, something, I don't exactly know what to call it. A good memory?"

"Left me naked on the bed."

"Just shut the hell up about it!" Cary yelled.

"He was good," Belle said with a smile.

Regardless of how crass Belle was being, Darla was beside herself with glee until she saw Edwin come out of the dining room. Edwin was carrying a file folder against his chest with one hand, but there was something in his other that she couldn't quite distinguish. It wasn't until he got halfway down the hall that she understood what he was up to. Edwin put the ice cream cone up to his mouth and began licking all around the sides, slowly and methodically.

"No, Edwin! Don't you dare go in there doing that!"

"Is she talking to Edwin? Bring him in here. I got a bone to pick with him."

Edwin pushed Darla aside, holding his ice cream out of Darla's reach as he walked through the door. Belle sat in her chair and gazed at him with a far-off look.

"Oh my God," Karen said, covering her mouth as she tried to suppress her laughter and embarrassment.

"Hello, Belle," Edwin said softly, continuing to slowly lick the smooth sides of the ice cream.

Belle smiled, showing her teeth and moving her head from side to side as if trying to show him her best angle. She cooed and used her fingers to try to manipulate her hair into curls, combing it this way and that. She was infatuated all over again.

"Belle, look! It's Edwin," Darla said desperately. "Tell him all those things you wanted to say!"

"Ooooh" was all Belle could muster, mesmerized by the man in running clothes standing in front of her. Her eyes raced over him from head to toe as she continued to smile and primp.

"For the love, Edwin! Stop doing that, take this seriously!"

"Good to see you again, Belle. And here, I brought this for you," Edwin said, taking a framed photograph of himself from the file folder and laying it in her lap. "I gotta run. Take care, Cary. You, too, Darla."

Edwin turned and began walking back down the hallway. Darla was seething, seeing him flash a grin at her as he walked by and rubbing all those years of revenge in her face.

"Where do you think you're going?" she said while standing at the door. She looked back at Belle, who was smiling and looking ahead as if Edwin were still standing in front of her. She clutched the framed photograph with a death grip as Cary tried to pull it away from her.

"Why don't both of you just forget about him? If it ain't one of you it's the other yammering away about him. You both got what you wanted, now get over it. At least it's shut her up for a few minutes."

"Cary, you're just jealous and I'll remind you that's sinful."

"Yeah, well what are you? You're a spiteful hussy is what you are, feeding on everyone else's shortcomings. 'Revenge is Mine, saith the Lord!' Remember that quote, Darla? Get the hell out of here."

"There'll come a day when you'll regret talking to one of God's messengers this way."

"Well, it ain't going to be today so get lost."

Darla walked back to the front desk, but Edwin was nowhere to be found. Eloise was rolling up the hallway in her wheelchair, straining her neck in all directions to see what was going on. Karen walked out, her eyes watering from suppressed laughter and her hand still covering her mouth.

"What did I miss?" Eloise asked.

"Nothing," Darla hissed. "Edwin went to see Belle, that's all."

"Oh my, what happened?"

"Nothing, I told you! That's what happened. Nothing, dammit!"

Karen grabbed the back of Eloise's wheelchair and pushed her back into her room.

"Did you see it?"

"I saw it," Karen replied. "I guess I can believe what everyone's been telling me about Mr. Kranz. He's smooth."

"Girl, you haven't seen anything."

Darla heard the exchange and charged into Eloise's room. Eloise began laughing and pointing a finger at Darla, knowing Darla hated to be mocked.

"I don't know what you two are laughing about, that was despicable. It's a sad day when someone is taken advantage of and everyone else thinks it's funny."

"This just isn't going to be your day, is it?" Eloise asked.

"What do you mean?"

"Sit down, I've got something to share with you."

"I'll give you two some privacy," Karen said.

"No, I would appreciate it if you would stay. I'm going to need a witness. Darla, let's talk about my purse."

Darla's look of anger suddenly changed to one of confusion.

*****

Jack peeked around the corner of the door into the dining room, hoping that he wouldn't run into either Joan or Eloise. His secret being discovered the day before still troubled him, but at the moment his hunger troubled him more. He grabbed a few cookies left over from lunch and walked into the galley for something to drink. He was barely able to pull the handle on the walk-in refrigerator but managed to get it open. The large stainless steel serving pitchers full of milk sat on a shelf at the same height as his little shoulders. He grabbed one, but the weight was more than he could handle, causing him to spill the contents all over himself and the floor.

"Uh oh. Did Mr. Jack have an accident?" Ramy asked. Jack spun around quickly, knowing he'd been caught. "Mr. Jack knows he ain't supposed to be in dat cooler. Dat door close on you and you'd freeze to death."

"Yes, sir, but I didn't break anything. I'll help clean it up," Jack replied with a hopeful smile. He liked Ramy but was afraid of him and didn't want to make him mad.

"You remember what Ramy said from now on, so you don't get in a fix in here. You go put some clean clothes on and Ramy'll get everythin' cleaned up."

Jack nodded and ran out of the kitchen. Ramy looked back at the handle on the door and decided he would have to make it a bit stiffer to open.

Jack found Ellie and within a few minutes they were taking his clothes off in the laundry. Jack was still pulling off his socks as Ellie began emptying the cargo pockets of his shorts. She grabbed what felt like a wad of paper and pulled out a roll of cash.

"Jack," she said while counting, "Where did you get this money?"

"I earned it," he said proudly.

"How do you... There's eighty-seven dollars here. Who would give you that much money?"

"Everybody gives me dollars, Grandma. I do things for them and they give me money,"

"Are you sure you didn't take this from anybody? You know, I can find out if you're not telling the truth."

"They give it to me when I'm making my rounds. Just like you, people pay me for making my rounds."

"Honey, you can't do that, you—" she began and then felt another piece of paper in the other pocket. It was neatly folded and she opened it to see the contents.

DARLA MCGEE WAS IN YOUR ROOM JUST BEFORE YOUR PURSE WAS STOLEN.

The writing looked similar to the other note she'd taken from Belle.

"Jack, where did you get this?"

"I can't tell, Grandma, it's a secret."

"Jack, you have to tell me."

"I can't. Then nobody would trust me. That's what my dad said. He said that you should never tell secrets. And Miss Eloise already made me say it."

Ellie felt a headache beginning to form.

"Jack, what this says can hurt Grandma. You've got to be honest with me."

"Miss Joan wouldn't hurt you, Grandma, she thinks you're the nicest lady here."

"Miss Joan wrote this?" Ellie asked. Jack turned red and realized it had happened again. "Listen, Jack, it's okay."

"It's not okay," Jack said in tears. "Now nobody will trust me and my dad will think I'm not good at keeping secrets."

"Come here," Ellie said, pulling him into her arms and hugging him. "I trust you. This turned out to be good."

"No, it didn't."

"Well, I know you don't think it did but someday you'll understand."

"I don't want to."

"I know. Look, I won't tell anybody else, but I have to talk to Miss Joan and I promise she won't be mad at you."

"Yes, she will," Jack said.

"Let's just wait and see what happens, okay?"

"I don't know. Can I go upstairs and lay down?"

"Sure, you run along. I'll send Grandpa up to check on you in a few minutes."

"Can I go to Miss Norma's room?"

"Sure, as long as you don't bother her."

"I won't. She likes me, she never asks me to tell secrets."

Ellie's heart sank as she watched Jack make his way to the elevator. There had been a lot of major changes in his very short life and now she felt as though she'd betrayed him instead of showing support and compassion. It wasn't just Jack she was neglecting, though, but the patients as well. They were getting what they needed physically, but emotionally she hadn't had the time or patience to give them the extra care that had made her agree to open Kranz Gardens in the first place.

Ellie slid the money and the note into her scrub jacket and sat down on one of the chairs to take some time to think. She decided to look in his backpack while she had it there and that's when she found the betting sheets and a racing form. Now all of his scurrying from room to room every day and the roll of cash made sense. It had kept him busy and entertained and she had to take it all away. Things just weren't getting any easier for either one of them.

Chapter 24

There was another night-shift nurse now that the second floor was nearly full and two more assistants to help Jenna. Karen could see the daily strain taking its toll on Ellie and decided she needed to take matters into her own hands.

"Hey, you," Karen said, standing in the doorway of Ellie's office. Ellie looked up, her eyes like those of a wild animal ready to take down its prey.

"Hi," she said with a heavy sigh.

"Let's go have a drink," Karen said.

Ellie looked down at all of the receipts, invoices, applications, resumes, and legal forms scattered across her desk and then looked back up at Karen. She thought about being a little snarky, maybe with a touch of snotty, while telling Karen how much work she needed to get done. But she felt a strange kinship with Karen and what actually came out of her mouth was "Sounds like a great idea."

"I'm buying, but you'll have to drive. I think my car gave up the ghost this morning," Karen said.

"You mean leave here?"

"Damn right, that's exactly what I mean. When's the last time you left this building?"

"I don't remember. I don't really know that I have."

"Let's go, I have to be back in two hours."

"Anything wrong?"

"No, that's when Ramy and I are going out on your dad's boat."

"You and Ramy?"

"On a boat, under the stars. And tonight, naked as jaybirds if I have my way about it."

"Oh my God!" Ellie said, covering her mouth. She grabbed her purse and locked the door behind her as they stepped out into the hall. "Well, I don't want to hold up romance. But Ramy?"

"Do you want me to spell it out for you?"

"At the bar, not here. I don't know if I can handle it without a drink."

The two left in Ellie's car and Karen decided to pitch an idea to her.

"You need a manager," Karen said.

"I am the manager."

"Yeah, but are you happy?"

"I'm miserable. There's so much to do, I never thought it would be like this. It probably wouldn't be so bad if I weren't dealing with all of Dad's shit all the time."

"Oh, come on, I'd love to have a dad like yours. He's a riot, and what a life he must have had. I don't think you know how lucky you are."

"Lucky? I'd have been better off without him. It's embarrassing to know your father is still running around like some Casanova at his age. I thought he would be an asset in all of this but every time I turn around, I'm dealing with another one of his messes. Unfortunately, I need the financing. It's the other stuff he brings to the table that's killing me."

"I never had a father. Trust me, you're lucky. I suppose we're coming at it from different directions, but I do find your dad to be such a character, I could fall for him in a minute if he were a bit closer to my age. Anyway, back to business. Look, I know the management aspect of this. I know the accounting, the HR, and the attitudes. I've seen what's on your desk and I've got a pretty good idea that you're buried in it."

Ellie drove silently, stinging from the words Karen said but also realizing she was right. If there was one thing she'd learned about Karen, it was that when she spoke her mind it was brutal but precise. Ellie also felt a flood of relief come over her with the notion that all the work in the office could be lifted from her shoulders. Ellie's mouth was moving as she tried to form a response, but nothing came out.

"I'm sorry if that came out wrong. I don't have a good bedside manner. But I want to see you do good. I want Kranz Gardens to do good. I love being here and I love working with you. This is like a dream job for me and I want it to last."

"Can you teach me?"

"Teach you what, the management part?"

"Yeah, I feel like I ought to know how to be a good manager."

"Is that why you got into all this? Because your heart doesn't seem to be in it at all."

"It isn't. It's in the caring part, or at least that's where I want it to be. I've been beating myself up about it since day one that I don't have the time to spend with the patients. By the time I've put out the fires that Dad started years ago, or whenever something goes wrong, I seem to lose that compassion and I get short with everyone."

"You need to let some of that crap go. You can't do anything about your dad's past, let them live with that drama. I actually think they like it. But you need to get someone else in to do the managing, get back to what you want to do, and maybe find some common ground with your dad."

"I agree, but I'm afraid he'll think I'm a failure. He's already been on my butt about the accounting. I thought it would be easy but I—"

"It's tough, Ellie. It's doable, but you gotta know how. And frankly, you gotta enjoy it. I do, you don't. Look, I can do all of that and devote about half my time to helping you with the nursing, too," Karen said. Ellie looked over at her, exasperated.

"Well, if you can do it, then why can't I?"

"It's just an ability, sweetheart, that's all I can tell you. Plus, I already know accounting and I'd gamble that you don't."

Ellie sat silently as she turned into the parking lot of the sports bar. She put the car in park, turned off the motor, and laid her forehead down on the steering wheel. Karen reached over and stroked her hair in reassurance.

"You know, I wanted to do this because I love taking care of people and I hated the way management treated the staff, the patients, and all of that. And now I've turned into one of those people and I want out. I just want to deal with the patients, that's all."

"And I'm just the opposite," Karen laughed. "I love the business part, that's why I went back to school. I just never got the chance to use it. But trust me, I can do it."

"I'll have to talk to dad and make sure he's onboard with this. And another thing; you can't boss me around."

"Nobody's going to boss you around, we don't need to boss anyone around. Everyone does their part and we all live happily ever after. Right?"

"C'mon," Ellie said as she opened the car door. "Come inside and try to convince me there's something attractive about Ramy."

*****

The next morning, Edwin came out of the elevator with no intention of sitting at the front desk. He was scheduled to be there again but the task of greeting and taking in new people had become irrelevant; everyone knew where they were supposed to go and who to see and the building was full.

"Dad," Edwin heard from behind him.

"Good morning, Ellie."

"I don't think we need anyone at the front desk anymore, do you?"

"Not really, no. I guess I hadn't thought of it until now."

"Yeah, well, look, I need to run something by you," Ellie said as Karen walked by looking disheveled and exhausted. "Karen, are you okay?"

"I'll give you one more reason to appreciate Ramy if you want to know."

"I'll pass."

"Cute couple, aren't they?" Edwin asked.

"You knew?"

"I know everything. I gotta go to the library, can we put off the conversation for a little while?"

"Yeah, that's fine. How about tonight?"

"Sounds good. That's going to be the first wedding here at Kranz Gardens."

"Who?"

"Karen and Ramy."

"Don't you think you're jumping the gun a little bit?"

"No. I just told you I know everything."

Ellie smiled and waved him off as she headed for the medication room. She felt good this morning, really good. She promised herself she wouldn't even go into her office today, feeling that anything that needed to be done could wait. By the looks of Karen, she wasn't going to get a lot done today either, but Ellie found that more amusing than a concern. And something else occurred to Ellie; she felt no animosity toward her father this morning. All of the pent-up anger toward him seemed to have vanished, making her conclude that perhaps her frustration was more a product of her job than of his antics. Regardless, she felt better and her new resolve was put to the test quickly as Joan walked by.

"Joan, can I speak to you a minute?"

"Oh, hello Ellie. How are you this morning?"

"Good, but listen, I need to ask you something. Do you know anything about Eloise's purse being taken?"

"Heaven's no, I don't have—" Joan began to say but then saw Ellie pull out the note she had given to Jack and her face turned red.

"You don't know anything? Did you really see Darla coming out of the room?"

"Yes, but you know, I can't be sure Darla did anything wrong. After all, she is a woman of God."

Ellie took a deep breath and closed her eyes for a moment, remembering how good she had felt moments earlier and put the note back in her pocket.

"No more notes, Joan, please. They aren't helpful. Deal?"

"Deal, I understand."

"And no more using Jack as a courier or you'll have to leave," Ellie said and then turned and walked away. Joan nodded and scurried to her room before she got into any more trouble.

As Ellie carried out her morning tasks, Edwin spent his time at the library looking at the microfiche newspaper stories about the retreat when it closed. He had his cellphone laying on the old oak table waiting for it to vibrate. He'd left a message for the reporter, Adrienne Parker, about the research he was doing and didn't think it would be long before she got back to him. It had been three minutes and the phone began to buzz.

"Adrienne?"

"Edwin, how are you? I thought I'd hear from you sooner."

"Sorry, I've been putting out fires at the nursing home. I've been meaning to call though. You got the flowers?"

"That's the only reason I returned your call."

"Yeah, listen, I need some info about the retreat and I don't know where to look. I've got some old newspapers that were found in a wall and some microfiche that I'm looking at in the library, but I think there's more. Got any ideas?" Edwin asked. The phone was silent for a few moments and then Adrienne replied.

"I think I can find some other interesting things. When is a good time for you?"

"Anytime, just say when."

"You're at the library now?"

"Yeah."

"I'm right across the street, I'll be right over," she said, and the phone went dead.

Edwin spent the next five hours with Adrienne, looking at old press clippings, talking to some of her contacts in the police evidence room and reviewing other documents at the newspaper office. What he learned from Adrienne, though, was distressing; she had copies of the videos of Darla as well as copies of other videos.

"How did you find out about these?"

"The video guy that copied the tapes is always looking to make extra money by selling people's secrets. He thought I might be interested in this for background. He's a snake, I wouldn't use him in the future."

"I'll take care of him. I'm sure I don't have to ask you not to use them for your research?"

"It'll cost you dinner."

"Sometimes, blackmail is the small price of doing business."

That night, Edwin watched the videos on his computer in his room with Adrienne. He couldn't bring himself to watch the ones with Darla but was astounded at how many people he knew from his past that were in the other films. None were more significant than Angus McGee, Darla's father, who was giving a woman everything but fire and brimstone.

"How did this asshole get hold of these tapes? These are evidence," Edwin asked.

"The police wanted them digitized and he kept a copy. Don't worry, he can't blab a peep about this or I'll turn him in for keeping a copy."

"I'll take your word for it," Edwin said and then let out a laugh. "I even saw my old boss in there. Good family man, go figure."

*****

"Darla! Darla! Darla, please... Darla!" Belle called out as Cary sat cringing in the chair next to her bed. The sound of her voice had become whiny lately and it made it difficult for him to concentrate on his reading. Besides her calls for Darla, Cary could hear a persistent banging on a door down a hall.

"She's busy, Belle, shut the hell up," he said.

"I need Darla," Belle said and began to sob.

Nothing Cary tried was pacifying Belle so he started for the dining room to see if there was leftover dessert that would take Belle's mind off of Darla. Cary could see Darla kicking a door at the other end of the hall.

"Darla," Cary called out, but she didn't respond. "Darla, hey, Darla!"

"What?"

"Belle's calling for you, I can't shut her up."

"Pretend you're Edwin," a voice said from a room across the hall, followed by laughter from several others.

"Shut up, Eloise."

Darla took one long hard look at Joan's door, vowing to herself that she'd return, and walked down the hall to Belle's room.

"What's wrong with her now?"

"Who the hell knows," Cary replied, not even bothering to look at her as they passed.

Darla entered Belle's room and found her clutching the photo of Edwin to her chest with tears rolling down her cheeks. Her hair was matted and she looked tired. Belle seemed to have changed over the last few days physically, and certainly mentally. She had deteriorated rapidly after Edwin visited her, as if she'd accomplished her final task in life.

"What's the matter, sweetheart?" Darla asked, her anger evaporating as she looked at Belle.

"I want to go see him."

"Who's that?" Darla asked. Belle pulled the frame away from her chest and pointed at it. "Edwin?"

"Yeah. He's my husband. I want to go see him."

"He's not—"

"I want to go see him. He died, you know. I want to go see him."

"You will, Belle, I promise you will. You'll see him soon, I'm sure."

"I'm going to go see him soon," Belle said and smiled.

Darla stroked Belle's hair, noticing that her face suddenly seemed radiant.

"Real soon."

"I'm going to go to sleep now."

"Good, you sleep well," Darla said and put a blanket over her as Belle curled up on her side.

Darla walked back down the hall to the dining room where Cary was walking out with the dessert.

"She's asleep now."

"Good, I'll eat this myself."

"Cary," she said as she grabbed the sleeve of his shirt, "Don't let the stuff she says about Edwin bother you."

"She's out of her mind. She doesn't know what she's saying half the time. What pisses me off is all the rumors running around here, other people knowing about my business and everything."

"They probably aren't all true, you know."

"Yeah, they are, she told me. I upset her one night and she told me all about it. I don't care what she did, just who she did it with. I always hated that bastard."

"Didn't we all, or at least I thought so until he came back. Seems there are a lot of people on his side around here. But I guess we all need to work together, right?"

"I suppose. She ain't gonna last long and then I don't have to be reminded anymore."

"Just don't let it get you down, not in whatever time she has left. Like you said, she doesn't know what she's saying."

"Whatever. You said she's asleep, right?"

"She said she was going to sleep, I'm not sure if she did. I don't hear her talking right now."

"I'll check on her and then I'm taking off for a while."

"Take care."

Cary peeked in the doorway and saw that Belle's eyes were closed and she looked peaceful. He walked quietly down the hall toward the exit, making sure to do nothing to wake her.

*****

Karen opened the door to her apartment to see Norma reading a book to Jack. When Jack saw Ramy, he squirmed a bit to get closer to Norma. Karen looked at the two of them sitting in Norma's wheelchair and smiled.

"We brought you a gift, Mom," Karen said as Ramy held out the small pastry box. Norma took the box and opened it and inside there was a cake with the words "Will you marry Ramy?" written on the top.

"You're asking me?" Norma asked.

"He's asking us," Karen said and Ramy nodded.

"Ramy get two pretty girls for one."

"I think it's wonderful," Norma said, choking on the last word as she teared up. "I began to wonder if she'd ever get married with an anchor like me around."

"What's it say?" Jack asked, trying to decipher the words.

"Ramy and I are getting married."

"Oh," Jack replied, looking sideways at Ramy.

"Karen a good woman, Ramy can't do no better."

"I think she's lucky to have found you," Norma said. "But I have an unusual request for Karen."

"What's that?"

"You've got to ask your father."

Karen looked at her mother in confusion, not sure what to say or how to say it.

"Ramy gonna ask 'em, already planned on it."

"Well, good fucking luck, I've never met the man." Karen said, and Norma covered Jack's ears with her hands. Norma looked at Ramy suspiciously.

"What do you know, Ramy?"

"Ramy gonna wait down in the dinin' room while Miss Norma talks to Karen. We'll ask him together."

"Mr. Jack might think about helpin' Miss Norma eat dat cake," Ramy said as he stood up and walked calmly out the door, leaving Karen with her mouth hanging open.

An hour later, Karen appeared in the dining room drained, confused, and irritated. Ramy brought her a cup of bayou coffee as Karen looked at him with contempt.

"How long have you known?"

"A few days. Ramy just started puttin' two and two together. Daddy said he knew right off the bat. He's always right 'bout dis kind of thing. How you feelin'?"

"I don't know. Numb. Everything I've been told about him all my life has been a lie. And now I have to deal with the fact that my dad is a pervert from way back."

"Your daddy ain't no pervert, Karen. Your daddy's a good man, Ramy knows dat. Dey ain't one person in dis here place he ain't helped."

"I know, I guess I'm just a little sensitive right now. Up until now I thought all of his bullshit was funny, but I see what Ellie's been going through. Oh, God, what do I say to her?"

"Let Mr. Kranz worry 'bout dat. You get along with Miss Ellie just fine. Everythin' gonna work out."

Karen stood up from her chair and then sat in Ramy's lap, laying her head on his shoulder. He wrapped his arms around her and she snuggled up to him.

"You ask him."

"To get married?"

"Yeah. I don't want all this to come out together. You ask him. I'll talk to him alone."

"Dat sounds good. Ramy likes dat."

"When are you going to do it?"

"Tonight. Ramy take some time after dinner and see him."

"Good. So, does Ramy have about twenty minutes?"

"Ramy can make twenty minutes."

"Good, take me upstairs," Karen said and then stuck her tongue in his ear.

"Miss Karen gettin' to be more like her daddy everyday," he teased as he took her by the hand and headed for the elevator.

Ramy had barely closed the door to his apartment and Karen already had her scrub top off when the rhythmic alarm began to blare in the hallway and the recorded voice repeated "Code Blue on first floor, Code Blue".

Chapter 25

Jenna found her. Belle lay peacefully while she held the photograph of Edwin tightly to her chest, her chin resting on the frame. She'd been dead for at least an hour.

There was a somber feeling around Kranz Gardens; the first resident to move in there had been the first to die. There was even a bit of a squabble, and fear, between others as to who had gotten there second. Regardless, it was Eloise who started the healing process by remembering events from Belle's past before Darla or Cary had made it back.

"She made this pastry one time, something to die for," Eloise said to the crowd that had gathered in the dining room. "I happened to be at her house for some stupid thing or another and I told her I wanted the recipe. She told us that she couldn't give it out, that it was a secret aphrodisiac."

"That sounds like Belle," Ruth said as the others lightly

chuckled. "Always looking for a way to shock all of us. I swear she was the female Edwin of the school."

"Well, then I asked her, I said, 'Is that why you had four kids, you kept making that for Cary?' and she said 'I wasn't making it for Cary!' and she let out that obnoxious laugh she had and made us all crack up until we lost our breath."

"She was ornery, alright, taking over the PTA meetings all by herself every time that boy of hers got kicked out of school for fighting," Al Cartwright said. "I wonder where he got that temper from?"

"Goes to figure that he's in prison right now. Well, let's not beat up on the dead, she wasn't all that bad. I never liked her that much because she was obnoxious, and maybe a little prettier than me, but I can't recall her ever doing anything wrong."

"Just that thing with Edwin we always hear about," Ruth said.

"I don't want to hear about that ever again," Cary said as he walked through the doorway. He had tears streaming down his cheeks and his voice shook as he spoke. "She was a good woman, goddammit! Ya'll making fun of her this past year and spreading rumors, well by God it's time for you to stop."

Cary turned and walked away, leaving the room speechless.

"He's grieving," Ruth said. "I didn't think that was possible."

"She's the only one that could have put up with him all these years," Eloise said.

"Can we all gather around and pray for Belle?" Darla asked as she walked into the room. Eloise rolled her eyes and started wheeling herself toward the door.

"I already did and I've got something else to do."

"Me, too," said Ruth, and the others followed suit.

"I don't believe it," Darla exclaimed. "You're telling me that all of you said a prayer together for Belle?"

"Not all together," Joan said, "But we don't need God's ordained busybody to show us how. Plus, your prayers take too long and most are full of bullshit, anyway."

Eloise stopped short of the door and waited for either Darla to explode or for a bolt of lightning to come down from the ceiling and strike Joan dead. Neither happened. Instead, Darla was left speechless.

"Ladies," Joan said, standing tall and with an air of authority, "I'll see you at dinner."

Joan walked past Eloise and exited the dining room. The others followed behind for no explicable reason other than being too stunned to do anything else.

Feeling faint, Darla reached behind her and found a chair just before her knees buckled. She'd been humiliated both personally and spiritually and she had nobody to turn to.

"Miss Darla needs a cup of coffee."

"Mind your own business," she replied. She was angry and embarrassed that he had obviously witnessed her public drubbing.

"Dis is Ramy's business. Folks look to Ramy to feed 'em good and take care of 'em. Ramy watches out for 'em, too."

"They're all going to hell, every one of 'em."

"Miss Darla don't know dat. Dey's some good in everyone. Dey's some bad in everyone, too. Ramy don't know everythin', but Ramy knows dat nobody gets to heaven usin' the Lord as a hatchet."

Darla glared at him but Ramy seemed unaffected.

"You don't know what you're talking about! Don't ever pretend—" Darla began to say, but Ramy ignored her rant.

"Are you sure Ramy can't bring you any coffee?"

Darla said nothing, got out of her chair and stormed out the door. Ramy calmly went back into the kitchen.

*****

A month later, Belle's shadow still loomed over Kranz Gardens. It no longer seemed to be the lively, tumultuous place it had been and Edwin went to Eloise's room to voice his

301

suspicions.

"It seems dead around here."

"Bad choice of words, Edwin. Besides, I like it quiet."

"Quiet is one thing, this is worse. Can't seem to put my finger on it. Maybe it's Belle, maybe that's what's missing. She didn't have a clue what was going on around her but perhaps she was the life of the party."

"Wasn't she always?"

"Maybe. Anyway, I was wondering if you wanted to have a movie day? We can round everyone up. I've got a new classic we can watch."

"That's a great idea. We haven't had a movie day since she died."

"Haven't had to. Darla hasn't come around to have a prayer meeting so there wasn't any need."

"Yeah, I didn't think about that. Who cares, go get the movie and I'll call everybody and get the word out."

"Good, and I'm gonna go upstairs and try to get Norma and Beau down here."

"Don't bring that Beau, he was trying to feel me up last time he came down. The man's a pervert."

"You didn't like it? I thought you might have found it a compliment."

"You're as bad as he is."

"I'll be there, don't worry about him. We still have plenty of booze?"

"Yeah, everybody has one drink and starts nodding off," she replied. "Go on, get all that stuff done and we'll meet down there."

Edwin nodded and left, and Eloise began dialing numbers. Ten minutes later a crowd had gathered outside the craft room, waiting for someone to unlock the door. Darla came in through the front door looking tired and despondent. She walked up to the back of the crowd quietly, not looking at anyone.

"Hello, Darla. How are you, honey?"

"Okay, I suppose. Still missing my friend."

"Ain't it funny? She wasn't making a damn bit of sense for the last year or so but just having her around was like having all those memories playing over and over in our head. God knows what y'all are gonna think about me when I'm gone."

"We'll all say you were the tough peacemaker," Al Cartwright said.

"Peacemaker?" Jenna asked as she waded through the crowd, jingling the keys to unlock the door. "Who's making trouble today?"

"Nobody, they're all full of shit."

Everyone filed in, finding a seat or adjusting their wheelchairs to face the screen. As soon as everyone got settled, Darla walked to the front of the room to address the crowd.

"Can I please take a moment..." was all she got out when Cary and Joan came through the door, hand in hand.

"What in Beelzebub's name are you two doing?" Darla asked. The rise in her blood pressure was noticeable as she watched them enter the room, unable to take her eyes off of their clasped hands. Joan looked at her in defiance and Cary looked guilty.

"What does it look like?"

"Cary, your wife just died a month ago! This is no way to remember her, parading this slut in front of all her old friends."

"Don't call her a slut. You know as well as I do that Belle's been gone in the head for a few years and I haven't had anyone to talk to."

"You could have talked to me! You don't need to go off whoring around for company."

"Well, I'd rather talk to whores than you!" Cary said, and Joan wasn't sure which one of the two she wanted to slap first.

"Well, maybe there's some things you need to know about Joan that might change your mind."

"Knock it off, Darla, that's none of your business," Edwin

303

said as he entered the room.

"Why don't you tell him what I'm talking about," Darla said to Joan, crossing her arms in defiance. Joan looked at the crowd, feeling anxious now.

"Darla, let it go now or I'm going to throw you out of here on that skinny butt of yours," Edwin said.

"Go ahead, I'll go to the papers and tell everyone about how someone is sabotaging this place with little notes and secrets," she replied. Jack and Larry had just walked in the door and when Jack heard what Darla said he ran out of the room.

"It's okay, Edwin, I'll let my own secret out. I'll tell it myself instead of letting her use it to endear herself and her gossip."

"I beg your pardon! I never gossip."

"Shut up, Darla. Everyone shut up because in a minute I'm gonna tell a story," Edwin said. "Larry, can you hook that computer up to the television in here?"

"Yeah. You sure you want to show that?"

"Damn sure, go get it if you would."

Larry left quickly and Darla looked at Edwin curiously. A smirk appeared on her face as everyone else in the room looked bewildered.

"I don't know what you think you're doing but you aren't scaring me a bit."

Edwin said nothing but looked at the floor while waiting impatiently for Larry.

"Come on," Cary said, guiding Joan over to a chair. "Nothing's gonna happen for a while and my hip hurts."

Joan said nothing but sat next to him, unsure of what was to come.

Within moments, Larry appeared with his computer and a cable. He hooked everything up and turned on the television.

"Here, put this in," Edwin said holding a flash drive. "Go to the image labeled 'house'."

Larry plugged the flash drive into the computer and pulled up the file. There was a picture of the charred remains of a house.

"Remember your old house, Darla? The one that burned down as if hellfire ran through it?"

"Edwin, that's a painful memory, why are you bringing that up?"

"Go to the image labeled 'nail', Larry," Edwin said. Larry pulled up the image showing the remnants of a singed board with a nail sticking out and wire wrapped around it. Larry looked horrified. "The fire department said this was what caused it."

"That was a science experiment, an accident!" Darla protested. "What does that have to do with anything? Where did you get these pictures?"

"Alright, Larry, show us the nail we had here." As the image came up, there was a gasp from the crowd. "See that wire wrapped around that nail? That was what caused the fire in the laundry room here recently."

"What? You think I had something to do with that? This is outrageous! Why would I want to burn this place down? It was a filthy, disgusting cesspool of sin, but why would I—"

"Maybe because it was a cesspool of sin. But maybe there was more here to get rid of. Larry, show the first video clip. Be ready to turn it off. You know which ones are which, right? Just show them in order, we'll see how far this goes."

"Okay," Larry said, looking pale as if he were about to set off a bomb.

"Sit down, Darla. Let me know when you want me to stop. Folks, I'm going to show you why Darla doesn't drink lemonade anymore."

Darla's eyes widened.

"I don't know what you mean," she said, trying to sound amused. "He's planned something disgusting. Some sort of crude trick. I'll warn you now, be ready for anything."

Darla's feigned laughter fell on deaf ears. All eyes were glued to the monitor as the blue screen appeared, the prompt in the upper right corner waiting on Larry to press 'play'.

The status bar showed ninety-seven percent, ninety-eight percent, and then the screen went black for a moment and the first seconds of the film began and the group gasped again. The camera had been trained on Darla, showing her standing at the bar with a look of anger.

"Dad, don't…" Ellie began. She had just walked in the room and Edwin held up his hand to silence her. Edwin knew that Larry must have shown her the video.

"Pause it, Larry," Edwin said, and as he did, he noticed the group looking longingly at the screen. It was as if they were recapturing time and their youth. They were vicariously remembering their own lives simply by looking at the youthful face they had known so long ago.

"That's you, Darla," Edwin said quietly, but Darla was looking away, tears running down her cheeks.

Edwin grabbed a nearby chair and pulled it close. He eased her into it and then laid a hand on her shoulder for support. She sat rigid, looking scared and guilty.

"Weren't you a beautiful woman? I used to marvel at how pretty you were and how much I thought you were missing out on all the fun. You know there probably wasn't a boy in our school that would have passed up an opportunity to take you out if they hadn't been so goddamn scared of you."

The group nodded in agreement.

"Look at you, Darla, you were so pretty. So smart, too," Eloise said. "And mean as shit, I might add."

The crowd laughed but the mood of the room was reflective as Darla covered her eyes.

"Please don't, Edwin," she begged.

"Let's drop this, Darla. We don't need all of this do we?"

"No," Darla replied, her other hand reaching up and grabbing Edwin's that was resting on her shoulder. "What do you want me to do?"

"Leave everyone alone. You go on and preach the good word without trying to beat people up with their past, that's all. Look at these people, they want to be your friends but they're afraid of you. After all these years, let someone, anyone, into your life."

Darla looked up at the group with shame on her face, only to see compassion and understanding on theirs.

"Don't hate me," Darla said. "When we were kids, all I ever heard was how much people hated my father and how they were scared that if they told me anything that I'd tell him. I had nobody to talk to. The only thing I knew how to do was what my father told me. He was the only one that wanted to get close to me. And if these tapes ever got out, I knew he'd disown me. I feel like he's been looking down on me from heaven everyday ashamed that I'm his daughter."

"Well, it damn sure ain't your fault, now is it? Your daddy driving you crazy with all of that Satan crap every time you got around him, no wonder you turned out to be a lunatic. And you know what? I love you anyway."

"Me, too," another voice said, and then another.

"You were a damn prude..." Cary began but Joan hushed him.

"I just wanted to be normal. And from where I came from, that was normal."

One by one, the people in the group either walked or wheeled their way up to where Darla sat. As they gathered around her, Joan stood and addressed them all.

"I have a confession to make: I stole Eloise's purse out of her room."

Ellie slapped her hands on the armrest of her chair and looked angrily at Joan. Joan shrugged her shoulders slightly as she looked back at Ellie with a guilty grin.

"What the hell for?" Eloise asked. "We thought Darla did that."

"I did it to get back at Darla."

"You stole my purse to get back at her? You're both lunatics."

"I did it and then wrote the note saying that I'd seen Darla coming out of your room while you were in the shower. I was just angry at her and, well, I'm sorry."

Darla reached over and grabbed Joan's hand.

"I'm sorry, too. I hurt you probably more than anybody in here."

"Well, I'm sorry, too, but where's my money you took out of there?" Eloise asked.

"Right here, all of it," Joan replied, pulling the cash from her pocket. "Please forgive me."

Ellie had a look of regret on her face and sent Larry to go find Jack. She had never accused him of stealing the money but had been suspicious, nonetheless. Now it was time to give him his money back. Meanwhile, the group continued to sort out their feelings.

"Forgive you? I think I'm gonna be sick," Eloise said. "Where's that coonass at, isn't he supposed to have some snacks out here for this? And where's the booze? That's the only reason I come to these God-forsaken things."

Darla closed her eyes tightly, seeming to smart at the comments from Eloise. Then she opened her eyes and looked at Joan.

"I've got your diaries in my purse. It's over there, I trust you to get them out yourself." Joan rushed over to the table by the counter and began going through the purse. "For the rest of you, I have some confessing to do myself. I want to tell you about these movies."

"Darla, you don't have to," Edwin said. "I'm not going to show the rest of them."

"You're a good man, Edwin. You turned out to be a very good man. I would have thought you'd ruin me. But it's time for me to have some peace within myself. I need to get this off of my chest."

"You're not a virgin, are you?" Eloise asked. "That's what you're going to tell us, ain't it? Something on those videos."

Darla took in a deep breath and let it out, trying her best to maintain her new identity and temperament.

"I was going to explain it a different way."

"So, now we know, what's to explain? Nobody needs to hear that shit, do they? And I certainly don't need to see it."

"I want to see it," Cary said.

"Shut up," Joan scolded.

Cary stood up and began shuffling to the door, grumbling and waving his arms.

Edwin sat down next to Darla and asked everyone to give them some privacy.

"There were other tapes, did you look at them?" Edwin asked.

"I ran through them real fast. I knew what I was looking for and didn't spend a lot of time on it. You know what was in there, that was just sick and sinful."

"The reason why I asked is that there were a lot of other people in those films that you'd probably recognize. People that were close to you. Very close."

"Edwin, I wasn't really close to anyone."

"I know, so think about that next time you feel like your daddy is looking down at you from the heavens. Everybody makes a mistake and he'd probably be asking you for forgiveness right now for making you feel the way you do for all these years."

"I don't understand."

"Just let it sink in and give yourself a break. You've got friends now," Edwin said and stood up.

Darla sat staring at him, confused but looking more at peace. The crowd began to gather around her again and Edwin backed away.

"Where is that damn coonass?" Eloise shouted.

"Right here, Miss Eloise," Ramy said as he rounded the corner. He was holding a tray full of miniature muffins and pretzels. There was one in the middle that had a lighted candle sticking out of it. Ramy set the tray down, then lifted the muffin with the candle from the center and walked over to where Karen was standing. He got down on one knee and held it up to her.

"Is it her birthday?" Eloise asked. Ramy ignored her.

"Miss Karen, Ramy knew the day he set eyes on you dat you was all Ramy wanted. You see dat ring?" he asked. He pointed to the diamond-encrusted engagement ring imbedded in the frosting in front of the candle. "If'n you blow out dat candle—" he started to say, but Karen didn't give him the chance to finish. She blew out the candle and quickly grabbed the ring, leaving a trail of icing as she slid it on her finger.

"I will," Karen replied. She grabbed him by the collar of the shirt and pulled him up, her lips meeting his with an overtly raunchy kiss. "We'll work out the details on my break."

Karen looked over at her mother and winked, watching her mother smile as Ramy walked back over to her. Karen grabbed Ellie by the arm but before she could get her out the door Ellie caught the attention of Edwin.

"I'm proud of you," she mouthed silently, and Edwin nodded in return.

"Alright, Miss Eloise, you better eat up 'fore you starve to death. Ramy's got some crawfish cookin' for later on if'n anybody wants some."

Larry returned with Jack, who had become quite the celebrity and adoptive grandson, although he knew his 'rounds' might be curtailed from now on. Joan motioned for him to come over and she hugged him.

Edwin walked over to Larry, who had already disconnected the computer from the TV.

"Erase that shit, will you?" Edwin asked.

"Are you sure? What if she backslides?"

"There's no more leverage for her, she's done. She'll be okay, just get rid of that stuff in case you get hijacked or something."

"Hacked," Larry said with a smile. "No problem, I'll delete 'em."

"I gotta talk to her in private and see if she had any other booby traps around this place. And I want to see if she knows who H.H. is."

"You weren't able to find out with that little reporter you've been seeing?"

"No, and I've spent a lot of money to find out. Nothing."

"Yeah, I'd kinda like to know that myself. Let me know."

"I will. I'm going out on the boat in a bit, I'll catch up to you this evening."

"Have fun."

Edwin walked out to the hallway and saw Cary sitting in one of the chairs in the lobby. He walked up and sat down by him.

"Cary, I never mentioned that I was sorry for Belle passing. I know you and I don't get along, but I thought I at least owed you my condolences."

"I appreciate it. You didn't do nothing wrong, I just got sick and tired of hearing about it."

"Can't say that I blame you. Look, I've got a proposition to offer you. We have a suite on the third floor that isn't being used right now and if you want to do your little horse operation out of there then that's fine. But no cigars or cigarettes and you gotta be just as quiet as you were down in the craft room."

"You're kidding, right?"

"Nope, just one catch. I get three percent of the house earnings."

"Three," Cary said with a frown. "Damned if you still ain't a son of a bitch in your old ways."

"I know, but I need some new running shoes."

"Deal. And I hate myself for saying this, but thanks."

"I'll get you a key."

Edwin watched as Cary rushed off. He smiled, knowing that sometimes all anybody needed was something to look forward to in order to want to live another day. He sat back in his chair as he waited to catch Darla by herself, but the others were keeping her busy. A few minutes later Eloise pushed her wheelchair over by him. It only took a few minutes to talk her and Norma into a boat ride just to get away and let the dust settle. He grabbed a few sandwiches from the refrigerator and some beer that Ramy had stashed away. They escaped to the boat where they spent the rest of the day talking about what Edwin had seen on the videos.

*****

The warm glow on the horizon was all that was left of the day and Edwin was happy about that. There had been too much pain today and he'd had to do the unspeakable: Letting Darla know what he knew. He didn't do it to hurt her, he did it to keep her from hurting others. Still, it bothered him. It was time for this day to be over. He was on his third glass of wine with only a little left in the bottle when Karen and Ellie walked up and sat on either side of him on the dock bench.

"Everyone settled in for the evening?" Edwin asked, trying not to slur his speech.

"Yeah, I think today was an emotional drain on everyone," Ellie replied. "How about you, are you doing okay?"

"A little tired. Maybe a little too much wine."

Ellie looked over at Karen, who was nervously rubbing her hands together. Karen looked back at her and nodded her head.

"My sister has a question for you," Ellie said.

Edwin sat up straight, his eyebrows raised as he looked first at Ellie, and then at Karen.

"Your mother told you?"

"About a month ago," Karen replied. "There's been so much happening around here and, well, I've been trying to get it all figured out in my head. That's why I haven't said anything before."

"I told her she should be horrified by now," Ellie said.

"Actually, Mom said that I take after you. A lot," Karen said.

312

"But to be honest, I don't see that as a bad thing, and I think she's starting to see you a little differently, too. What you did today with Darla? I was proud of you. Anyway, sorry it took so long to come talk to you about this."

"That's alright, we've all got plenty of time, right?"

"I don't know, it's a gamble with you. Darla seemed like she wanted to kill you at one time and Ellie looks like she wants to strangle you on most days."

Edwin turned his head and looked at Ellie with a grin and patted her knee. Ellie smiled and took his hand in hers.

"Anyway, Mom told me all about it. She took all the pieces of the monster apart that I thought was you. I'm not really sad for me, I'm sad for her and from what I hear I'm sad for you. It's difficult for me to feel this way after all these years."

"How's that?" Edwin asked.

"I used to fantasize that someday I would meet my father and that everything would be set straight and we could make up for lost time and all of that. I thought about how exciting that would be and how I'd do the romantic thing and cry. I don't know. Over the years that just faded and drifted off into some obscure little place and now I'm fifty-seven years old and I happened to wind up in that obscure little place. Right here, I'm feeling all those old feelings. I'm too old to have those feelings!" she shouted, laughing at herself while tears kept forming in her eyes.

"And you think eighty is too old for that, too?" he asked.

"No, at your age you're reverting back to childhood anyway." Ellie laughed out loud and Edwin smiled and shook his head.

"I knew from the first time I saw your resume and application. I had a gut feeling, only at the time it tore the guts out of me. I knew what it meant for both you and your mother."

"Just so you know, I don't blame you. I want to blame both of you, but I can't. You didn't know so you didn't do anything wrong and I think Mom's paid enough. The only thing I know is that you can't go back and fix things."

"Sure you can, or at least you can try. You can't change the past, but you can always start something fresh, something that will hopefully last. That's what I'm trying to do here, that's what all of this is about, I think. I know that I've trying to fix things with Ellie," Edwin said. "But you're miserable, though, aren't you?"

Ellie nodded.

"I guess we never know what our actions or good intentions are going to lead to, and sometimes it all blows up in your face. As for you and your mother, I didn't try or do anything special by bringing you here, it just happened."

"I can help Ellie and we wanted to talk to you about that."

"I'm not cut out for this, Dad," Ellie said, her voice shaking as she spoke. "I'm ready to run away from here tomorrow if I have to, but I can't stand the management part of this. I just want to be a nurse, that's all. Everything's slipping through the cracks and we're going to be in real trouble, legal trouble, if we don't get a grip on things and I don't know what to do."

"I'm proud of you," Edwin said to Ellie, and her tears began to roll down her cheeks. "Don't think you're the first person that has started a company that grew so fast they had to step aside and let others take the reins of managing. You keep your focus on what you want the business to be. Your goal was to provide people with the best care in the last season of their lives, right?"

"Yeah," Ellie replied.

"She doesn't have the business skills for this and she doesn't want that part of it," Karen said. "She just wants to provide the care and comfort."

"Do that, then. Look, I want you to do what you want and be happy about it. You've done the hard work, now enjoy what you've created."

"You're okay with that?"

"Hell yes, we'll get someone to take over the management part. They'll continue to carry out your vision and you get to do what you like."

"We talked about that already," Karen said. "You saw my resume, I can do the administrative part and Ellie can do the nursing. I can still help her at times. Would you be comfortable with me trying my hand at running things?"

"Can't hurt to try. You certainly seem to have the instinct for it."

"Good, that's all we've been waiting for. Ellie's been afraid to talk to you about it and with all that's gone on for the last few weeks it's been even more stressful."

"I was afraid that you'd see me as a failure," Ellie said.

"Never. You've put up with me, you can put up with anything."

"Putting up with you and your past is enough for anyone."

"We need more staff, is that possible?" Karen asked.

"That's fine, we'll hammer out all the details in the morning. Is that the question that you wanted to ask me?"

"Not exactly, it's something a little more personal in nature."

"Is it about men? If it is, you'll have to ask Ramy."

"No," Karen laughed. "Something even more along the father-daughter lines."

Edwin braced himself for what might be coming.

"Fire away," Edwin said. Karen hesitated and Ellie began poking him lightly in the ribs.

"She needs a new car," Ellie said.

"Yeah, I need a new car," Karen said and then batted her eyes at him, "Daddy."